Julia Redesigned

Kyle Hunter

P. O. Box 30981
Raleigh, NC 27622
www.Kyle-Hunter.com

Cover design by Erika Alyana Sañga Duran.

ISBN: 978-1-7330294-3-8

Books by Kyle Hunter that will take you places

Circle Back Around

One December

Provence Series

Prodigals in Provence (Book I)

A Promise in Provence (Book II)

Second Chance Series

Marissa Rewritten (A Novella- Book I)

Julia Redesigned (Book II)

Chapter One

It had been a matter of time. But that knowledge didn't lessen the hollow ache that welled up inside Julia De Luca as the mourners dropped roses into the hole where her mother's coffin lay. The priest's pale, lined face appeared white against his dark robe. Head tilted skyward, he lifted his eyes and one hand as he pronounced his final prayer for Gianna De Luca.

Julia's fingers, moist under the August sun, clutched the slick stem. She stepped forward and let her rose fall to join the others. Silently, the petals hit the wooden coffin. She lifted her eyes from under a wide-brim straw hat and panned the small cluster of mourners. Her mother's friends from church, some long-ago colleagues. No relatives. Only her.

"She's in a better place, Julia, you know that," came the soft words from Sylvia, her mother's former best friend. *No.* Julia corrected herself. *My mother's best friend.* Just because her mother's last years had slipped away as a result of Alzheimer's didn't make Sylvia any less of a friend. The woman had visited her mother at least monthly over the last three years.

Julia offered a half smile and a nod. The women leaned toward each other for a tight, lingering hug. When they pulled apart, Julia said, "Thank you for being there for her, Sylvia." From experience, she knew it was hard to visit the memory care center and make conversation with someone who stared at the wall without speaking or slept through the visit. It was required of a daughter, but not of a friend, bless her. Sylvia had been her mother's faithful friend for over thirty years.

Sylvia shook her head, as if dismissing the gratitude. "*You* were there nearly every day, Julia, especially toward the end, despite running a successful business. I don't know how you did it."

Julia shrugged. It hadn't been a choice. It was her mother. "We all do what we have to. I knew we didn't have much time together and I wanted to be there as much as I could. I have competent employees who kept the ship afloat on the business side of my life. They were very understanding, too."

Despite the cold block still weighing down her insides, a stray thread of contentment pushed through her sadness like a stubborn seedling. Her interior design business had kept her sane over the last years of her mother's decline. She'd thrown herself into projects and new designs, her sadness driving her to risky, out-of-box creativity, and it had paid off. Her reputation had shot well above obscurity in the last year and a half, to the point that she was sought by local celebrities, big hotel chains, museums, and event spaces.

Her work was a satisfying anesthesia, an effective pain-blocker, at least during working hours, which extended far into the evening on most days. "I'll be taking the next couple of weeks off to regroup and go through Mom's storage unit." She swallowed. What would *that* be like without her anesthesia for two weeks?

Sylvia nodded, but her brows knitted with sympathy and concern. "I hope you'll get some rest as well. And don't be alone too much, Julia. I know you do that sometimes. Call me if you want to talk or be with someone."

"I will." She laid her hand gently on Sylvia's shoulder. "Thanks for the reception you prepared. You didn't have to arrange all that. It was a lot of trouble."

"No, not really. And it was my honor. For Gianna. She was a treasure to me for over thirty years. Friends like that don't come along every day. I'll miss her. I *have* missed her." As she looked away, her eyes filled and her face took on a misty expression that suddenly made her appear older. She looked back at Julia and the upbeat thrust of her voice seemed forced. "And don't feel like you have to stay at the reception for too long. I think people will understand."

Julia was grateful for Sylvia's acknowledgement of an accepted fact, that post-graveside receptions were difficult for family members. She'd have to spend a minimum of time, nonetheless.

She hugged Sylvia more tightly the second time. "See you in a bit."

Turning away from Sylvia, Julia stared at the hole where her mother lay, a last gaze before she closed her eyes. "Bye, Mom," she whispered. When she opened them, several tears spilled down her cheeks. Her mouth and throat were dry and perspiration trickled between her shoulder blades. She shifted her gaze to the stone alongside her mother's fresh grave. A grave for Joe Connelly, the disembodied name of a father she'd never met. Her mother had wanted to be buried next to Joe, concluding the ending chapter of the Joe Connelly thread of their lives.

It was about time.

Julia's gaze roved over the remaining guests in Sylvia's living room. They chatted quietly or refilled their paper plates from a table with canapes, quiche, fruit, and mixed nuts. During nearly two agonizing hours of the reception, she'd hugged mourners and answered questions about her mother. Some attendees hadn't seen her mother much since her retirement over ten years earlier. Most hadn't seen her at all in the three years since she'd moved to the memory care facility.

"Wasn't your mother really young to have Alzheimer's?" The question came from one of her mother's former hospital colleagues whose name escaped her.

"Not really. It was within the normal range. She was seventy-five when she was diagnosed and seventy-eight when she passed." Julia swallowed on the hard words, still too fresh. She'd done research on the disease and none of it had been encouraging. "My mother also struggled with emphysema, which likely made everything worse." And sped up her departure.

When the woman wandered away back to the food table, Sylvia sidled up to Julia and said, "You need rest, Julia. You've been through a lot. Why don't you go on home? Of course, I don't mind if you stay. It's up to you, but don't feel obligated to stay."

"Thanks, I am pretty tired." She gave Sylvia a grateful smile and didn't wait for the suggestion to come again. Soon on the freeway, she put distance between herself and sadness. Just then, home wasn't the destination in view nor a place where her heart would receive solace.

Instead, she wove through the suburb into the next town and sought the familiar brick building. A few shoppers and strollers roamed the sidewalks. She parked along the street and unlocked the metal door of her shop, De Luca Interiors. She stepped through the doorway, leaving the busy sounds of Saturday out on the streets. The air inside was stuffy, since the shop had been closed for a couple of days. Just being within its walls lifted a weight from her chest.

Her design shop was a world apart from the cemetery and from her mother's memory care center, where she'd spent countless hours over the last year. In the gray dimness, her fingers fumbled and found the switch. Light flooded the space. It had the feel of a living room, with comfortable beige chairs in soft leather around a low table covered with design books. Underneath the seating area sprawled a huge oriental rug in beige and navy blue. Off-white counters, tables, and racks displayed samples of color, texture, and patterns. One entire wall built from multicolored used brick created a trendy yet vintage-looking backdrop for framed photos of Julia's designs of homes, hotels, and offices.

Julia crossed the store to the color palettes on the far wall. She stood and stared at them. Sighing from a deep place inside her, she allowed the soft turquoise and dusty rose to penetrate her like a balm. She smiled and relaxed her shoulders as tension released like a metal lock suddenly opened.

Her appreciation of color was cheaper than a therapist and more effective. It had always been healing for her, going back to her childhood. She'd grown up the only child of a single mother who'd immigrated from Italy in her twenties. Even then, Julia had been the one to decorate their sequence of small apartments in New York. She remembered clearly how much she'd craved the virtual "excitement" that color could bring to a drab, inexpensive urban dwelling. Her mother had often taken her to fabric stores where she chose bright patterned lengths of cloth to cover their shabby furniture, the coffee and dining tables, the windows. Every surface she could beautify. If it wasn't suitable for fabric, she used paint.

She'd also put together outfits from her mom's thrift store purchases. "You have the flair, my Giulia," her mother would say, her still-strong Italian accent so familiar and charming to her. "You can make anything out of everything, my amazing child." No one was surprised when Julia attended design school in New York and began working at a large design firm there while still in her twenties.

A lifetime ago. The memories turned like pages of a scrapbook, those of a rising career, a failed marriage, friends come and gone—

these were filmy images, no longer sharp in her mind. Her mom had always been there in the background, supporting her, offering sage advice when asked. She'd been a solid presence during some hard experiences, both for herself and for Julia.

Julia could say she'd miss her mom, but Gianna had been "gone" for the last three years. It was as though she'd lost her back then, gradually. Of course, along with mourning there was relief. Relief that the indignity and waste of her mom's final state were over. And if Julia were honest, it would take *her* time to recover from the rhythm she'd had to keep, stretched between her mother's needs and her own company and employees. But taking off two weeks might not have been the best idea.

"Seemed like a good idea at the time, Mom." Her words filled the quiet of the empty shop. She'd have to go through her mother's storage unit, something she should have done ages ago. Her mother hadn't needed anything inside it for years, but Julia had put off the task of emptying it out. That was one thing she could do during her time off, which would likely be much too long.

In the pocket of her linen dress, she felt a vibration. Someone had just texted her. For the last few days, she'd received sporadic showers of emails and text messages—condolence from her employees, acquaintances, and friends. Those messages did bring comfort, diluting the sting of her aloneness. Especially consoling were the frequent messages from Marissa, Eden, and Sydney, women who'd become like sisters. The four of them had been friends in college twenty-five years earlier. Years of sparse contact followed, threaded together only by Christmas cards and Facebook updates and the occasional phone call. But in the last couple of years, following the loss of their marriages, whether through widowhood or divorce, they'd begun getting together twice annually for a girls' weekend. That bi-annual retreat was a lifeline for each one of them. Too bad the next one wouldn't be for another three months at Thanksgiving.

She'd heard from her friends at least three times each that week. The current text was possibly one of them checking in on her, aware that her mom's service had taken place that day. Julia typed the code into her smartphone and scanned her text messages. Two from her employees, Crystal and Jake, one from Billy, a suitor who wouldn't take no for an answer, and Eden. She clicked on Eden's message.

You are right now at this very moment in our thoughts and prayers, Julia, with truckloads of virtual hugs and kisses. A thread of warmth snaked through her grief as she read Eden's message. She couldn't stop a slow smile from stretching across her face. Especially now, their friendship was vital. She kept reading: *But that's not quite enough for our Julia. So, we're all coming to see you. Tomorrow, in fact.*

Julia's mouth dropped open. "What? They're coming tomorrow?" Her eyes kept scanning the message. *I hope that's okay with you. We've been on the phone together discussing what we can do to support you during this time and we decided there was no substitute for hands-on hugs and loving on you! So, let me know when you get this. Eden.*

She let the welcome news sink in. As she did, the weight rolled away and was replaced by an airy, carefree lift she hadn't experienced in over a year. A chuckle escaped her throat as she typed, *Yes! That's okay! Let me know when you're coming and I'll be ready. I took off some time, so this is perfect!*

A perfect way to put off the inevitable. Only a weekend, but she'd take what she could get. If ever there was a time when she needed to see Eden, Sydney, and Marissa, this was it.

Chapter Two

Julia stood by the full-length window in the dining room and scanned the street. The "girls" should be there any time. Eden had flown in to Dulles Airport from Indianapolis that morning. Marissa and Sydney were driving together, since they both lived in North Carolina. They'd picked Eden up at the airport so they could arrive together. Eden had artfully and passionately coordinated every detail to fit like a well-engineered machine.

Somewhere, a car door slammed but the street outside Julia's suburban D.C. home was deserted, save two children on bikes. Truthfully, her mind had been in such a cloudbank yesterday, she'd had trouble remembering exactly what Eden had told her. But now, it was as clear as a mountain lake as she awaited their arrival. She'd at least gotten the time right, since Eden texted the details to her again the evening before. She was grateful for Eden's efficiency, which was never without a healthy dose of humor and thoughtfulness. It had likely been her idea to pull this whole thing off. They'd all just been together at Marissa's in May, a month before Julia's mother had gone into a coma. The two months following that event were a painful blur. Now, the unscheduled arrival of her dearest friends was nothing short of an emergency heart intervention.

Just as she glanced through the wooden blinds again, Sydney's blue-gray SUV came into view and pulled into her driveway. In an instant, Julia was outside, almost tripping down the porch as she hurried. The car doors flung open and out spilled Eden, her petite form rushing across the yard, her blond hair flying loose and longer than Julia remembered it.

Eden quickly closed the space between them and wrapped her arms around Julia's shoulders. "Our Julia! Dear Julia! We're here to totally distract you!" Julia shut her eyes and returned Eden's heartfelt squeeze.

She heard Marissa's calm voice beside her. "If that's what you want, that is." Julia opened her eyes and smiled at Marissa, who had joined them on the sidewalk. She, too, enveloped Julia in a hug. When they pulled apart, Marissa gently added, "Of course, Eden has good intentions, but it's *your* time, Julia. Maybe you'll want a more solemn weekend. You've been through a loss, after all."

Compassion shadowed Marissa's face as she touched Julia's cheek. Marissa understood loss, but for her it had been worse. She'd lost her husband two years earlier. Somehow for Julia, her mother's long illness had allowed her to let go more slowly, as her heart adjusted day by day. And her mother had been seventy-eight.

Julia touched Marissa's arm. Her friend's pale face, framed with dark wavy hair, showed kindness and compassion. "It's okay, Marissa. I've had enough sadness for a while."

Sydney joined them. "Nope, no solemn weekend. Not with us, you don't. Uh-uh." She wore a straw hat—fashionably, as only Sydney could—her sun-tinted straight brown hair brushing her shoulders in a blunt cut. She flipped the hat back so that it hung down her back on a string and hugged Julia tightly, swaying her side to side. "We think you need some cheer, joy, and red wine."

"Hear, hear!" Eden clapped. "And we brought all the food. I know you're supposed to do that after a loss but, well, we went overboard."

"Yeah, check the trunk," Sydney said. "No, better still, let's buy another fridge. We'll need it."

"I love your house, Julia!" Marissa scanned the front façade and corner porch. "I can't wait to see the inside of our interior decorator's home."

"Don't expect *too* much." Better tamp down their expectations. Julia loved her home, but it wasn't the five-star elegance of some she designed. "I went for comfort, comfort, and more comfort." Her home was small, but in a stylish neighborhood on the Maryland side of D.C. After her divorce from Nick almost eight years earlier, she'd wanted a house, not an apartment, to call her own. Not only had she spent her whole life in apartments up to then, but with a house, there would be more to decorate.

"There's lots more in the car—" began Eden.

"Come on in first." Julia gestured to them and walked toward the house. "We can unload the car together in a little while."

"I'll just bring a handful of fridge stuff." Eden rounded the vehicle and pulled out a thermal tote and a paper grocery bag. The other women murmured agreement and filled their arms before heading inside.

As the women moved en masse toward the porch, Eden recounted her less-than-smooth flight and Sydney threw out one-liners. By the time they entered the house only seconds later, they were all laughing. What good medicine her friends were.

"Oh, Julia, it's lovely," Eden said, her eyes roving up and down through the foyer and open-space living room. "Your house looks so homey and comfy, just like you said. Yet, everything blends together perfectly. I'm enjoying just looking at your colors and special touches. If I disappear on you all, it's because I'm taking the liberty to tour every room." Eden touched the hand-woven tapestry from

Morocco that hung on the entry wall. "This must be from one of your trips."

Julia nodded. She hadn't taken many trips since separating from Nick. She'd always intended to start traveling again, but her default had become prioritizing her work to the point that the months flew by in a flurry of projects and obligations. That needed to change. One day.

"Feel free to look around. I don't mind." Julia grinned as Marissa and Eden peered into the kitchen and wandered over to Julia's study in the next room of her single-story home.

Sydney had collapsed into an overstuffed chair. "I know I've been seated in my car all day, but I had to try this deliciously comfy chair before taking the tour or bringing in our junk. And I do like your home, too."

Julia's personal tastes and favorite artifacts were everywhere, in subtle earth tones and bold, colorful accents with lots of natural fibers. Alpaca, jute, Berber. It was the first time her friends had been to her home. That thought made her feel vulnerable and proud at the same time. The first visit was always a rite of passage, whether one was a designer or not. All the girlfriends had to admire and approve the first time they came to each other's homes. Such a female trait, and she loved it, even more because it was her profession to make home spaces beautiful and welcoming.

Within a short time, the women lounged around a burled wood table now covered with snacks, mineral water, and wine glasses. "Try this aged cheddar on rice crackers. It's my new addiction." Eden slid the plate across the table.

"It's wonderful to have you all here. I really appreciate your efforts." Julia looked at each of her friends.

"Aww, efforts, schmefforts! Julia, that's what we do for each other, especially at a time like this."

Though Eden's tone was upbeat, her statement touched a fragile place deep inside and Julia's eyes stung. She blinked at her tears but they didn't obey, silently pouring down her cheeks unexpectedly, as if released from a dam.

Eden looked up from slicing the cheddar and froze. She laid down her knife, rose from her armchair, and squeezed onto the couch next to Julia. Without a word, she slipped her arms around Julia's shuddering shoulders and pulled her close. Though Julia had no intention of letting the weekend be a maudlin display of grief, Eden's arms felt warm and solid around her. She needed that moment of silent recognition.

Sydney spoke, her voice soft, lacking its usual jocular tone. "For a minute I forgot that this wasn't our usual get-together. I'm sorry, Julia. I'm sorry for your loss and I hope you know how much we love you."

Julia gave her a mute nod through a smear of tears. Marissa and Sydney both joined Julia on the couch and gave her a long hug, one at a time. It was healing, nourishing. Afterward, Julia looked around at their red faces and eyes. "I made you all cry. Now, stop it!" She smiled, deeply grateful for their care, but also ready to move on. "How about some of that Malbec?"

"I'll pour." Eden, who had returned to her chair, reached for the bottle and expertly removed the cork.

Sydney grinned and gestured to Eden. "You did that so fast, Eden. Takes me a while every time, even though I have loads of experience."

The women laughed. Eden said, "I own a restaurant, remember? Anything to do with food, I'm all over it." After she'd poured the wine, she turned her attention back to Julia. "How was the service, Julia? That is, if you feel like talking about it."

"No, I'm fine. Much better now, really. I'm so grateful to you all." Julia reached for a tissue and the glass Eden had poured for her. She took a deep breath as if to shake off her display of grief. She felt like she'd just had an hour of therapy. Lighter, more hopeful. "It was a short graveside service. Not too many people came, but a few. People who'd worked with my mom or been members of her church. Some former neighbors. Her best friend did a little reception afterward. It was nice, considering the circumstances. I didn't want to have a service or a viewing at the church. I didn't see the point. She wanted to be buried next to Joe."

"Oh, the famous Joe," Sydney said.

"Who is Joe?" asked Marissa. "I don't think I've heard about him."

Julia sighed. "He's my biological dad. He was killed before I was born and my mom never got over him. She even gave me his last name."

"De Luca?"

"No, Connelly. Joe Connelly." Julia leaned back against the woven cushions of the couch, not sure if she was in the mood to talk about Joe. "They met at the Catholic church they both attended. Fell in love. A few months later, they got pregnant with me, then engaged. Then when my mother was just a few months along, Joe was killed in a car accident on his way home from a work trip. My mom didn't know for weeks that he'd been killed. She thought he'd just abandoned her because of her pregnancy."

"Oh, that's terrible!" Marissa's hands flew to her cheeks. "How awful for your mother."

"Yes, it was. I wasn't born yet when it happened, but when I got older, she told me she' d been beside herself, thinking he'd gotten cold feet and was backing out. But it was even worse when she learned he'd been killed."

"Such a shame." Marissa leaned forward. "So, back to your name. Did she name you Julia Connelly?" Marissa was a novelist, so maybe she was thinking of creating a story around the tale of Joe Connelly. Which would be fine, since poor Joe hadn't had a chance to live his own story.

Julia swallowed, stifling a grimace. She hadn't wanted to dig up ancient history. So many doors better left closed. "Yes. I was born Julia Connelly. I should have told you all that at some point, but it didn't cross my mind."

"Julia Connelly is a beautiful name, too. Connelly is Irish. But you look Italian, not Irish. Bet that was confusing for a lot of people." Sydney grinned.

"Except for the beautiful blue eyes." Eden smiled, playfully lifting her eyebrows.

"I did get my blue eyes, apparently, from Joe's mother, and Joe had them, too. My mom told me that." Julia shrugged. "I never even met Joe and I certainly didn't want a name that had nothing to do with me."

"Were you angry about your name?" asked Sydney.

Julia let out a laugh that was sharper than she intended. "Yes, as a matter of fact. Very angry. My mom and I bickered about it frequently. I wanted to be a De Luca. That's what my relatives in Italy were called. That was my mom's name. Why didn't she just name me De Luca, I used to ask her."

"What did she say?" Marissa asked.

Julia paused, wishing she could erase this whole conversation. Why had she even mentioned Joe Connelly? Yet, it was right that her closest friends know her background. "She told me I was all she had left of him, so she wanted me to have his name."

"Did you change it to De Luca after your divorce?" Sydney propped her crossed arms on her knees.

"Before then. When I met you all in college, I told you my name was De Luca because I'd planned to change it as soon as I could. Thought I'd save you some confusion that way. Since we didn't have classes together, none of you learned about my fib back then. And I really didn't think of it as a fib, because I'd internalized the De Luca name. I secretly had it changed as soon as I turned twenty-one. When my mom found out, she cried. But it was *her* history, not mine. I didn't want the name of a man I'd never known."

"I can understand that. Really, I can." Marissa nodded and clasped her hands around her knees.

"But I get your mom's point, too, especially since he was your bio dad and she loved him. To her, he was a real person." Sydney said. "But she shouldn't have gotten so upset. You'd spent your life with this guy's name and he meant nothing to you."

Julia felt the pressure rising in her chest from that old argument, her mom's firm position about Joe. She took another sip of wine, too large a sip, and swallowed. There was a comfort in the burn that coated her throat. "The hardest thing for me was living with the ghost of Joe Connelly. My mother never went on with her life, never wanted to remarry." Except for Doctor Sam. Another buried story better left alone. If her mom *had* remarried, it might have meant brothers, sisters, a dad, a family. Maybe her mother had desired it, but Joe's memory had been a sufficiently compelling life purpose. Until she simply gave up.

The lonely years were suddenly current and just as painful, just as empty. Julia pushed them away to the back of her memory. In their place weighed a metal clamp of guilt for thinking and speaking of her mother negatively. Her mother who'd dedicated her life to raising her young daughter, giving her what she could. The mother she'd just buried. She blinked away the sting that began in her eyes.

If only the conversation would move on.

"Hmm. I wonder why she never married anyone. You showed me that photo you carry in your wallet. Your mother was so pretty. Just like you are," Eden said. "Do you look like her?"

Julia nodded and her smile returned. "Everyone in my Italian family always said I was a smaller version of my mom." She heard it often, from Nonna Lucia, Uncle Giuseppe, and the other Italian relatives whose names she forgot, as well as her mother's friends.

"Do you still see your Italian relatives?" Sydney reached for the wine bottle.

Another closed box that hadn't been opened in years. "Uh, no, I haven't seen them since I was a child. We—we've lost touch."

"That's too bad. Just don't follow in your mother's footsteps and refuse to remarry." Eden leaned forward and swatted Julia's knee across the table.

"Look who's talking, Eden!" Sydney laughed. "You're the one who's been widowed *forever* and never remarried. What's it been, ten years already? You're so darned adorable, you *have* to bite the bullet and make some man deliriously happy."

Eden looked flustered at the turn of the conversation. "Well, I've had my hands full with the restaurant—"

"Which you're about to sell, or so you've told us. After that, you'll have time for other pursuits, like finding some male companionship." Sydney cocked her head with a knowing smile then, with a laugh, threw a small cushion at Eden. "I'm just teasing you, Eden. Mostly, but a little bit *not*."

Julia was relieved that the conversation had moved onto Eden's love life instead of hers, though they'd followed the same path of avoiding the whole thing. She'd also had her hands full, between establishing a design business, which ended up being more successful than she'd imagined, and her mother's declining health.

"I'll have a couple more of those rice crackers, Eden." Marissa's voice was soft. Maybe she wanted to change the subject to rescue Julia and Eden both. Marissa would do that. Her well-timed sensitivity balanced clear appraisal and firm decision-making. "You're right, this cheese is really good." She lifted her head to Julia. "Do you have a church that you like, Julia? I was thinking it could provide some support for you."

Julia fought the urge to create a distraction and change the subject, turn it to someone else. It was too late to deflect. Might as well come clean on her failure. "There's a church near me I've attended several times. I like it pretty well." She paused to gather her thoughts, her words. "I guess I can tell you all that I don't feel comfortable going there. First, it's horribly lonely to sit on a pew alone in the midst of several hundred people who are all connected to someone."

"Oh, I understand completely!" Eden's hands fluttered in the air. "Totally. Widows don't have their place either. At least it sometimes feels that way."

Julia sighed. "I tried a women's activity once, thinking I could get to know some people, but the fact that I didn't have a husband or kids made me feel like I had two heads. I think some of the women had no idea what to talk to me about." She recalled the uncomfortable silence and expression of either shock or sympathy, she hadn't known which, when she answered the polite questions that always came at women's events. Husband. Children. No, and no. And she wasn't widowed, she was *divorced*. Even worse. Those conversations didn't evoke pain anymore, just the nagging sense that somehow, she'd made a wrong turn in the pursuit of the kind of life she was supposed to have.

"Yeah, I feel that way sometimes." Sydney nodded, a reflective look on her face. "I'm part of an "older singles" group, which is helpful. I like it. We can all be misfits together. Maybe you could find one of those in your church."

Julia chuckled. "Yeah, maybe. Once things get settled again for me, I'll check it out. I'll look on the church website for the middle-aged misfit group and tell them I want to sign up." Everyone laughed, though she sensed that for all of them the humor held a thread of painful truth.

Online church was a lot simpler. Of course, it lacked a lot, and if loneliness was already a burden, watching church on her computer didn't solve anything. But it did provide the comfort of coffee and slippers while tuning in for spiritual inspiration. Julia couldn't complain about isolation from believers. It was her own fault.

"Sydney, your turn. How has your summer been, you unemployed bum?" Eden reached for a slice of chorizo and another rice cracker.

"Not all the fun in the sun that you'd imagine." Sydney blew out a puff of air and stretched her long, tanned legs onto the end of the coffee table. "After I finished the school year and turned in my grades, I took Jessie to the beach but would rather have been with *you* all. A week at the beach with a sixteen-year-old isn't what it's cracked up to be. And now, I'm an unpaid taxi driver, to swim practice, to the mall, the movies."

"Jessie will get her license soon, won't she?" Julia asked.

"Gosh, I hope so! At the same time, I'm afraid to let her out on the streets. It seems like she's still a child. So, you see, my life's not that exciting. One day, maybe after Jessie's in college, I'll quit teaching and travel the world. Or maybe just go back to the beach and be a *real* bum."

"That's what you always say!" Marissa laughed.

"One day, one day. I want to hear from you, Marissa. You have some interesting news. What's his name?" Sydney prompted.

Marissa's normally pale complexion colored but she smiled. "Jarrod. It's new, so all I can say is, so far so good."

"Have you seen him much?" Julia reached for the carafe of water and poured a tall glass.

"Well, he lives in Asheville but he's been to Raleigh twice." Marissa paused and smiled shyly. "I really like him."

"That's wonderful, Marissa." Julia turned to her friend. "At least one of us has some love life potential going on. And you have a new novel, too, don't you?" Marissa's book was likely a more comfortable topic for her than her budding love interest. She and Julia were more reserved than Sydney and Eden, so she recognized and understood Marissa's subtle signs of discomfort.

As expected, Marissa brightened up. "I'm working hard on my new one. It takes place during the Civil War. It's my first novel since my long writer's block after Robert's death. But it's going well. I'm almost finished with the first draft." The women murmured their affirmation.

"I can't wait to read it," Sydney said. "*And* to hear more about Jarrod. But we have all weekend. We'll get it out of you sooner or later." She sent Marissa an evil grin with a wink and they all laughed.

The sound of their mingled laughter pushed something airy and hopeful up through Julia's sadness, like a fragile sprout. It softened her childhood disquiet about Joe Connelly and her mother's decisions, whisking them back to their shelf in the distant past.

Her friends could only stay a few days, but it would boost her like a year of therapy and help her hobble more gracefully into the next phase of her life, one without Gianna De Luca.

Chapter Three

She was putting it off. As she poured a second cup of coffee and contemplated a second blueberry bran muffin, Julia knew that she was killing time, avoiding going to the storage unit. Not only would it unearth layers of memories when her grief was still too fresh, but it would be a long, tedious project. Boxes on boxes to the top of the storage unit. She could always just have them hauled away to a dumpster, couldn't she?

Not even a question she'd entertained. She'd have to at least pry open each cardboard box and plastic bin to determine what should go where and to whom. Likely, the boxes didn't contain much that she would want in terms of décor, jewelry, or clothing. If she didn't at least *see* everything, though, she'd always wonder if a special keepsake had gone to the thrift store by mistake.

Julia reached to her throat and touched her necklace, a heart-shaped gold locket with delicate swirls carved into the surface. It was a perfect example of why she needed to open every box. Her mother had given it to her for her sixteenth birthday. It had belonged to Nonna Lucia, and her mother before her. It reminded her that she was part of a larger family, as distant as they seemed. There might be other treasures in those boxes, as well as links with her mother, clues to her life, even if their discovery was painful.

Minutes later, Julia drove toward the storage building. Speed and the wide-open road lifted her spirits slightly, as the balmy morning air slipped through a partly open window. All too soon, she had to flick her turn signal and turn toward the ramp. As she sat at a light, her phone rang. She hit the Bluetooth button and saw the name of Crystal, her star employee. The efficient young woman who was currently holding everything together. "Hi, Crystal. Thanks for your sympathy message. It was very sweet."

"Oh, of course, Julia. I hope you're doing okay. I know it's hard to lose a parent, even an elderly one."

Did Crystal know anything about that? She was about twenty-seven. She was kind, nonetheless. Though the call from her employee probably signaled a snag somewhere in the business.

"Thank you, Crystal. I appreciate the thoughtfulness of all of you. Everyone's been really sweet. I'm doing okay, really. I had a visit for a few days from some dear friends and that perked me up." She'd spoken no truer words. Sydney, Marissa, and Eden had landed on her doorstep at the perfect time. They'd given her the strength to head to her current destination. "Is everything okay at the store?"

"Yes, everything's fine, don't worry about a thing. We'll keep the building from burning down in your absence." Crystal chuckled and Julia winced. "Just kidding, of course. I wanted to let you know that Pearson decided that to save money on the rehab of the lobby, they'd keep the same chandeliers."

Julia bit her lip. "Yuck. Their chandeliers are hideous. And they have about sixty years of filth on them, too."

"Yes, I agree. Totally. It will save them some money, but will possibly kill your design. I know you're off work now, but I had to ask about that so I can get back to them. Sorry to bother you with it."

Julia parked in front of the storage company. She made an effort to silence the deep sigh that escaped from her chest. Pearson

Hotel was a big account, but she'd known they'd be difficult. They'd been pinching pennies from the start.

"That's okay, Crystal. It's an issue for our design, but I think I can convince them to agree on an alternate idea. When I get home later, I'll send you a link for a line of chandeliers that are modern but in a better price range. They'll see that it won't be a lot more expensive to update. We can cut down the cost on something else, maybe reduce the size of the waterfall or something, so it won't be much of an overall increase for them."

"You're so smart, Julia. It's no wonder you got where you did with your company. I'm learning a lot from you."

"I appreciate that, Crystal. With all the years and different situations, the solutions get easier."

If only they'd get easier in other parts of her life. Julia hung up and stepped out of the car to face her next challenge. The two-story storage unit had always reminded her of a Soviet era hotel, like a large, square box lacking any design whatsoever. The key to her mother's unit dangled from her hand. If she had siblings, they could all do this together. Or uncles, or *anybody.* It would provide a moment of shared remembrance, but also divide the workload. She wouldn't ask friends to help. It was too laborious. She alone was the one to make those decisions, to evaluate each item and choose its fate. And it would take days.

Julia set three large plastic bins near the doorway of the storage unit. One for things she'd give or throw away, one for items she wasn't sure about, and the third for what she'd definitely keep. She was fairly certain she wouldn't keep much, if anything, aside from a token or two. She'd probably have to trash entire boxes of things. At least there was a dumpster in the parking lot where she could empty trash right away. For the rest, it would be handy to have Sydney's SUV for a trip to Goodwill instead of her sporty Honda.

She stared at the first box, sure to contain fresh reminders of her mother. Her stomach tightened. Maybe it had been too soon to come here after losing her mother. On the other hand, it might be therapeutic to open each box and comb through the past. One thing was sure, she'd come this far and she wouldn't walk away until the job was done. Then she could do something fun to reward herself. Such as paint a bathroom.

Exacto knife in hand, she went to work. The first boxes held old papers and files. Likely, they could all be trashed. A box of her mother's nursing uniforms. Why had her mother saved them after she retired? Her mother had put herself through nursing school while working full-time. Those years had been even more barren for Julia, because she saw her mother so little. But it was for both of them, Gianna would say. To have a better life. And they did. But it had been hard. Very hard.

Then there were tablecloths and cloth napkins, faded from many washings. Julia should have given those away years ago when she'd donated so many of her mother's clothes. The black marker she'd brought came in handy. She wrote a big "T" for "toss" on the top of the carton.

She slit the packing tape on the next box and removed carefully-wrapped knick-knacks and dishes. Memories trickled from the past, images of dinners with her mother night after night until her mother started nursing school. Then, she shared more meals with a neighbor, Regina.

Julia touched the brass candle holders that had always sat on the sideboard in the dining room, unless they had company, which wasn't often. Framed photos of her as a child, both alone and with her mother, then as an adolescent. All of those, she'd keep.

She lifted another frame from the stack and stared down at a photo of Joe. Her father. Her mother had kept the photo in her bedroom. He'd been handsome, with clear blue eyes, curly brown hair, cropped close, and a deep dimple which, unfortunately, Julia hadn't inherited. Should she feel something for this man whose genes she carried in her body? She couldn't. She turned the frame over and placed it back into the box. Then an impulse overtook her and she removed it, pried off the back of the frame, and slid out the photo. She didn't value it, but maybe one day would wish she had one photo of the man whose bloodlines she shared. For most of her life, it had been a sore subject for her. But if she discarded the only photo she had—well, one just never knew.

Why don't you date someone, Mom? You might find someone like Joe.

Why do you want me to marry someone? You have me all to yourself now! Her mother would grin playfully, as if that would please Julia.

I wouldn't mind having a dad.

You have a dad, my Giulia.

At that point, Julia would roll her eyes as only an adolescent could do. Her frustration would thrust out of her. *I don't care about Joe! I don't know him. He's gone! You need to go on with your life.*

Then her mother would get a sullen look and shake her head. She'd never understood Joe's lack of relevance for her daughter. And Julia had never grasped how her young, beautiful mother could be satisfied with only a memory of love rather than the real thing.

That was before Dr. Sam. Julia's mother had started working at the hospital as part of her nursing practicum when Julia was about eight. Dr. Sam noticed Gianna right away and his attention must have touched a hungry place inside her creating a happy fantasy until it all abruptly evaporated in a cloud of pain. After that, her mother closed her heart to love. Twice was enough.

Julia's sigh billowed out from a deep cavern. They never talked about Dr. Sam again. But her mother used to tell her to guard her heart. It was too risky not to.

She swallowed the hard lump that had formed in her throat. Maybe the next box would distract her from those memories. When she neatly cut through the packing tape and pulled open the flaps, she saw the Christmas decorations and realized there was little chance of that. She'd trade one set of painful memories for another.

The ornaments, she'd keep for sure. After removing crumpled tissue paper, Julia fingered the delicate Italian hand-blown glass angel that had survived the years. It unleashed a new stream of memories, taking her mind vividly back to childhood. There were several more ornaments with different designs in a wooden box. She set it aside next to the doorway where the ornaments wouldn't get damaged.

Christmas had been the hardest time of year. Julia had envied her classmates who had so many relatives, so many gifts. Not so much for the gifts, but for the number of people who cared enough to give them. She'd been a shy child. Having relatives might have helped her out of her shell.

Several times during her childhood, her mother took her to Italy where she'd grown up. There were lots of relatives there. Nonna Lucia, Uncle Giuseppe, Uncle Flavio. She couldn't remember the other names because they stopped going there when Julia was about ten. Probably too far and too expensive, or her mother had too much work at the hospital. Those relatives were the closest Julia ever got to having a real extended family, but she hadn't seen them in nearly forty years. Now, she was alone. No Gianna, no husband or kids, no siblings or extended family. Alone.

Julia closed her eyes as that realization washed over her like polluted water. A surge of old anger trickled in, but just for a moment. How could she be angry with her mother when she'd just lost her? Tears stung her eyes then silently slid down her cheeks. "I'm sorry, Mom. I know you did the best you could. And I miss you."

A fresh wave of grief came with a shudder then quietly left. Julia fished a tissue from her purse and mopped her face. Her childhood was what it was. And she'd choose the memories of her mother she wanted to keep. Like these dusty heirlooms.

Two hours later, Julia pulled into her driveway with a long sigh. The first day was done. Though emotionally difficult, she'd accomplished more than she'd expected and tomorrow would be easier. She'd confronted the past and felt stronger to encounter it again before being able to fold it up and put it away for another decade or so. She might finish the whole project in just a day or so more. Then she'd have to decide what to do with the remaining time she'd taken off from work. She was determined not to go back early, though it would be tempting if she felt at loose ends around her house. She needed a break, that was sure. But beyond taking care of her mother's affairs, she hadn't planned out this blank period of time.

In her backseat and trunk were the three labeled bins. She would put their contents in her guest room until she finished then haul everything to the Goodwill. Before leaving the storage unit, she'd also grabbed two smaller, lightweight boxes labeled *Italia*, which she could easily sort through in the comfort of her living room.

Back home, her house felt empty, silent. She'd finished her scheduled chore for that day but the lack of a new focus weighed on her. She recalled Sylvia's words at her mother's graveside and dialed her number. "Hi, Sylvia. Just wanted to hear a human voice. You said to give you a call if I felt too alone. I've been at the storage unit all day."

"Oh?" Sylvia's voice was tentative. "And how did that go? Are you okay?"

Julia swallowed. "Yes, I'm fine. There were some hard moments and a bunch of memories, of course, but I got a lot accomplished. It had to be done, so I thought I'd get it over with."

"You could have waited, you know. You'd have been . . . how do I say . . . not as close to the time of loss. Also, I could have helped you." Her voice faded. Julia would never have permitted that, at Sylvia's age.

"That's so sweet of you, Sylvia. I appreciate the thought. It's not really something anyone besides me can do." Julia regretted calling her mother's friend. Aside from probably disturbing Sylvia's dinner hour, her phone call made her sound so needy. "Just thought I'd touch base. Are you making something good for supper?" She'd only meant to change the subject, but feared she'd just invited herself over. Another misstep.

Sylvia laughed an elderly rasp. "I don't cook anymore, ever since Howard died. I do cook some for the grandkids when they come. No, I've discovered the Crock Pot, the Pressure pot, the InstaPot and all kinds of other pots." She laughed again.

"Just avoid the kind you smoke." That was a stupid joke, but had been the first thing she could think of to lighten the moment.

Sylvia laughed louder. "Oh, my, that's funny! I don't even take aspirin, let alone touch that stuff."

Julia smiled in spite of her heavy mood. She added a lift to her voice. "Cooking pots are a good idea, though. I should do the same thing, instead of takeout. I'll leave you to your various Pots, then. Have a nice evening, Sylvia."

A toasted bagel with smoked salmon and cucumbers would be perfect for a light supper. Julia prepared the meal, added a glass of cold herbal tea and set them on her coffee table. First, she'd send an email. She flopped down on her comfortable couch and grabbed her phone. Her friends had left only the day before, but she couldn't let the connection break so soon. She needed it.

Just wanted to tell you all again how wonderful it was to see you. Thank you so much for coming and bringing your love, your care, and all the food! She added an emoji with its tongue hanging out. *It was wonderful and healing for me. I love you all. I survived my first day of cleaning out the storage unit. Don't worry, I will do something fun with my days off. Love you, Julia.*

Something fun. What would that look like, exactly? Billy Wetherill would certainly have some ideas if she asked him. Billy, her persistent suitor-slash-client, the one with the airline and money to burn. In early summer, she'd begged off an invitation to fly her to New York for dinner. Might have been fun, but she didn't want to encourage him. He was sweet. Sweet and not her type, if she even had a type anymore. Everyone told her she needed to get "out there" again. She and Nick had split up long before and for the first few years after, dating didn't interest her. Her desire to meet someone was just beginning to percolate again. Or maybe it was just loneliness.

Her phone rang. It was Marissa. Julia's cloud lifted instantly. "Hi, Marissa. What a pleasure!"

"Just got your text. How are you doing today, Julia? Are you okay?"

Julia smiled. "Sweet Marissa. You are a dear, you know? I'm doing okay in a sad kind of way, to be honest. But it's so good to hear from you."

"That's totally normal, Julia. You've just had a big loss. And I'm sure going through the storage unit stirred up a lot of grief as well."

"That's true. This is going to sound strange to you, but I'm realizing something. I lost my mom, which is sad, but I was prepared. Actually, it's kind of a relief, because she was in the end stages of Alzheimer's and her life was pretty lousy. But even though she didn't really know me for the last year, I felt like I still had family, you know?"

"And now you don't." Marissa's voice grew quiet.

"No, I don't." Once voiced, the truth fell like a heavy weight inside Julia's chest.

"Did you ever meet Joe's parents or any of his family? Did your mom tell them about you when you were born?"

Julia frowned. "She told me she tried. She hadn't met them yet, because his family was prejudiced against Italians. Imagine that. Irish immigrants against Italian immigrants."

"I guess that's human nature, unfortunately. I've heard that some people quickly forget their origins. They immigrate, but then quickly feel the right to look down on others." She clicked her tongue in disapproval. "I think this was worse in the last century, though it still sometimes happens. Thankfully, most people aren't like that."

"Both Joe and my mom believed his parents would accept her in time, especially with a new baby. But she'd never met them and didn't have their contact information before his death. She tried to find them but their name was so common, she wasn't able to locate them."

"What a shame. They're your grandparents but you never knew them. What about on your mom's side? Didn't you say you had relatives in Italy?"

"I guess I still do, but I haven't been there in almost forty years."

"Oh, I see. There may be someone there who still remembers you." Marissa's voice sounded hopeful.

Julia stretched out her legs on the coffee table. "I used to go with my mom every couple of years or so, but then we stopped going. She basically lost touch with them, aside from an occasional Christmas card."

Marissa was silent for a moment. Then, "How odd. You mean she lost touch with her own parents and siblings?"

"Apparently. I don't know why. She never wanted to talk about it, so I wonder if there was a falling out of some kind."

"A big one, since it was never resolved." After another brief silence, Marissa said, "Could you try to write to them to tell them of your mom's passing? It would give you a very reasonable excuse to contact them. What do you think?"

Julia's breath hitched. Marissa was right. Why hadn't she thought of that? They'd want to know, wouldn't they, that Gianna had died? "That makes sense. I should have thought about that. But I have no idea how I'd ever get in touch with them. Remember, it's been almost forty years."

"Oh, right. That is a long time. I wonder if any of them are on Facebook."

"If I can even remember all of their names." Mild frustration simmered inside Julia. Years had passed without her thinking too much of the De Lucas, but now she had an important reason to reach them, to let them know about her mother. And possibly open a door for herself. But it seemed like a long shot. "I remember a couple of the older siblings, but I doubt they'd be on Facebook. They'd be in their seventies or older by now if they're still living."

Marissa sighed. "I'll be your sister, then. You now have family!"

Julia laughed. "Marissa, you were *already* family. You and Eden and Sydney."

The women chatted a while longer then hung up. Julia stared for a moment at her bagel, but her thoughts were elsewhere. How could she get in touch with her Italian family? At the very least, she needed to let them know of her mom's passing. Maybe it could open up a correspondence of some kind. And with time, perhaps a visit.

But they were strangers. It was so long ago.

A hunger pang pushed the thoughts aside and she reached for the bagel. After she ate and showered off the dust of the day, she remembered the boxes in her car. Her mother had labeled them *Italia* when she first moved into assisted living. Or maybe she'd done it many years prior.

Julia slid into her flip flops and headed for the garage. Maybe there would be clues in those boxes as to how to contact her Italian relatives. She carried the two boxes into the house and set them on the coffee table. The aging tape barely held the box closed. She gently pried open each dusty flap of cardboard.

The first box contained two shoe boxes. Maybe these held small items. Or even shoes. She pulled out one of the shoe boxes. On the side was printed the words *De Luca Scarpe.* "Shoes," she said aloud. Where did that word come from? She didn't speak Italian, since, unfortunately, her mother had always spoken to her in English. But somehow, Julia knew that the inscription was about shoes. And, of course, it was a shoe box.

Something was coming back to her. There was a family business involving shoes. The De Lucas in Italy *made* shoes. A big shoe factory or a small atelier, she didn't know, couldn't remember. She must have recorded that Italian word and others in her subconscious when she visited as a child.

She'd found the first clue to the Italian De Lucas. They were shoemakers. Maybe this information would lead her to another clue about the De Lucas and how to contact them.

Julia lifted the lid from the first shoebox. Inside lay what used to be an elegant pair of red and black leather shoes with a skinny heel and a strap on the top. She'd never seen her mother wear them, unless she'd simply forgotten. The second box held a black pair, just as dressy, with a black patent leather toe. She pictured her mother wearing these shoes the day she met Joe Connelly. Maybe that was the reason Julia couldn't remember her mother ever wearing them. Just like Joe's memory, the shoes were embalmed and hidden away in a box, preserved like a relic frozen in time.

A layer of heaviness seeped through her. Her eyes stung for a moment as she recalled her mother expressing her sadness about Joe. She blinked the tears away and reached for the second box. It, too, had a shoebox tucked inside it and a couple of inexpensive ceramic figurines her mother had always liked. She pulled out the shoebox and opened it. Instead of shoes, she saw a pile of letters and drew them out. When she examined the postmark, her heart began to race. The postmarks and stamps were from Italy.

Julia leaned back on the couch cushion with the letters in her lap. She scanned the addresses. She guessed that most of them were from her mother's relatives in Italy, since the letters bore the same address, but showed no name. It was unlikely that the family still lived in the same house.

She tried to make out the dates on the postmarks. Some were clear, while others had been smudged or faded with age. They all seemed to be from the same time period. It was the year following Julia's last visit with her mother to Italy.

The letters must contain clues to why she and her mother never returned to Italy, never spoke again of the family. Nonna Lucia,

Uncle Giuseppe, Uncle Flavio. Why didn't they return? Something must have happened. As Marissa had said, it must have been something big.

The thought triggered a vague memory that became sharper like a telephoto lens. She suddenly remembered her mother shouting on the phone in Italian and spending days afterward crying. Julia had been about ten, shortly after their trip to Italy. She'd pleaded with her mother to stop crying, to tell her why she was sad, but her mother hadn't told her anything. There was a link between the loss of contact with the family, the letters, and the phone call.

The letters themselves would hold the truth.

Chapter Four

Julia awakened with a jolt. Lying still, her eyes roamed her bedroom, dark though streaked with milky moonlight soaking through the filmy curtains. She was no longer sleepy. The energy that flowed through her thoughts told her she wouldn't get drowsy again for a while. She turned her head to the bedside clock. It read two-thirty.

Her bare feet touched down on the nubby surface of the Berber rug. She slipped into her flip flops, groped for the hall light, and went down the hall into the kitchen. Outside the kitchen window, the backyard was black, pierced only by distant pinpoints from street lamps.

She made a mug of almond milk laced with turmeric and cardamom and carried the steaming brew into the living room. Scanning the darkened room, she saw them: the letters. She'd planned to read them the night before, but exhaustion had overtaken her. Now, her curiosity had thrust through the unconscious layers of sleep and dreams.

Julia turned on a lamp and settled onto the couch. Only the hum of the refrigerator broke through the silence of the dark house. She reached for the stack of letters, really only three, and took the first one. She had arranged them in chronological date order the evening before. She slipped two sheets of stationery out of the yellowed envelope. Each one was covered on one side with large, looping letters.

Which were written in Italian.

Her heart sank. Why hadn't it occurred to her that, of course, they'd be in Italian? Letters from Lucia to her daughter.

Julia skimmed the lines, hoping that more Italian vocabulary would emerge from her subconscious, but most of the writing wasn't clear enough to distinguish a string of words. Only certain isolated words were legibly written. It was as though the letter's sender had been angry, overwhelmed, outraged. *Cativa . . . familia. . . lavoro . . .* She didn't know what the words meant, but like a puzzle, she might be able to piece them into a coherent message.

She padded into her office next to the living room and turned on her computer. When it had powered up, she opened a translation site and inserted some of the words from the first letter. *Cativa* meant bad. *Lavoro* was work. *Familia*, family. A few lines later there were others. *Promessa*, promise. *Filia*, daughter. One full line looked legible so she typed it into the translation site and hit "enter". Translation: Forever stolen stirring black ostrich. She fell back in frustration against the desk chair. This was futile. There weren't enough words she could decipher to enable her to grasp the conflict that had exploded in the De Luca family forty years earlier.

She sat in that position for several minutes, her mind churning. How could she reach them? That was her first goal, to find the De Lucas. It was no use mailing a letter to the address on the envelope. Forty years later, they wouldn't be living at the same house, would they? She didn't even know where in Italy they were. The town on the envelope told her nothing. It was likely a smaller town outside of one she'd heard of, but at that moment, that was of no help. She'd Google it if she could decipher the whole city name. When she used to go there with her mother, they flew into a large city and were usually picked up by a family member in a car. What city, she didn't know. Another dead end.

Julia shut her eyes and forced her memory back through the fog of years. In her mind's eye, she saw a large, white house with mature trees in front. In a separate mental photo, she saw a river with a lovely covered bridge, tall with several stories atop one another, like a city street on top of a bridge. The waters had been greenish after a rain. Ornate bridges were spaced along the river's length. Disjointed images emerged, barely visible as if through a long tunnel. She could almost see Nonna Lucia's face in her mind. Julia's grandmother would have passed away by now, along with Nonno Flavio, her grandfather.

How would she reach them? Marissa had suggested Facebook, but without specific names of living relatives, where would she start? De Luca . . . *scarpe*. Shoes. They had a shoe store, so maybe they had a website. Julia quickly typed De Luca Shoes into the subject line of the browser. Several options scrolled out before her, but fairly close to the top she saw it and clicked. Hopefully, there weren't other De Lucas who made shoes.

Their website was professional-looking and, fortunately, bilingual. Maybe the company had gotten much larger and more successful over the last forty years. Out of curiosity, she clicked on the online catalogue and saw a vast array of shoes in many styles for men and women. Of course, she had to look. She was a woman and therefore needed to see the shoes first. Julia grinned to herself. It would only take a minute. She marveled at several styles but only for a few seconds. There were also boots, kids' shoes, purses, and belts. Impressive. They even had an option for hand-made "bespoke" shoes. Having gotten her curiosity out of the way, she could get down to business.

Quickly, her hand went to the About Us tab. She skimmed through the information there, which only explained what products the company made and the fact that they distributed their shoes internationally. Apparently, they had a presence at all of the main trade shows. The page didn't give much in the way of history, except to say the company had begun in 1938 and was still family-owned. *That* was something. If the company had been sold to another entity, she'd be sunk. It wasn't yet a dead end. But what she had found so far wasn't going to help her to find the De Lucas.

She scrolled down further and saw photos of the employees of De Luca Shoes, rows of photos three across. Julia didn't recognize the first man, a distinguished-looking older man, Sergio Regio, who was the CEO. The photo next to his was Emilia De Luca, her mother's younger sister. Her pulse quickened. Emilia, her *aunt*. She remembered Emilia's name, but not her face. Though Emilia was quite an attractive woman, her expression was cool, with a forced-looking smile for the photo. She was the vice president of *De Luca Scarpe*. Maybe she and Sergio were married. They both seemed to be close to sixty years old.

Then Giuseppe De Luca. She *did* remember him. He seemed to still play an active role in the company, although he must be in his seventies. She peered more closely at the photo. Giuseppe looked elderly but well-presented in a crisp suit jacket and tie. From the alert sparkle in his dark eyes and the determined set of his jaw, he appeared to be a man who had tabs on everything. She remembered his full Stalin-like mustache, now gray to match a full head of wavy, gray hair. On the next row of photos was dark-haired Luca Regio, probably Sergio's son, who was a *rappresentente commerciale*. A sales rep.

There were several employees who didn't bear the De Luca name, who could have been family or not. Or in-laws. Her eyes fell to the photo of a pretty blonde, Valentina Regio, who was also a European sales rep. Julia's eyes darted back to Emilia's photo on the previous row. Clearly, they were mother and daughter. If Emilia was a De Luca, then Valentina likely was, too. Emilia was probably married to Sergio, but had kept her maiden name.

Which made Valentina her cousin. Julia's pulse hammered with excitement. Cousin Valentina. She looked to be in her early thirties or younger, which increased her chances of being on Facebook. In the photo, Valentina wore a tailored light pink blazer and a cluster of large beads at her throat. Her makeup was somewhat heavy, but her beauty was still obvious. She had a warm, soft smile in the photo. Would she welcome a new cousin she hadn't previously known about? Would Valentina be a good contact person for her? Julia scrolled down and saw an address on the website footer, but, of course, it was a general one for the company. She'd use it if she had no other option. A message through Facebook would be more private.

Valentina was less intimidating than Emilia or Sergio because of her age and the warm smile in her photo. Julia swallowed, suddenly aware she was perspiring. She opened up Facebook. Her hands were clammy as she fingered the mouse and clicked. She typed "Valentina Regio" into the search bar. Several photos came up, but none of them resembled the woman on the De Luca website. Julia typed in Valentina De Luca. *Bingo*. On the header stretched a photo of Valentina on a ski slope with snow-covered pointed peaks in the background. She wore a feminine-looking pink snow jumper with fur around the hood and a matching ski cap with goggles atop her head. Her site was in Italian but some parts had been translated.

Julia scanned through her cousin's photos. In one of them, she stood in an affectionate pose with a handsome dark-haired man Julia had seen on the company website. She clicked back to the site.

Marco Esposito. A company romance, apparently. There were other photos of Valentina with other people. She seemed like she enjoyed a good time and had plenty of friends. But then, everyone on Facebook tried to appear that way.

Julia found the message button and stopped. Her heart pounded against her chest. She lifted her hands to the keyboard and typed with moist fingers. *Dear Valentina.* She stopped again. What would she say to a cousin she'd never met? Best thing was to get right to the point, which was usually her preference. All Valentina could do was ignore her. But she hoped her cousin wouldn't. What would she do then?

You don't know me, but I am your cousin Julia, daughter of Gianna De Luca, who is the daughter of Flavio Sr. and Lucia De Luca. My mother, Gianna, left Italy fifty years ago and moved to the USA. That is where I live, near Washington D.C. Sadly, my mother passed away one week ago. I wanted to let the family know, but I do not know how to reach them. I hope you'll respond to me, Valentina.

Julia stopped and reread her message. Sounded factual, cold, except for her last line. Something full and hopeful welled up inside her. Her eyes burned. Blinking, she continued typing. "I'm so happy to know that I have a cousin." She stared at it then shook her head and backspaced. No, it was too soon to be so transparent and grasping. She wouldn't want to come on too strong before meeting her cousin or at least hearing back from her.

Her finger hovered for almost a full minute before she shut her eyes and pressed "send". Almost as an afterthought, she said, "Lord, let your will be done. I'm sorry I haven't asked you before now." She'd rushed headlong into her need to find the De Lucas without asking for open doors, divine direction.

Don't get your hopes up, Julia. The voice in her head wasn't a response from God, she knew. It was a knee-jerk reaction, a voice from the past, of Gianna herself, despite Julia's prayer. It had been a prayer of ritual more than faith. Yet, so far, he'd led her to Valentina. And who could say where *that* would lead?

The following morning, Julia awakened to the sun blazing through her sheer curtains. She lay still, allowed herself several minutes to come fully alert then leaned over to look at the clock. Eight fifteen. Much later than she usually got up. Then she remembered her two-a.m. quest to locate the De Lucas. And her message to Valentina.

The younger woman would likely not answer right away, so Julia needed to be patient and focus on something else that day. Her original plan had been to return to the storage unit and hopefully finish up but her thoughts were in freefall. She tamped down her eagerness to hear from Valentina as she washed her face and made breakfast.

She made a cheddar and arugula omelet, which she ate slowly as her mind drifted again and again to the message she hoped to receive. Finally, she couldn't stand it any longer. She left her dishes where they were and padded into her home office. She sat at her desk and powered up her computer. No return message appeared from Valentina. It wasn't a surprise, but disappointment still pooled inside her. What to do next? Of course, she had to go on with her day, since she might not *ever* hear from Valentina. In that case, she could message Luca, who was also her cousin. Or eventually, Emilia, her mother's sister.

She returned to the kitchen to empty the dishwasher then started a load of laundry, forcing herself to stay away from her

Facebook page. She thought she heard a ping from her phone, which also had Facebook, and returned to her computer screen. The notification she'd heard was from an acquaintance who had a birthday. Maybe Valentina was off that day or on a trip.

As Julia sat still staring at the screen, willing it to produce a message from Valentina, the message icon popped up again. Julia clicked on it. Valentina! She'd responded. She was online at that very moment.

Ciao, Julia! I was very excited to read your message! I didn't know I had a cousin in America. What good news! I love America and have visited several times for work and for vacations. I am sorry to hear of Aunt Gianna. How very sad.

Julia cried out, "Yes!" and pumped her fist, something she never did. She almost wiggled in her chair from excitement. *Thank you, Lord!* Valentina was open, even glad to hear from her. What should she say next? *Ciao, Valentina! How happy I am to hear from you.* She paused. What to say next? *Yes, it is so sad my beloved mother died. She was sick for three years. I wanted to let you know. We lost touch with the family for many years.*

A moment or two passed. Then from Valentina, *Yes, it is sad that we haven't seen you or your mother in so long. I never met her, but I have heard of her from my mother, Emilia, who was her sister. Do you live near the capital? What do you do in America? I have so many questions for you! I hope it's okay!*

Julia grinned and her shoulders relaxed. Cousin Valentina was responding just as she'd hoped. A relationship had begun. *I live close to the nation's capital in a state called Maryland. It is near the city, though. I am an interior designer. I design décor for homes and businesses. You can ask as many questions as you want! I don't mind. It is so nice to meet you, my cousin!*

She gave herself permission to add the final phrase, sure that Valentina would welcome it. A message popped up. *Oh, your work sounds very interesting and artistic. I will come visit you someday!* Yes, yes, please do, Valentina. *Do you come to Italy sometimes? Do you want to come visit us? I'm sure the family would love to see you again.*

Julia fell back against her chair and her mouth fell open. She had vaguely hoped she could work them up to inviting her one day, but there it was, an invitation from Valentina herself. The response from her cousin was better than she'd even dreamed. She typed, *I haven't been to Italy in many years, but have wanted to return. I would love to visit one day. It would be wonderful to reunite with the family after so many years.*

She shook her head as a smile emerged on her lips. Ten minutes ago, she was alone with no family. Now, she had an invitation to travel to Europe and meet her entire Italian family. She'd get to know them as an adult, just her without her mother by her side translating everything for her while she sat silently. She could sign up for a class in Italian and maybe travel next summer. Giddy with joy, she murmured again, *Thank you, Lord! You've answered abundantly!*

A new message popped up. *How soon can you come to Italy, Julia? I know your work must keep you busy, but we have waited so long to see you! Please think about coming soon! I must get back to work now, but write to me soon! Yours, Cousin Valentina. (la tua cugina)*

Julia grinned and kept grinning on and off as she did her yoga routine and made a cup of coffee. Returning to the storage unit was no drudgery because her thoughts were far from her task all day. Her mind played a movie where she saw herself returning to Italy, meeting her cousin and all the De Lucas, finding her own place in her extended Italian family.

Hours later, she returned home, satisfied to have almost completely emptied the storage unit. In the end, it hadn't taken too long. She'd give away most of it. Now, she only needed to sweep it clean and return the keys.

As she entered her house, a wave of contentment contrasted with her angst of the previous day. How much could change in twenty-four hours! She prepared a simple meal with broiled salmon and considered how and when she could get away to visit the family. She was already taking time off from her business, so she wouldn't be able to do it again until after the New Year or the late spring.

Her phone rang. Might be one of her girlfriends. She hadn't yet texted them to tell her news. She glanced at her phone and sighed. Billy Wetherill, probably asking her out again. He didn't give up.

"Hi, Billy. What are you up to this evening?" She tried to sound friendly in a cool, cordial way that promised nothing. After all, he was her client. But she wished he'd just stick to their business dealings and accept the fact that she didn't want to date him.

"Hello, Julia. I'm between meetings and the next one is running late."

She glanced up at the kitchen clock and continued stir-frying colorful vegetables to go with her fish. "At seven in the evening? Don't you ever go home after work?" Another reason why they weren't meant for each other. The guy was a workaholic. Of course, she could be too. Quite often.

"Clients on the west coast, what can I do?" Billy said cheerfully. "It doesn't happen every day. In fact, you'd have been proud of me yesterday. I went to the gym at six."

Julia nodded. She could picture his boyish blond curls and black rimmed glasses, though he was around fifty years old. "Is there something, uh, I can help you with?" She cringed, knowing it sounded almost cold but wanting to send a message about dividing work and home.

"Yeah, sorry to bother you at home. There's a wonderful dinner for donors of the Museum of Modern Art in New York the weekend after next. I'd like to invite you to be my date. It'll be amazing. The food and entertainment are always top-notch. I've only been once, but it was unforgettable—"

Julia's mind groped for a response. She had turned him down so many times, it was almost embarrassing. She should just tell him straight out. Why was it so hard? "Billy, I really appreciate your invitation, but—"

"And some very important people will be there. Your company will get some great exposure with the movers and shakers of New York. We can fly there on Saturday morning and spend the weekend. It'll be a good getaway from the stress of work."

"I was going to tell you that I'll be in Italy then." Her hand flew to her mouth. What had she just said?

Billy paused. "Really? That's great, Julia. Is this for business or pleasure?"

"Pleasure, actually. I have some relatives there and I haven't seen them in a long time." As she spoke, she shook her head. She should have simply reminded him that she'd just lost her mother. He would have accepted that and stopped pushing. But Italy?

After hanging up, Julia sat still at the kitchen table for a long moment. It had just slipped out, maybe a subconscious desire or the result of her obsessive thoughts about contacting the family.

Valentina wanted her to come as soon as possible, or at least, that's what she'd said. Julia had the next two weeks off and had already finished with the storage shed. Could she just up and go to Italy to see the De Lucas to reconnect with her long-lost family?

Julia laughed aloud as the idea sent out tender roots that began to burrow into her heart.

Why not?

Chapter Five

The musical chatter of Italian conversations swirled around Julia as she perched on the edge of her seat in the city bus. Despite little sleep on her overnight flight, a surprising stream of energy flowed through her and she felt alert. She didn't want to miss a thing. Only yesterday, she was at home wondering how she'd spend the next two weeks. Today she was in *Italy*. Birthplace of the Renaissance. She'd actually done it. Unbelievable.

The bus rumbled through the narrow streets of Florence, turning corners sharply, narrowly missing bicyclists and curbs. Every few minutes, a few passengers stood and filled in the aisle near the door. She'd learned that meant a stop was coming up. Julia braced her hand on the seat in front of her as the bus lurched around another corner and screeched to a stop. Other passengers filed past her and joined those crowding around the door before stepping down into the street.

As the bus lurched into motion once again, she stared through the smudged window and greedily absorbed the ochre and rust-colored facades of buildings, flower boxes, and Italian script on the signs as they went by. Across the aisle through the facing windows, she glimpsed the terracotta domed roof of the famed Duomo cathedral, the tallest structure in Florence.

She hadn't been to Florence since she was a child. Yet, something was achingly familiar and the old-world charm triggered shadowy memories too distant to grasp. All that remained was a wave of something she couldn't identify, rich and promising. Almost a feeling of belonging there.

The paper she clutched in her hand was moist with perspiration. *Borgi della Scala*, number fourteen. With Valentina's help, she'd found an available hotel room rented by an elderly lady, Signora Vecchietti, across the bridge from the Old Town. She'd planned to stay two weeks, but at Valentina's suggestion, added a couple more days to make up for travel time. That was pushing it, since she'd already taken a few days for her mother. Such an un-Julia thing to do, deserting her business for over two weeks. But she'd hardly taken even a week's vacation in the last five years.

Her business would be fine without her. She could keep tabs on everything by email, with Crystal's help. She recognized that this impulsive excursion was an opportunity she wouldn't easily get again. An open door from Valentina to come and restore her family connection with the De Lucas. If she'd waited, maybe Valentina would cool off to the idea of welcoming her American cousin into the family. For now, she was rolling out the red carpet. It was also an ideal time in Julia's business, during the last sluggish days of summer before the frenetic igniting of the fall season.

And a key factor that she couldn't dispute, if she hadn't reserved time to take care of her mother's affairs, the feasibility of the trip would never have crossed her mind. That, combined with Valentina's urging *and* Julia's intense desire to see her relatives made her decision a no-brainer. As she gazed out on the ancient city unfolding before her, she knew there was another reason to have come. Florence was fabulous.

She shook her head as a chuckle lodged in her throat. Two days ago, she'd contacted Valentina for the first time on Facebook. Later the same day, she made hasty flight and hotel reservations, miraculously, given the season. Now, in just a few hours, she'd meet her cousin and step into her next chapter in Italy. If Valentina was shocked that Julia had immediately taken her up on her invitation, she hadn't shown it in her messages. She'd insisted, *My family will be as happy as I am as soon as they see you!*

Julia hoped so. A needle of tension poked through her euphoria at being in Florence. They were strangers to her, as she was to them. Were they wondering what she was thinking, landing on their doorstep out of the blue? By that time, the family would know that the long-lost De Luca was on her way to reconnect with them. She prayed it would be a happy reunion.

Valentina had written, *You should stay in central Florence, across the river in the Oltrarno neighborhood. It's very popular, but is more local than the other side of the river, which overflows with tourists. That way, you can enjoy seeing everything while you are here.*

Julia didn't need to be convinced. Any time she wasn't with the family, she'd have plenty to see and do in Florence following her forty-year absence.

The bus passed through what she assumed was the Old Town. She leaned closer to the window to drink in everything in front of her. Tall buildings and narrow streets suddenly fell away from view as the bus approached a bridge covering the wide, swirling Arno River. While crossing the bridge, her eyes followed the river. In the distance, she saw the famed Ponte Vecchio Bridge, which adorned every website, brochure, and map she'd seen during her turbo-research session the previous day. She'd seen the bridge before. It was the same one in her foggy memory of her childhood visits to Florence.

A wave of comfortable familiarity flowed through her senses. Multi colored layers of shops on the covered bridge gave the appearance of having been tossed into place over the centuries. As indeed they had been. She resisted the temptation to take a photo. She'd be there long enough to get a better view, instead of through a bus window, as well as to visit the jewelry shops that had been doing business on that very bridge for five centuries. Apparently, there had been butchers and fish shops back in the day until the 16th century when Duke Ferdinand I forcibly replaced them with jewelers, whose daily commerce smelled much better.

Once on the other side of the river, the bus turned and paralleled the riverfront. Soon, it was time for Julia to leave the safety of the bus. *"Grazie"*, she called to the bus driver after he helped her lug her suitcase from the storage compartment. Map in hand and feet on the ground, she set about locating *Borgi della Scala*, which she found to be a narrow alley several blocks away from the river. Perfect. She'd get settled then explore and eat something before meeting Valentina for a drink after her work day. Excitement mounted up inside her. *Thank you for bringing me here, Lord.* She was in a wonderful place about to meet her relatives.

Julia rang the buzzer at number fourteen. After several minutes, she heard slowly approaching footsteps then the massive wooden door pulled open. Signora Vecchietti, an elderly woman with wispy gray hair tucked into a bun, grinned broadly. *"Buongiorno, Signorina De Luca."* That was about all Julia understood, but the warmth that poured from the woman's eyes and partly toothless smile put her at ease and assured her she'd feel at home during her stay in Italy.

"*Buongiorno, Signora Vecchietti. Piacere.*" Julia hoped she'd pronounced everything correctly. She'd spent her overseas flight cramming in beginner Italian with an app she'd hastily purchased. At least Valentina seemed to have an advanced level of English. She would have to, as a European sales rep for De Luca Shoes.

Through the woman's gestures and a few words that slipped from ancient archives into Julia's mind, she understood that Signora Vecchietti lived on the ground floor and the rooms she rented were up a circular, wooden staircase.

"*Grazie, Signora.*" Key in one hand and suitcase in the other, Julia climbed up the stairs to her simple room on the second floor. A heavy red cotton bedspread, faded with years of washing, covered the double bed. The cream-colored walls were unadorned, but the view from the tall, narrow window made up for it. She looked out over the terracotta rooftops and down into the narrow streets as a thrill shuddered through her.

Julia quickly unpacked then, not wanting to waste a minute. She placed her clothes into a carved wooden armoire that appeared to be several centuries old. It could easily hold six times the amount of clothing she'd brought.

She'd also brought the letters so that at some point during her trip Valentina could translate them for her. For now, she tucked them back into the pocket of her suitcase, along with her photos of her mother, and slipped it under the bed. Fatigue from her overnight flight played a tug-of-war with anticipation inside her. She changed her shoes and was out the door before her eyes could become too heavy, eager to explore the neighborhood for a while before meeting Valentina.

Although Valentina had told her the family lived in a town several miles southwest of Florence, she herself preferred to live in the city for its nightlife, shopping, and culture. Made sense to Julia, but more importantly, provided a sense of relief and security, since she wasn't completely alone in a foreign city. Her cousin and ally lived there as well.

Two hours later, she'd scoped the nearby streets, observed the shops and people-watched. She ended up in Santo Spirito Square, the location of her appointment with Valentina. Immediately, she loved it and felt drawn by the atmosphere. Noisy, lively, and crowded, it also seemed a good place to find a snack before her cousin arrived.

Julia checked her watch as her pulse accelerated. Wouldn't be long now. She found a sandwich shop with an outdoor window and ordered a panini in English, feeling slightly ashamed of not being able to speak Italian. Not yet. She'd order in Italian her next trip, she'd already decided. Hopefully, she'd pick up a lot and start developing her ear for it during her trip.

She'd finished her panini and couldn't resist gelato for dessert. It would be all too easy to eat the decadent stuff daily and end up taking ten extra pounds back home with her. Better be disciplined with that but for now, a "welcome to Florence" sample wouldn't hurt.

She didn't expect Valentina for another half-hour, but still nervously scanned the crowds. She'd forgotten to send a current photo of herself, but was confident she could pick out her beautiful blond cousin in the crowd of tourists and locals who milled around Santo Spirito Square.

"Julia!"

The voice pierced through the rumble of the crowd around her. Julia's head shot up and her eyes darted through the crowd around her. She spotted Valentina. Her glossy, blond hair swung from a high ponytail as she jogged toward Julia. She wore jeans and a sleeveless turquoise top. She closed the space between them and stopped in front of Julia. She planted a kiss on each of Julia's cheeks. "I knew it was you. You look just like your mother." Her English was nearly perfect, laced with an appealing Italian accent.

"It's so good to see you, Valentina!" Here she was in person, her cousin Valentina. Her large blue eyes sparkled as she smiled. Her cousin. Her family. A gush of emotion welled up and a surprising sting began in Julia's eyes. She blinked it away.

"I left my work early so I could stop at my flat and be ready to meet you. I'm so happy, Julia!" Valentina slipped one arm through Julia's and drew her forward. "I know a little place that is very – um, how do you say, trendy? Is that the word?"

Julia laughed. "Yes, I can already tell that this whole area is trendy. You were right. It's very popular and energetic. I love it."

Valentina's laughter joined her own. "So, we will go there and have a drink or a coffee, whatever you want. I invite you. Have you eaten something yet?"

"Yes, I just had a panini and some gelato. A cappuccino would be nice."

"Perfect! Let's go to that street over there." She pointed down a curved pedestrian street filled with boutiques, restaurants, and shoppers.

Minutes later the women were seated outdoors on the terrace of a busy café, its warm orange and beige décor inviting, its noise and motion energetic. "Mostly locals who come here. It's one of my favorite places." Valentina settled into her seat and scanned the terrace for a waiter.

Julia sat quietly while Valentina ordered a cappuccino for her and glass of wine for herself in enviable Italian. When the waiter left, she asked, "Valentina, you said I looked like my mother. You haven't ever met my mother and any photos would be forty years old."

"We De Lucas have a family resemblance." Valentina nodded for emphasis. Her blond hair glowed like gold in the mellow light of the café. "Does not matter if we are blond or brunette, does not matter if we are young or old. It is distinct, as you will see. I saw photos of your mother and you look much like her."

"I guess I do. Everyone says so. I should look at photos of her when she was my age. I brought a few photos with me of my mother when she was younger, but they're at my hotel."

"That's fine, we'll have a lot of time to see them. Just don't forget about them. My mother, especially, would like to see them, I am sure."

"Oh, and I also brought some letters with me from Nonna Lucia to my mother and I'd like you to translate them sometime before I leave, if you don't mind." Good thing she remembered to mention the letters. They were a catalyst to her coming to Italy.

"No problem, Julia. I will be happy to do that."

The next thirty minutes flew by as Valentina and Julia talked about their lives, interests, and routines. Valentina talked about her role in the company and her relationship with Marco. Her face softened and flushed when she talked about him. It triggered in Julia a surprising stir of longing to experience those sweet, euphoric emotions for someone. It had been so long.

Julia was glad Valentina had felt open enough with her to talk about Marco. She enjoyed getting to know her cousin, hungry to know more, to picture her daily life and discover several things they had in common. Valentina ordered a second glass of wine and a sandwich while Julia declined the offer of a second cappuccino. She wanted to sleep off her jet lag that night. She was determined to waste no time by being sluggish.

"Are you married, Julia? Or do you have someone? You never said anything about a man in your life, but you are so beautiful, that would surprise me if you didn't."

Julia flushed at the compliment, which always made her feel awkward. "You're sweet, Valentina. And you are beautiful, too. No, I'm not married. I was married for ten years but I've been divorced for the last eight years. I guess I'm too picky, maybe too busy. I don't know. I haven't met anyone special." She didn't want to talk about her marital failure. At least that part of her life had been covered in the conversation and could be checked off the list. She'd likely have to do the same thing with the family once she met them.

A question had burned in Julia's mind for several days. Now, she had the prospect of a response. "Valentina, do you know why my mother never came back to Italy?"

Valentina frowned and shook her head. "No, I don't, except that I guess she must have changed her mind. I know that everyone in the family wanted her to move back to Italy but she seemed very happy in America."

Disappointment dropped like a rock inside. Valentina didn't know the cause of the seismic rupture that had occurred between Gianna and her mother, Lucia. And Valentina's guess that Gianna had simply changed her mind wouldn't account for such a dramatic event.

"Your mother never married, did she?"

That subject again. "No, she didn't. As a child, I wasn't very happy about her choice. I wanted to have a dad and siblings. Then when we stopped coming here, I lost touch with everyone in the family, too. I was only a child, so I wasn't able, of course, to visit on my own." *I would have come back if I could have.*

Julia hoped she hadn't said too much. It felt good, though, to open up to someone who could understand the situation, even if

Valentina was in the dark about why Julia and her mother never returned to Italy.

"Sounds like a lonely childhood. I'm sorry, Julia. I have my brother, Luca, my sister, Isabelle, and tons of other relatives. You may have a chance to meet everyone, and you'll wish you hadn't!"

Julia laughed. "I'm sure that's not true. I just wish I spoke Italian. I remember a word here and there from my childhood, but most of it is gone."

"Your mother didn't speak to you in Italian? Ever?"

"No, unfortunately. I didn't think too much about it until this week. Now, I really wish I had at least a few words."

"That will come, maybe while you are here. You'll go back to the States with a little Italian and a bunch of new relatives."

The women laughed. The waiter returned with Valentina's meal and second glass of wine. "I'm so hungry." She bit into her sandwich and briefly closed her eyes with pleasure.

"I did miss having relatives," Julia said, "but I have some very good friends, and now I've met you. It's so nice to have a new cousin." She smiled at Valentina.

Valentina reached across the table and squeezed Julia's forearm. "Yes, it is. So nice! Soon, you'll meet the whole family." She wiped her mouth with a paper napkin. "I'll tell them tonight that you are here."

Julia's smile fell. "They don't know I'm here? Did they at least know that I was coming? Didn't you—" she stopped herself and pressed her lips together. The last thing she wanted was for Valentina to think she was criticizing. "I'm afraid they won't be prepared to meet me. They'll be very surprised, won't they?" She should have known not to be too optimistic. Unprepared, the family could react to her with shock, indifference, or even anger.

Valentina waved the air dismissively. "It will be fine. We sometimes have the midday meal together as a family, just to stay up to date on everyone, though we see each other *constantly* at the office and factory." She gave a slight roll of her eyes. "We often end up talking about business anyway. Shoes, shoes. Always, shoes. This competitor, that leather vendor. I will tell them tonight about you and you will come to lunch tomorrow. *D'accordo?* It's okay?"

A thread of discomfort wrapped around Julia's stomach. It would have to be okay. Her arrival would be an even bigger surprise than she thought for the De Luca clan. They likely hadn't thought of Gianna or Julia for at least three decades. "I know you didn't have much time to prepare everyone, I came so quickly. Yes, it's good if they are willing to meet me."

"Willing?" Valentina hitched her head back as if shocked. "You are family! They'll be overjoyed, you'll see. And I'm so very glad you came quickly, my Julia. I was so eager to meet my American cousin. I'm sure we will become great friends."

Again, tears sprang into Julia's eyes. "Yes, I'm sure as well." She touched Valentina's arm and blinked the sting away.

Two hours later, the urgency of sleep fell on Julia like a stone as she changed clothes and washed her face. The last twenty-four hours had been like a dream. Her evening with Valentina, the pinnacle of the dream. Her cousin who, despite their age difference, accepted her completely and joyfully, would be her ambassador into the rest of the family. She couldn't have asked for more.

Her phone buzzed. Valentina had texted. *I hope you are not sleeping, Giulia! You can come tomorrow for the midday meal at the house. You will take a train and a bus. I'm sorry I cannot pick you up, because I will be coming from the factory, which is close to the villa. I will give you the instructions below including the name of the stop where you will get off the bus. I will meet you at this bus stop. You should allow about one hour to come here. Take the 11:10 train from the Santa Maria Novella train station in the direction of Chianti. I know you can drink Chianti, but it is also a region near Florence!* Smiley emoji.

Below her message was a small paragraph of instructions about the bus number and the name of the bus stop. A bolt of excitement stabbed through Julia's fatigue. Tomorrow she'd meet the rest of the De Luca family. *Her* family.

Chapter Six

Julia shaded her eyes against the midday sun with one hand as she watched the bus rumble away. She stood still and alone, surrounded by green and golden hills covered with vineyards and distant manor homes, each one perched on its own hill surveying the rolling land on every side. When the bus grew smaller and disappeared, the silence grew louder. She shifted her weight and cast a glance in every direction as she listened for the faint sound of a motor.

Where was Valentina?

Julia stole a glance at her watch then kicked the dirt roadside beside the asphalt, trying to calm her nerves. At least she'd slept long and well and had enjoyed wonderful Italian coffee and a *cornetta* at a corner café she'd discovered. Well worth the pound or so it had likely put on her.

When she saw a car, a speck in the distance, she uttered a prayer. As it approached, she saw Valentina's blond head through the windshield. She waved an arm out the window and pulled up beside Julia. "*Buongiorno*, Cousin. I hope your journey this morning went smoothly. I'm just now coming from the factory. I had some meetings this morning. Did you sleep well?"

Julia slid into the passenger seat and tucked her woven purse between her feet, along with a bouquet of flowers for Emilia.

Valentina wore skinny beige pants and a dressy matching print top with elegant folds down the front.

Before Julia could respond to Valentina's question, Valentina continued talking. "So, today we will be six at lunch. There will be my parents, Sergio and Emilia, you and me, and then Uncle Giuseppe and his wife, Paola. You may remember them. They live at the villa. We won't have Luca with us today. He has out of town meetings all week. Even when he is in town and is a part of the family, he doesn't socialize with us too much. I guess my brother thinks he sees everyone plenty at work." She laughed and turned down a rural street flocked with grape vineyards on either side. "He has his own family. His wife, Sofia, and they have two kids, Diego, who is twelve, and Alessandra, who is nine."

When Valentina paused, Julia asked, "What about Uncle Flavio? Is he still alive?"

"No, unfortunately he died about ten years ago from a heart attack. We miss him. He was your mother's youngest brother."

"I remember him. He used to make funny faces and jokes. I'm sorry he's gone. I guess my mother was the oldest of the four kids. Your mother is much younger than the other siblings, isn't she?"

Valentina set her arm along the open car window. "She was the surprise baby who came much later. I was a surprise baby, too. My sister, Isabelle, is ten years older than I am."

"How old are you?"

"I'm thirty-two. Isabelle is forty-two. And you?"

"I'm forty-eight."

"You and Isabelle are closer in age, then."

That probably didn't matter. Julia couldn't imagine feeling closer to Isabelle than she already did to Valentina. "I didn't know there was another cousin. I must have forgotten. So, there are three of you." Three cousins at once. Julia suppressed a smile.

"Three in my family. Then you can add Giuseppe's kids, Edouardo and Martina. They are your cousins, too, but they don't live in Florence. Flavio was divorced and didn't have any children. Isabelle is divorced and has a daughter, Mia. Mia is at university, so we don't see her much. We hardly see Isabelle, either, although she works in the office of the shoe factory. You won't meet her today because she's on a trip."

"Does everyone have their own homes, like you do? I mean, how many family members live in the house we're going to today?" Julia had a thousand questions, but she hoped she wasn't revealing her near complete ignorance of Italian culture.

Valentina didn't seem to mind. "Most of us have our own homes. Giuseppe and Paola live at the big house with my parents because they are elderly. Though Giuseppe would argue with me, because he insists he isn't elderly." She laughed. "The house is big enough for all of them, as you'll see. Isabelle and her daughter live in a small town nearby. My parents have a lot of company out to the house. Dinners with industry people, vendors. Lots of people all the time. It's nice sometimes, but I need a break and a separate life, so I live in Firenze. In Florence, I mean."

"And Marco? Where does he live?"

"Marco lives on the other side of Florence, so it's not hard for us to see each other when we have time. Which we don't often have, unfortunately." The car slowed in front of a small road where Valentina turned. "Here we are."

Julia's stomach tightened as a stately peach-colored villa with terracotta roof came into view. As Valentina had said, it was big. Seemed like a lot of house for four people. It wasn't the same home that Julia saw in her cloudy memories, but as she'd noticed, her memory wasn't sharp about those days.

Valentina pulled the car into a broad, circular driveway where two cars were already parked. They got out of the car and Valentina led the way through a wrought iron gate into a small, sunny courtyard where several large clay pots overflowed with flowers and vines. She pushed through a tall set of coffered wooden doors into the villa. They entered a long, tiled hallway, empty and cool. A breeze flowed in from an open window at the other end of the hall and an appealing roasted meat aroma hung in the air. To the left stood a wide stone staircase.

"Mamma, noi siama qui con Giulia!" called Valentina.

After a few moments of silence, Julia heard slow footsteps. In the doorway on her right appeared the woman she'd seen on the company website. Aunt Emilia.

She wore stylish and professional-looking gray pants and a coordinating floral blouse. Her graying hair was cropped short. A slight half-smile curved her lips, but her eyes didn't reflect the welcome. Rather, they retained the same coolness that Julia had seen in her photo.

Emilia's eyes roved over Julia. What must she be thinking? *Is this really Julia? What's she doing here, coming to Italy out of the blue?*

Julia smiled as her heart pounded in her chest. She felt she was being examined for fitness at a slave auction or a livestock sale. She mustered one of the phrases she'd learned on the flight. *"Buongiorno, Zia Emilia. Non parlo molto Italiano."* May as well apologize up front for her lack of Italian language. From a sweaty grip, she extended the bouquet of flowers to Emilia, holding her smile as if affixed with glue.

The woman waved off her apology and stepped forward. "Thank you." She took the flowers without looking at them and set them on a small table beside her. "Let me see you, Julia. I remember your face as a child, but you are grown now. You have your mother's face." After a brief silence during which she stared at Julia's face, she said softly, as if to herself, "It's almost like looking at her."

Her gaze fell to Julia's necklace. Julia couldn't interpret the sober expression that sculpted her aunt's face, like a wistful sadness. Her voice softened. "I remember this necklace from my mother." When her eyes lifted again to Julia's she extended her hands and, without smiling, grasped both Julia's in hers. "At last, you have come to see us."

Was her aunt glad she'd come, or reprimanding her for not coming sooner? Julia couldn't decipher Emilia's tone. A faint gnawing of discomfort began in her gut. "I didn't know your address or have any information all these years. I'm so sorry we lost touch." *But I'm here now.* She had a childish urge to defend herself, but held it back. It was the first five minutes and she shouldn't expect all of the family members to be as warm and accepting as Valentina had been. After all, it had been nearly four decades. Almost Julia's entire life. They were strangers, yet had a lot of catching up to do.

Emilia might be wondering why Julia had chosen *that* time for a visit. Maybe with the success of De Luca Shoes, the sudden arrival of a distant relative was suspicious. Did she think Julia was after their money? She cringed. That would be the *last* thing she'd come for.

Julia pushed her doubts and questions aside. She *had* come and would make the best of it. Whatever the outcome. "Yes, Zia Emilia. It has been much too long. I'm so blessed to be here, finally, with all of you, even though it's a sad event that made me realize how important family is."

Emilia's stern lips widened ever so slightly then her expression clouded. "I'm saddened to hear about Gianna's passing. You will tell us what happened during lunch. Come with me to the patio." She walked slowly like an old woman or one with a burden, although she seemed only in her late fifties or early sixties. Julia exchanged glances with Valentina, who had been silent since their arrival.

"Mamma, where is everyone?" she asked.

"They are coming. *Ascolti, Giuseppe, lui vene.*" Giuseppe was coming.

Julia heard footsteps in the adjoining room before she saw him. Uncle Giuseppe. For some reason, his face had remained in her mind's eye while all the others had disappeared. Same Stalin-like mustache, now white. Julia launched into her prepared greeting. *"Zio Giuseppe, Buongiorno. Ce Giulia."*

He shuffled toward her, hands outstretched, and said something in Italian. His smile stretched wide under his mustache and his eyes glistened with tears as he grasped her hands in his. He raised her hands to his lips and kissed them. His tears and his gesture caused her throat to tighten. Her eyes filled. She blinked. Her Uncle Giuseppe remembered her and was glad to see her.

"My English not good. It get better. Happy you are here, Julia."

"Thank you, Uncle. I'm happy, too." She grinned at him and squeezed his hands which still held hers.

"Come." Emilia interrupted the exchange and marched ahead toward the patio. Everyone fell into step behind her like humble soldiers in training.

They all stepped down from the house to a large flagstone patio topped with wide strips of canvas shades and tangled grape vines. A large glass table was already set for a meal. Beyond the patio, gentle green hills and vineyards rolled out as far as her eyes could see. "This is beautiful. Stunning." The majestic scene invaded Julia's senses. She glimpsed an inviting stone path and a garden beyond it. The scene brought to mind a travel magazine.

Minutes after they sat down at the table, a young woman wearing a long, beige apron brought out a large platter of various meats and raw vegetables and placed it on the table. Antipasto. Julia's stomach growled. Her morning *cornetto* and coffee were long gone, though her anxiety had distracted her until that moment.

"*Grazie*, Amara," Valentina and Emilia told the girl. For the last half hour, Valentina had been uncharacteristically quiet. Was bubbly Valentina intimidated around her mother?

Just as Julia wondered about the other two lunch guests, they both arrived, a man and a woman. They must be Paola and Sergio, Giuseppe's wife and Emilia's husband. Julia stood and approached them. Sergio, clad in a crisp summer suit that was perfectly tailored, stood several inches taller than her own five-foot seven. His graying hair and direct gaze matched his generally authoritative bearing.

He held out his hands as Emilia had and grasped Julia's, but unlike Emilia, gave her a warm smile. "Welcome to Italy, Julia. We are happy for your visit." His English was almost as good as Valentina's. It was possible Julia had met him years before, but couldn't remember and certainly wasn't going to admit it.

Paola approached Julia with a shy smile and kind, light blue eyes, a network of wrinkles around them. The older woman leaned forward to kiss Julia's cheeks. She said something in Italian then took her seat next to Giuseppe.

Once they were seated around the glass patio table, Emilia wasted no time. "Tell us about your mother, Julia." She reached for the carafe of water. "What was her life like? Why did she pass away? Was she ill?" She frowned. "We've had no news for thirty-eight years, aside from a card at holidays."

Julia swallowed and considered her words while everyone at the table waited for her response. "I know that's a long time and I'm sorry about that." Julia glanced at each person then settled her gaze back on Emilia. "I don't know the reason why she stopped visiting. I was really sad that she did, because I missed all of you."

Emilia nodded, seeming disinterested in Julia's apology on behalf of her mother, but silently waited for an answer to the mystery of Gianna De Luca.

Julia served herself from the plate of antipasto that came her way then passed it to Giuseppe, seated next to her. "For most of my childhood, we lived in a suburb of New York city. There were a lot of Italians in that region and my mother had some Italian friends." Julia smiled at a mental picture that floated into her mind, that of her mother sitting at their kitchen table talking in animated Italian with two girlfriends. It must have given her comfort to be able to communicate in her mother tongue and make friends from her homeland. Julia had almost forgotten that memory. "Some time after our last trip to Italy, my mother started nursing school. She completed a three-year program but she worked at the same time, so she was very busy. I didn't even see her much." She managed a conciliatory smile. "Then she worked at our local hospital until retiring about fifteen years ago."

"She not marry?" Giuseppe leaned forward.

Julia shook her head. "No, she never got married. She almost did once, but it didn't work out. After that, I guess she didn't meet anyone she loved like my father." She hated to mention Joe Connelly, but he would provide a reasonable explanation for Gianna's choice to remain single.

Amara brought in a plate of pasta, which looked and smelled delicious, though seemed heavy for a noon meal. "*Il primo piatto,*" she announced as she placed the platter on the table. Julia made a mental note to ask Valentina what that meant.

Paola asked Julia a question in Italian. Sergio leaned forward. "She wants to know what happened to your mother. Why did she die?"

Julia flinched at Sergio's words. "Unfortunately, she had a lung problem called emphysema, then on top of that, about three years ago, she developed Alzheimer's." Sergio and Emilia both nodded and exchanged glances. Sergio turned to Paola and translated into Italian. Paolo shook her head in sympathy. She said something to Julia in Italian.

"She says she's sorry about your mother and is very sad. She remembers your beautiful mother very well."

"She lost her mother and we lost our sister." Emilia's tone was hard. "Of course, we lost her many years ago. It was as though she had died back then."

Julia stared at Emilia, sensing the wall surrounding her. Though her aunt's anger and hurt over Gianna's desertion of the family was understandable, her tone cut into Julia's fragile optimism. Emilia wouldn't be easy to win over.

Sergio didn't respond to his wife or look at her. "Tell us more about your life and your work in America, Julia. Where do you live?"

"I live in a town near Washington, D.C. You probably know it's the nation's capital. I have my own business as an interior designer. I design the décor in houses, office buildings, hotels, different places."

"Sounds very interesting," Sergio said.

Might be a good time to set their minds at rest that she was not after their money. "It has become very successful, I'm happy to say. I have four full-time employees and a store. We have a lot of work right now and a good income." She smiled around the table but saw Emilia stiffen slightly. Hard to say, because she'd looked stiff since

Julia's arrival. Maybe she'd said too much. *I'm not after anything from you. Just some family connection.*

"It's amazing that you have time to come see us." Emilia's tone was cool.

"Julia took time off when Gianna died." Valentina finally spoke up. She reached for the bowl of pasta. "She wrote to me on Facebook to try to contact the family to let us know about her passing, but I was able to convince her to come visit."

Julia relaxed her shoulders. Cousin Valentina was finally helping her out. They would know now that her original desire was only to notify them about her mother's death. They wouldn't need to know how desperate a need *she* had to find them.

"We're glad you did, Valentina. Good job." Sergio sent an approving nod in Valentina's direction.

"After you and your mother stopped coming to Italy, my mother, your Nonna Lucia, became so ill with grief that she died."

Julia gasped at Emilia's words. "Oh, I'm so sorry. That's very sad. As I said, I don't know the reasons she stopped coming. She worked a lot at the hospital and was a single mother. That's all I can tell you." Defending again. Which she should stop doing. But this time, on behalf of her mother. So, Emilia had a second reason for the sour expression on her face.

"*Anche, nostra madre era malata,*" offered Giuseppe, who had only been listening and observing.

"True, true." Sergio wiped his mouth with a large cloth napkin. "He says that Lucia, their mother, was also sick. Meaning, she was already sick with a heart problem. The situation with your mother may have aggravated her condition, but didn't cause her death."

Julia nodded with a thread of relief, but still wanted to squirm in her seat. She had unsuspectingly walked into a family minefield in which her mother had been the primary protagonist. But had her mother's decision been the cause of some deeper family trauma or the result?

"Does anyone mind if we change the subject?" Valentina suggested cheerfully.

Julia felt grateful to Valentina for the prospect of a break in the tension. She focused on her pasta, which was delicious. She wouldn't need dinner that evening. Just more gelato. She set down her fork and Amara whisked in to clear the dishes away. Five minutes later, she returned with a large platter of meat and a bowl of vegetables. It appeared to be a second main course. "*Il piatto secondo,*" Amara announced. "*Vitello primavera.*" Sergio began passing the platter.

"I might be too full to eat more," Julia confessed. "Though the pasta was very good."

Valentina and Sergio laughed. Valentina said, "You're not used to the way we do things here in Italy. The pasta dish is only the first course. Sometimes the first course is lighter than pasta, but you are our special guest today, so it's fancier. *Il primo piatto* means the first course, meaning there's another one coming. This one is veal."

"*Il secundo* . . . the second," Julia and Valentia said at the same time as the meaning registered. Julia hadn't paced herself and hoped she wouldn't offend anyone if she only picked at her veal. Emilia's frown didn't budge as she stared past her family to the hills beyond the patio.

"Paola says to stop arguing about Gianna. She wants to tell you about her family," Sergio said. "I quite agree. We are grieved about Gianna's passing but we don't need to dig up the old wounds."

Julia felt a mixture of relief and curiosity, because she was certain the conflict went deeper. Paola might not have followed much of the verbal communication, but she seemed to understand the tension and outdated frustrations revolving around Gianna. *Thank you, Paola, for changing the subject.*

As the older woman spoke, Sergio translated for her. "She says she and Giuseppe are over seventy years old and they have two grown children, Martina and Edouardo. Martina is married to Francisco. They live in Verona and they have two grown sons, Cosimo and Federico. Edouardo was married to Carmina. She died three years ago and he is remarried to Stella. He and Carmina had three children, Jacopo, Livia, and Luciana. They live in Bergamo, which is not far from Verona in the north near the lake district. All of the grandchildren are in their twenties or thirties. She says that she's proud of all of her children and grandchildren, though they don't visit enough."

The string of Italian names evaporated from Julia's memory a moment after they were spoken. She smiled and said to Paola, "Sounds like a lovely family. *Una bella familia.*" Paola smiled and nodded back at her. The poor woman either couldn't or didn't want to weigh in on the saga of Gianna's desertion of the family, so she chose to talk about her favorite topic. A safe choice.

Julia smiled at Paola and Sergio. "I'm sure all grandmothers think their children and grandchildren don't visit often enough."

"*Exactamento.*" Sergio let out a hearty laugh. "The kids, they have their own lives. Just like Gianna had hers. She wanted to live in America, so let her live in America. We loved her but she didn't belong to us." Emilia didn't respond.

After lunch, Sergio, Giuseppe, and Valentina escorted Julia to the gardens in back of the villa to give her a tour of the grounds. The visit gave her another chance to drink in the beauty of the estate. The two men seemed warm and accepting, so maybe it was just a matter of time before she'd receive the same from Emilia. Clearly, there were many wounds that still ached and plenty of turbulent water under the De Luca family bridge. She hoped her presence would begin to put a salve on the wounds that were apparent that day.

After a delicate chocolate cake and sorbet, Valentina stood up and announced, "Well, Julia, are you ready to return to Florence? I'm going there now and can give you a ride so you don't have to take the bus."

Abrupt as it seemed, Julia was ready to leave. Hopefully, her subsequent visits would go more smoothly, that is, if she were even invited to return. By the look on Emilia's face, she wasn't so sure.

Julia said goodbye to the family members, who all responded, "*A presto, Julia.*" Emilia accompanied Valentina and Julia to the front door.

Valentina gave her mother a kiss on one cheek. "*A domani, mamma.*"

"*Alora*, Julia, we forgot to ask how long you'll be in Italy. Two weeks, I think Valentina told us, *vero*?"

"Yes, two weeks in Italy plus two additional days for traveling. I'm enjoying this region of Italy already. It's so beautiful." Julia smiled, hoping Emilia's features would soften before she left.

"After that, will you disappear in America and we'll never hear from you again?" The edge had returned to Emilia's voice and her face took on a sudden distracted air.

Time to give some reassurance. Julia's eyes boldly pinned her aunt's as she took her hands. "Now that I have found you again, I want to stay in touch. We are family and time doesn't change this." She hoped her words penetrated her aunt's brittle wounds. More softly she added, "I loved my mother and respect her memory, but I am my own person. I made the choice to come here, so I hope that counts."

Then she saw it. A flicker in Emilia's eyes, a shadowy smile that stretched a bit further. "*Bene*," was all she said.
Good.

Chapter Seven

"There you are. Sorry I'm late, Julia." Valentina looked flushed, though gorgeous, as she slipped into the seat across from Julia at the Lorenzo Café in Old Town. She wore a gray pencil skirt, a red, scoop-neck sleeveless top, and black stiletto heels with long, pointy toes. Her sunglasses pulled her hair away from her face.

"You look like a fashion model, Valentina. Are those De Luca shoes you're wearing?" Julia grinned. It was as though Valentina had already become a friend instead of only a cousin she'd known nothing about a week earlier. She took a deep sip of cappuccino, savoring the rich flavor. Even though the summer sun sweltered already at ten in the morning, hot Italian coffee had quickly become a daily craving.

Valentina pulled a mischievous expression. "I'd never hear the end of it if I didn't wear De Luca shoes. If a woman admires them, I can tell her they're from De Luca." She caught the eyes of the waitress in hers and nodded before turning back to Julia. "I have some meetings here in the city this afternoon, which is why I had some time this morning to meet you. By the way, I have scheduled a tour of the factory for you tomorrow, if you like."

"Yes, I'd love that. Thank you, Valentina." That must be a sign that she was being accepted by the family. Or maybe Valentina was acting on her own and they'd all wonder what she was doing there.

A waitress set a tiny espresso cup in front of Valentina. *"Grazie."* She smiled at her and picked up the demitasse. Valentina must be a regular, since the waitress knew just what she wanted.

She took a delicate sip. "I thought you'd enjoy seeing what happens at De Luca Shoes. Those of us who are commercial reps travel a lot and are rarely in the factory. I'm glad I wasn't scheduled to travel much this month during your visit. It's August, which is when everything slows down in Europe. Everything will be busier next month when the trade shows start. After the factory tour, of course you will stay for dinner, *si?"*

"Si." Julia wouldn't miss that for anything. She'd been invited back. Another good indication of her status as part of the family. "Will there be other family members at the dinner?" Given the long list of names she'd heard, though not retained, she'd likely meet more family members before returning home.

"The same as yesterday, but also a few people in the shoe business."

"Maybe your mother will be in a better mood." Julia had hesitated to dive into the subject of the family meal the day before.

Valentina's face clouded. "Yes, she wasn't very friendly, was she? She is still angry with your mother. More hurt than angry. I hoped she'd get over it when she found out Gianna had died. But maybe now she feels worse because of the years she lost."

"I understand her sadness. It must have been very painful for her, regardless of the reason." Julia's curiosity tugged at her mind. "Were they close as children? They were quite a few years apart in age."

Valentina frowned and pursed her lips. "They were eleven years apart. I don't know if they were close, since she never spoke about Gianna very much after she stopped coming to Italy. I think my mother may have admired Gianna, as her older sister who was grown up. But they were in different generations. I know she feels strongly about family and felt your mother, in a way, broke up the family." She shrugged and waved the air. "My mother will get over it and she will like you just fine. You shouldn't worry about the family, especially my mother. Everyone seems to like you. You are family, but we still need to get to know you." She chuckled then. "They'll know you're not a boastful American."

Julia's coffee cup stopped halfway to her mouth. "What do you mean?"

"People in Europe don't talk about their success the way Americans do. It is a cultural thing."

"Oh, no!" A cold wave flowed through Julia's chest. What had she done? "I am totally the opposite, Valentina. If you knew me better, you would know I'm telling the truth, that I'm very discreet about my success." She put a hand to her forehead. This was terrible, the opposite impression she'd wanted to make on her "new" family. "I feel horrified. I sensed your mother didn't like me so I thought she was afraid I had shown up out of nowhere to get money or something. I wanted her to know that I don't need De Luca money. I only wanted a connection with the family." Her efforts to reassure the family of her motivations had just blown up in her face. And on the first day.

Valentina laughed and reached out a hand to squeeze Julia's forearm. "Oh, don't worry, my Julia! I understand what you're saying. It wasn't really as bad as you think. They admire what you've been able to do by yourself. It's the spirit of business success, which they share."

Julia frowned. "Well, it's too late now. At least they know I'm not after their money."

"I don't know if that even crossed anyone's mind. As I said, don't worry. You've been invited back for dinner, so my mother is not afraid of your reasons for coming to Italy." She dabbed her lips with a napkin and pulled a tube of lipstick from her purse. "So, that's tomorrow. You can come to the same bus stop as yesterday, but come later, around three in the afternoon. You'll have some time to yourself tonight and tomorrow morning. You should visit the city while you're here. I don't think you've had much time to see anything yet. The Duomo, L'Uffizi, Palazzo Pitti, Palazzo Vecchio. Have you gone to the bridge, the Ponte Vecchio?"

"No, I haven't done anything but wander around Oltrarno. I've been very happy doing that, but I do want to see the important sites of Florence, too. Feels like I've never been here before, even though I have a couple of vague memories from my childhood."

"Good, you'll have a chance to do that. You can't go back to America just seeing the family house and my sour mamma! I insist you enjoy your stay in Florence."

As soon as both women left the coffee shop, Julia decided to take Valentina's advice. She'd gotten a city map from her landlady, Signora Vecchietti, and it led her down narrow one-lane streets overshadowed by apartment buildings. She couldn't stop staring at the architecture, so distinctly European, wanting to soak in the fact that she was standing there in Florence, Italy. For sure, she'd be inspired by everything she saw and could incorporate new ideas into her designs. She was unable to hold back from stopping into attractive stores to observe the layout, the displays, and the structure. She hadn't left her designer's mind at home, but aside from observing and taking a few notes and photos, she wouldn't think too much about work. Her task was simply to absorb the present moment and keep all other thoughts at bay.

The shadows brightened as the streets gave way to a large square crammed with tourists gawking at the most important site in Florence, the Duomo. The thirteen-century church could only be called immense. Its façade, unlike many sculptured stone or concrete churches she'd seen around Europe, was of green, white, and rose marble, which gave the impression of a monstrously large but stunning wedding cake.

If she'd planned to go inside the edifice, the miles of tourists in a line that snaked around the square deterred her. Instead, she took several photos with her phone then found a perch nearby to observe the Piazza del Duomo square and its crowds. Since meeting the De Luca family the day before, the prospect of being by herself in one of the world's most beautiful cities didn't overwhelm her with solitude, as it might otherwise have done. She was a De Luca, connected to a family rooted in Tuscany for generations. And tomorrow she'd see their shoe factory. Her mild interest in the fabrication of shoes was heightened by the family's involvement in it.

After people-watching for thirty more minutes, it was time for a gelato, her first of the day. Yesterday, she'd had Stracciatella, or chocolate chip. Today, she'd try *Arancia*, orange. Maybe she'd be able to get through all the flavors available in Italy before she boarded the plane in two weeks.

She gazed back at the imposing Duomo, with its immense brick dome, while she licked the creamy treat. Her mind wandered to the thousands of people who'd passed through those doors to seek God over the last seven centuries.

A wave of melancholy swept over her as she considered her own faith, currently a barren hole, due quite simply to neglect. She'd first encountered God in college when she'd roomed with Eden and later met Marissa and Sydney. Eden had brought her to some Christian activities and she'd slowly been won over by the promise of a heavenly Father who could love her so much and always be present, unlike Joe, who'd been nothing more than a name and a photo. She later understood that the very pain she felt growing up from *not* having a father had prepared her to whole-heartedly acknowledge a perfect heavenly Father.

She'd embraced him with joy, along with so many new faith siblings. Her closed-down heart began to unfurl like a spring flower. For a while. Years after her initial growth spurt, her elation had somehow seeped away. After college and design school, she'd worked for a few years, met Nick and married him. Her faith was diluted year by year until it sat like a pale, neglected puddle inside her. It had been a while since she'd thought about those first glorious days filled with her love for God and her wonder at his love for her.

To Julia's surprise, her eyes filled and her throat ached. How had she drifted so far? She missed those days. Missed him. Now, she had little connection, given the occasional snatches of online church she found time for. The aloneness of her in-person visits had been unbearable amidst a noisy, thrumming crowd of thousands.

She ought to find a smaller church. And face her part in letting her heart become cold. Distant. *Lord, where do I start? Maybe I'm here in beautiful Florence so I can reach out to you again.* She flicked at the tears that hovered on her cheeks. She'd just had two major turning points in her life, the loss of a parent and the gaining of an extended family. Maybe it was time to nudge another vital pivot into existence with baby steps in *his* direction. She'd planned on the rediscovery of her extended family, but maybe God meant her to rediscover him as well.

Those thoughts stayed with her, like God's presence itself, as her afternoon unfolded. Her wanderings took her to the *Piazza della Signoria*, where dozens of marble statues decorated the square. Along one side was the Uffizi Museum, a "must-see destination containing matchless works of art—", according to her late-night research before the trip. A few blocks away was the Galleria dell'Academia, where the famed sculpture of Michelangelo's David resided. There'd been no time to buy tickets online for either one. But really, she wouldn't spend hours to see sculptures and paintings when her real reason for coming to Florence was completely different. One day there'd be time for museums and tours. Nevertheless, a copy of the David statue stood in naked grandeur in the square, so for now, she'd be satisfied with that and the many other statues in the open air.

At the Ponte Vecchio, she browsed the centuries-old jewelry shop windows and bought a small cross-body bag from a leather vendor. Then she continued across the bridge toward Oltrarno. The neighborhood where she put her temporary roots already felt like home.

As she approached her street, she rounded a corner and encountered a festive explosion of color. Fresh flowers of all shades and shapes spilled from pots and trays. Like a special gift for her alone, she stood and absorbed the beauty of creation, the soothing quality of color, until tears sprang into her eyes. A gentle touch from God saying, *I see you, Julia. I heard your heart cry for Me. Here, I made these just for you. I know you'll enjoy them.*

Julia blinked and smiled at the words that had come into her mind. She bought a small multicolored bouquet and simple glass vase to keep in her rented room. To fill her heart with color. To remind her of his voice every time she looked at it.

The following day when the bus dropped Julia off in the middle of nowhere for the second time, her jittery nerves had been replaced by anticipation. The worst was behind her. Along with that hope, her reawakened faith placed an extra layer of confidence she could experience, like a warm embrace around her.

As she waited for Valentina to arrive, she scrolled through her emails, which she'd neglected since landing in Florence. One email from Crystal, who had promised to keep her up to date only as much as she wanted. Of course, she did want occasional news of the store, just to be assured that all was going smoothly in her absence, but found that hours would elapse without her even thinking of the business it had taken years to establish. The previous day, she'd had a short note from Eden saying simply, *Hope you are having a blast, Julia! You're in my thoughts and prayers*!

Just today, Sydney had sent a longer email. *Hey, Julie-Baby! I assume you arrived safely and already met the fam. So, did they fall in love with you? I'm sure they did! Let me know all is well so I won't worry. As for me, summer was way too short and I've already started a new school year. My new students seem surly and disinterested in math. You know, it gets harder every year to go back after the summer. I should probably think of making a change, but no idea what I'd do. I still have a teenager to support for a couple years, so I can't be too fancy-free. (Otherwise, I would have hidden in your suitcase!) Sorry to complain. I admit, I'm a bit super-jealous of you! But lovingly, of course. You deserve it and I hope it's fabulous! Love ya, Sydney.*

Julia chuckled. Despite Sydney's dead-end situation, just hearing from her in her humorous way had brought to mind her valued connection with her friends, who were like sisters. She hadn't updated them since her arrival. It would have to wait, though, because she spotted Valentina's car in the distance on the deserted country road.

Twenty minutes later, they arrived at an imposing brick building with a large, modern sign in front, *De Luca Scarpe*

Internazionale. De Luca Shoes. So, this was it. The De Luca empire. Finally, she'd see what went on inside, the trade that had defined the De Lucas for decades.

Valentina was dressed more casually than Julia had yet seen her, in faded jeans and a sleeveless blouse. Her hair swung from a high ponytail, suitable to make her a relaxed tour guide for Julia's factory visit. Julia had worn her favorite tunic and capris with sandals. Hopefully, she'd look appropriate for both the factory tour and the dinner with distinguished shoe industry guests later on that evening.

Julia got out of the car and followed Valentina into the building. A flutter of excitement began as they entered the De Luca shoe empire.

Valentina greeted a receptionist and said something to her in Italian. She gestured to Julia, probably explaining who she was and why they were there. The receptionist smiled at Julia and said something. Julia understood *"Benvenuto—"*, welcome, though the remainder of the woman's sentence disappeared in a musical blur of sound. Julia was starting to get used to that.

"I think I told you that I'm not here in the factory very often." Valentina lowered her voice. "Once the fall begins, I travel about sixty percent of the time." She led Julia through a doorway into a large room where several women worked at desks arranged in rows. On either wall, doors to private offices were mostly closed. "Our administrative staff works here in this area." She gestured to the group of women. "The management employees' offices are behind those doors along each wall, but most of us aren't at our desks too much. People either travel or visit the different departments to check on everything."

Julia scanned the room before they headed to another set of doors. Most of the women didn't glance up from their work as

Valentina and Julia went into the next room, where the décor changed to resemble a workshop more than a factory. Several men and women stood around tables and along counters working by hand with what appeared to be tissue paper and wooden shoe molds.

Valentina stopped walking and lowered her voice. "This is where the process begins, you could say. It's a pattern room where the design is put onto this paper and worked out before the leather is cut."

"I can see why that would be important." Julia remembered her mother's admonishment to measure twice and cut once, when she'd been young and crafting clothing and décor out of fabric.

"After that, it's measured against a block of wood in the shape of the shoe they're making. In English, that block is called a *last*. It's the basic shape the shoe will have. Once the leather has been able to sit on the last for a few days, it can be removed and the leather will maintain the shape. Many types of shoes begin with the upper. That's the most complex part to build, then the sole is added as one of the last things. If a woman's shoe has a tall heel, that is added sooner."

"I had no idea that any of this was still done by hand." Julia watched as the employees worked silently.

"Not all shoes you see or buy in stores are made this way. Many are manufactured almost entirely by automation and assembly line. Of course, this is reflected in the price. Ours are made with a combination of hand work and machines run by employees."

A nearby door swung open and a tall man with frizzy reddish hair strode through, barking orders to the workers at the table nearest him. Then he leaned over and showed something to one of the men working on the *last*. As he murmured to the artisan and pointed things out in his work, Valentina leaned in toward Julia.

"That's Fabrizio. He's our designer. He is a very central part of the factory. We have other designers, too, but he has been with De Luca for a long time and has a lot of authority."

Fabrizio toured the room and surveyed the workers before acknowledging Valentina. He nodded to her and said, "*Buon pomeriggio,*" but kept walking before she could say anything or introduce Julia.

"Let's continue on to the next phase." She led Julia toward the open doorway, which had no door, to the next room, an open space where large hides of leather covered every surface. "This room is where the leather is cut. They use a very sharp knife to cut around the patterns that were made. The knives make a clicking noise, so some people call this the clicking room." She smiled. Julia hadn't noticed before but heard clicking like metallic insects in the otherwise quiet room. For a moment, Valentina and Julia observed the artisans cutting the leather and shaping it against the *last*.

Valentina led Julia to some of the tables so that she could see the process, then toward the next doorway. Keeping her voice low, she said, "In Tuscany, we have a lot of small to medium-sized shoe factories that are family-owned. This area has always had a lot of tanneries and is a central place for shoes and accessories. There is another large center of shoe companies in a town called Le Marche, to the northeast of Florence near the coast. Shoe making in Italy began there over one hundred years ago. Come, let's continue."

They walked through a double door and immediately, Julia understood why the doors were in place. Machine noise filled the air as employees worked at stations around the room on a variety of equipment.

Valentina stopped again and whispered, "This is the closing room, where the shoe is closed. In other words, the pieces are put together. We don't do everything by hand, of course, but quite a bit of the work is still done by hand. At De Luca, we are very typical in this way. You will see many people working by hand on things, but others using machines, as you see here. Of course, all of these machines are still run by people, not automation. I think a bit more automation could increase our output, but my parents are old-fashioned about that. Here, we don't have a large manufacturing process."

"Would you want the factory to be more automated?"

"Certain parts, yes. I'd like to maintain the quality, but some of the processes are slow. We can't hire more people, but in today's world, we should take advantage of some automation that's available without sacrificing quality. We'd be able to grow the company." She frowned. "As it is, we'll always be a mid-sized company, never a large one with worldwide influence."

Julia didn't know how to respond to that so she kept silent. Seemed Valentina wasn't entirely satisfied with the way the company was run.

Valentina explained some of the machines, those that stitched the upper together, others that stitched the sole to the upper, and others that added an embossed design to the surface of the leather. Finally, they entered another room resembling an atelier where employees painted dye on the leather.

"At the end of the process, the sole is glued then stitched on, then a heel is added if the style has one, that is, of course, unless it's already been added earlier in the process." They passed a tall machine that stitched a sole onto an upper. Nearby, a man nailed small tacks into the sole of a shoe. "We put in brass nails on the heels of some models because they wear at the same rate as leather on the bottoms," Valentina said as they passed by the table. "A lot of foreign imports use rubber for the sole. Some of ours do, too, but other models have leather on the sole. It depends on the style."

"How many people work on one pair of shoes?" Julia marveled, staring around her as every person buzzed around the room for his or her specific task, ignoring the visitors in their midst.

Valentina's gaze panned the workers in the room and shrugged. "Could be as many as twenty or more people doing their small task for each pair. There are a lot of components to a shoe, more than for a belt or a purse. Everyone has their special job. Stitching the upper together, dying the leather, preparing the sole, and so on."

Julia and Valentina returned through a hallway following the tour and stepped back into the warm sunlight of the parking lot. "Thank you so much, Valentina. This has been so interesting."

"It's my pleasure, Cousin Julia. You need to be initiated, since the last time you were here you were too young to know anything about shoes." She laughed, having recovered her cheery mood. "Now you know more than you ever wanted to know about how shoes are made. We'll go back to the villa and relax a little bit before dinner is served. As I told you, we'll have some company tonight so the meal will be very lively," She looked happy about that. Would Marco be eating with them?

"I'm glad that was interesting for you." Valentina pulled her sunglasses down from her head once they were back in her tiny Fiat.

"Very interesting. It feels good to know much better what the company does and how they do it." Julia spoke with sincerity, though she was glad *she* didn't have to work in the factory, which seemed like a large bee hive with every person executing a specific and limited task in the goal of making a pair of shoes. She had the ideal job, to immerse herself in beauty and design and provide this to other people.

Julia chuckled as she looked down at her own leather sandals. All the shoes she'd bought over her adult life and it had never once crossed her mind what went into making a pair. Getting it to market was another story, more of Valentina's specialty.

When they arrived at the sprawling house, there were several additional cars in the driveway than for her previous visit. As soon as they entered the foyer, an animated discussion in Italian studded with laughter reached their ears from another room down the hall. Valentina turned to her and said in a hushed voice, "Some of our guests are already here. There are a couple of online distributors and my parents are working up a deal with them to make our shoes available on their site. We also have a couple who own a large chain of stores around Italy. They already stock our shoes, but are personal friends of my parents. We'll also have one or two reps from other locations here tonight."

Julia nodded and moistened her lips. Sounded like a big group and she'd need to prepare herself to drown in a sea of Italian. With so many important guests, no one would likely take the time to translate for her. Actually, she was surprised to have been included that evening, but maybe one more guest wasn't a burden. Even one who didn't speak a lick of Italian and would be as mute as a piece of furniture during the meal. She sighed. If she listened carefully, she might pick up a few more words. Maybe by the time she left Italy, she'd be able to talk like a toddler.

"Seems like they'll be talking business for another hour." Valentina kept her voice low as they passed the door where the lively conversation rumbled. Some voices were very loud, and there was frequent laughter. Must be a relaxed business meeting.

Valentina led her past the door toward the terrace where she'd eaten lunch two days earlier. The table held additional place settings, stemmed glasses of varying sizes, and a floral centerpiece Julia hadn't seen before. Must be an important dinner.

"If you want to, we can visit the gardens while they finish their meeting. Of course, that doesn't mean that their discussion won't continue during the meal, so I hope you're in a patient mood." She winked at Julia and led her down the flagstone path to the gardens Julia had seen the first day. They strolled through the manicured paths past a fragrant bed of red and yellow roses and sat down on a shaded bench.

"Is Marco coming tonight?" Julia wanted to learn more about Valentina's man, since her cousin hadn't told her much about him.

Valentina frowned and shook her head. "No, unfortunately. I don't really see him very much because we both travel for the company. We don't see each other often at the factory, either, though he spends more time there than I do."

"How long have you been together?"

A shy smile crept across Valentina's lips. Her eyes seemed to sparkle. "We were friends for a year or so first. We've been together as a couple for eight months. Not so very long. He had a bad experience with his last girlfriend, so it took him a while to commit to a new relationship."

"Understandable. As long as you're not in a hurry, he'll come around." Julia grinned. "How could he not? You're such a lovely person inside and out, Valentina." Her cousin flushed and smiled at Julia's compliment, which was utterly sincere. "Do you think it will become serious, or is it too early to tell?"

Valentina shrugged. "I'm serious already, but he is hesitant. I'll give him time, though. How about you? You told me you were divorced and you weren't seeing anyone right now. Is there anyone you are interested in?"

Julia shook her head. "I've had a couple of casual relationships since my marriage ended, but I also work a lot. I probably don't give myself enough time to meet someone." It was the bald truth. Maybe she considered starting with a new relationship to be just too much trouble, too disappointing, or too . . . uncertain. Like it had been for her mother.

As if reading her mind, Valentina asked, "Is that what your mother did? Worked so hard she didn't have time to meet someone?" Her voice and gaze were soft. "Is that why she never married?"

The question caused Julia to pause. Was she following in her mother's footsteps, as Eden had suggested the last time she'd been with her friends? Was working too much an easy way to stay out of the emotional fray, avoiding both hurt and fulfilment?

She took a breath. "It's a good question. I should probably think more about that. My mom was hurt when she lost my father. She also worked a lot, often with crazy shifts, and might have felt too tired afterward to make the effort to meet someone." She shrugged. "I do the same thing. I say to myself, I'm not attached so I can do more work for my company. But if I do more in my company, I lower my chances of ever becoming attached, right?" She looked back to Valentina, not really expecting an answer.

Valentina nodded slowly. "Seems you've said it yourself, Cousin. Maybe you're afraid and that's why you work so much."

Julia swallowed. Was she afraid? When she and Nick had broken up, it had been amicable. Things had gone stale between them in the later years of the marriage and they'd agreed to separate. Not an ideal ending in a relationship that was supposed to last forever. Was she afraid she'd never find something worth fighting harder for? Was she afraid to be wholly invested then devastated as her mother had been? "Maybe. I get focused and don't always realize I'm not balanced in my life."

Suddenly Valentina lifted her chin and grinned. "I have a couple of men in my mind who may be perfect for you. You'll have to stay longer so you can meet them"

Julia laughed and shook her head. She laid a hand on Valentina's arm. "Thanks for your concern, but really, I'll be able to find my own boyfriend when I return to America. But you *have* inspired me to be more open." When she returned to the U.S., she'd get involved in a few things to give her more of the missing balance in her life, *not* in order to meet someone. She could take salsa lessons, play more tennis, take an art class. Then, if God wanted her to meet someone one day, he was perfectly capable of making it happen.

Sergio appeared on the path. "There you both are. Hello, Julia. I'm glad to see you again and happy you could join us for dinner. We're ready to eat now, so please come to the terrace. We have a special treat tonight."

Chapter Eight

Sergio, Valentina, and Julia left the garden and followed the path back to the terrace. Emilia stood at one end of the table talking in Italian with a couple Julia didn't know. It took her several seconds to acknowledge Julia and Valentina, but to Julia's surprise, she left her conversation and came to them, kissing them both on each cheek. Despite her gesture, her voice was cool. "*Buona sera.* Julia, you were able to visit the factory today, *vero*? What was your opinion?"

"I found it so interesting to see the stages of making shoes." The scope of the family business still lingered in Julia's mind. "And I feel honored to see the De Luca factory in particular. It was so much more meaningful to me than tours I have taken on other trips."

A faint smile stretched Emilia's cool but cordial face. "I'm glad you enjoyed it." Her gaze then included Valentina, who stood next to Julia. "You can both sit. We are ready to be served." As they moved to take their seats, Emilia added to Valentina, "Stefano arrived in Florence this afternoon, but we won't hold the meal for him. He is likely running late."

Valentina broke into a grin. "*Ah, molto bene.* It will be nice to see him again."

Emilia raised her voice. "I present you my colleagues and friends." She introduced Julia to the two couples who, she guessed, had joined them for the earlier meeting. Their names passed in a musical-sounding blur she was sure she'd never remember. Each person greeted her in English with a slight nod and a warm smile.

"*Piacerre.*" Julia nodded back to each one, glad the polite vocabulary she'd studied had stuck. *Pleased to meet you.*

Giuseppe came through the hall door onto the terrace, with Paola following close behind him. "*Buona sera.*" He nodded to the group and everyone settled around the elegantly prepared table. The guests and family resumed their animated discussion in Italian, too fast for Julia to do any more than pull out a word here and there. Valentina caught her eye across the table and gave her a grin and a shrug. Amara came out to the terrace from the house and set one platter of antipasto at each end of the table. With a small bow and a subdued smile, she left the room and the platters made the rounds among the guests.

The sun gradually slipped down from a band of azure, creating a puddle of orange and pink across the sky. A faint breeze and cooler temperatures made a perfect summer evening. Julia shivered with contentment, despite her inability to follow the conversation at the table. It would be fine with her to observe the family dynamics while she enjoyed the lovely setting and a delicious Italian meal.

The seat next to her was empty but set with dishes and stemmed glasses, likely for the latecomer, Stefano. Just as Amara and another young woman came in to clear away the dirty plates, a tall man with wavy salt-and-pepper hair came from the house and stepped down onto the terrace. "*Buona sera, tutti!*" he called. "*Scusa sono in ritardo.*"

Immediately, Sergio and Emilia rose from their seats and gave the man an Italian greeting, a kiss on each cheek. Valentina did the same, standing on tip toe to reach him. Giuseppe remained seated, but smiled and extended a hand to shake that of the newcomer.

Emilia introduced him to the two couples from the shoe industry. "*Vi presento Stefano.*" She said the name of each person around the table. The man smiled and nodded his greetings as the room became noisy once again. Amara and her assistant quietly waited near the doorway until the commotion subsided before continuing to clear the table for the next course.

Julia was surprised when Emilia said to the man in English, "You can sit there next to my niece, Julia." Stefano made his way around the table and nodded a greeting to Julia as he sat down.

"*Buona sera.*" She greeted the man with a smile. She hadn't missed the fact that Emilia had presented her as her *niece.*

When the pasta bowl came by, Julia took a modest spoonful, having learned her lesson from the previous family meal. What she really wanted was more antipasto, but the platter had been whisked away. Amara paced the room, filling wine glasses and replacing water carafes. Just as Valentina had warned, most of the guests lapsed into Italian. On Julia's other side sat Signora Benetti, who preferred to interact with Emilia and Sergio across the table. Her aunt and uncle sat next to one another, but there was little warmth between them.

Julia wanted to address Stefano, since it felt awkward to say nothing all evening and he appeared to speak some English. She turned to him. "*Dove—*" she began. "Oh, shoot. What is that . . . *Dove Lei—*" That might be right, but it did her little good now that she remembered. Her face grew warm.

Stefano laughed, a warm, infectious sound, and Julia had to smile. He said, "I totally understand what you're going through." He spoke in perfect English as if he lived next door to her in Maryland.

Julia opened her mouth then closed it then cocked her head. "I'm confused. Are you American?"

"Yes, *sono americano*. I'm a rep for De Luca in the States. My territory is the east coast." He grinned at her then carefully folded the cuffs of his dress shirt partway up his arms. "I can understand your confusion. I don't really speak Italian well, although I've made a mighty and futile effort."

"But you sounded so authentic." Julia leaned forward on her elbows. "How do you pull that off?"

He shrugged. "I say the same things over and over whenever I meet people, so it's easy to perfect the accent on a few phrases."

"That makes sense. Maybe that's where I should start, perfecting a few phrases at a time. So, you don't understand what their conversation is about?" She waved a couple of fingers toward the loud discussion that continued to her left.

His gaze followed her gesture. "Sergio briefed me earlier by phone so I'd be in the loop, but their discussion doesn't involve what I do." He raised his eyes toward the doorway where Amara was returning with a platter. "I'm in town for a regular visit. I come here two or three times a year to check in, meet with the De Lucas and have some literal face time. Of course, we talk on the phone, text, email, but Europeans like having in-person time, too, especially over food. And the De Lucas definitely do." As he spoke his green eyes engaged with hers. Julia couldn't help but notice how attractive he was and how often he smiled or laughed. She wanted to talk more to him, drawn by his cheerful, friendly demeanor. Or maybe it was just his command of English.

"Did I hear your name is Julia?" He reached for a carafe of water and topped off her glass before filling his own.

She nodded. "Julia De Luca."

"Sounds like you're in the right place, this being the De Luca kingdom." He chuckled. "My name's Craig."

For the second time in their short conversation, she was puzzled. "I thought your name was Stefano."

He laughed again. "That's my Italian name. Well, not really. Stefano is a name the De Lucas gave me because they had trouble pronouncing 'Craig'. Valentina calls me Craig sometimes but the whole family calls me Stefano so even she forgets. It's easier, too, when they need to refer to me when talking with Italian vendors."

The antipasto plate returned for Craig's sake and circled the table for the second time. Julia was glad to see it and took a slice of prosciutto, some tomatoes, and some olives. "That makes sense, I guess. As long as *you* can remember who you are." She grinned. "How long have you known the De Lucas? How long have you worked for them?"

He served himself a few pepperoncini and some olives from the platter just as the pasta platter also arrived again at his end of the table. "Two different answers. I've known them for six years and worked for them for the last five. Long story, but I'll give you the shorter version. I was repping for another shoe company in Chicago but I was unhappy in the company. I'd had some contact with the De Lucas through that job. One year I took a vacation to Florence and other parts of Italy and looked up the De Lucas. We got to talking and it turns out they needed a U.S. rep for the east coast right about the time I was about to resign from my other job. Perfect timing."

"I'll say. And you've been happier working for De Luca Shoes than the previous company, I guess."

"Quite. Less micromanaging, for one. It would be hard to micromanage someone in another country, but that's not even their style. The best thing is the De Lucas have become like family."

That caught her interest. "Really? That's wonderful. You certainly got a warm welcome when you came in this evening. Like a long-lost brother."

His face softened. "Yeah. It's so cool, the way they accept me, and I don't even speak their language. Not well, anyway."

After five years, they accepted him as one of their own. How long would it take her? Their long-lost niece welcome had been more reserved. "Are you visiting for long?"

"Almost three weeks this time. I might be able to extend that because of the trade shows coming up in September. It's kind of like my second home now. I come, like I said, a few times a year."

Lucky guy. "And you don't speak Italian yet?" She hoped she hadn't offended him, though he didn't seem like someone easily offended.

He sighed and leaned back in his chair. "I can get by. I took a class at a community college when I was first hired, then I've continued some with online resources." He shrugged. "Everyone in the family speaks English pretty well, so that's probably the main reason I don't improve."

"Understandable." Julia relaxed against the wicker chair. "It must be nice to come to Italy so often, though. You seem to have an ideal job."

Craig turned to her. "It sure is. I love my job. How about you, do you have an ideal job, Julia De Luca?"

She smiled. "Yes, I do. I'm an interior designer."

He lifted his eyes and cocked his head appreciatively. "Sounds very creative. Homes? Offices?"

"Both. And hotels, convention centers. Whoever needs design."

"Where do you live in the States?"

"I'm in the D.C. area, Maryland side."

"I imagine being so near the capital would offer an abundance of hotels and other public places for you to make stylish and beautiful." He emphasized his words with a flick of his hand.

Valentina had been listening to the conversation between her parents and the Italian couple from the internet shoe company. She broke her attention away and leaned forward from her seat and said to Craig, "*Alora*, at last you have come to see us, Stefano. *Cosa c'è di nuovo?*"

"*Non molto.*" He grinned at her. "See, I've been practicing."

"*Non tanto*," she corrected. "Isabelle is out of town but should be back in a few days. She's bringing Mia with her but has to help her get ready to go back to school first."

To this, Craig simply nodded. "And you, what's new with you? Are you engaged yet?"

Valentina's eyes widened and she glanced around as if checking to see if anyone had heard. "Shh. Don't tell my secrets. I haven't convinced Marco yet that I'm the woman for him."

Though Julia had known Valentina only a short time, her cousin seemed like a prize many men would ardently pursue. She deserved someone who was crazy about her and maybe Marco wasn't that man. But, as a new cousin, what did she know about their relationship?

As if summoned by their words, the door opened and Marco strode through. Or maybe it was more of a strut. He was even more handsome than he'd appeared on the De Luca website photo, wearing a stylish black blazer which matched his black hair and eyes. He called out something in Italian to the group. Everyone responded in laughter, except the two Americans who hadn't understood a word. Julia glanced at Craig, who was observing the scene with the ghost of an amused smile.

Sergio rose from his chair and conferred privately for a few moments with Marco. When the older man sat down, Valentina slid her chair back and got up. She moved toward Marco and he went to her, a warm smile on his face. He slipped one arm around her waist, pulled her close and kissed her on one cheek. She giggled and smiled up at him. Their faces were close together as they spoke softly, privately. Then Valentina pulled away and sat down but followed him with her eyes, a soft smile curving her lips.

Marco waved to the group and said, "*Buon appetito, tutti.*"

Valentina replaced her napkin in her lap. She leaned forward toward Julia and Craig. "He can't stay, but he needed to talk to my father about something." Her explanation seemed unnecessary, as though she wanted to excuse his absence. Julia would have assumed that he would be present for the dinner, given his relationship to Valentina and the family. "That's too bad. I wonder why he couldn't stay for dinner tonight. You would have enjoyed that."

Valentina shrugged. "That's the way it is. He works a lot."

Julia wanted to ask why, but it was really none of her business. Maybe Marco was trying to rise in the company to impress Valentina. Or maybe there were other reasons.

Amara came out of the house to check on everyone and refill wine and water glasses. Julia had only taken one spoonful of pasta, craving more, but knowing what was coming. She wouldn't make that mistake again.

Craig leaned toward her. His voice was conspiratorial. "You aren't eating much, Julia. They can't fatten you up that way."

"Ha." Julia lifted her head, unable to stop a grin from spreading across her face. "I'm *sure* I'll be sufficiently fattened by the time I get on the return flight. In fact, I hope they have extra fuel on board." She leaned back and crossed her arms. "I learned my lesson about *primo piatto* the other day. I now leave room for the *rest* of the meal. I'm pacing myself."

He laughed heartily. "Yes, I have done that a couple of times too, eaten too much pasta and regretted having no more room for the rest of the meal. The trick is something the Europeans have down to an art form. They spread out the meal for hours, drink wine, and talk a lot. That's how you can put away a lot of food like it's nothing."

Julia glanced to the other end of the table. Emilia seemed oblivious of her and Craig's presence, focusing all of her energy on her Italian guests. Either the same conversation continued or a new one had erupted, but it seemed to her like one long strand of indiscernible sounds.

Valentina leaned forward again. "They're talking about the trade shows in September. That's when they start. There were a couple of shows earlier in the summer, like the leather trade show, but things get going in the shoe industry in the fall." Of course, her explanation would be for Julia's benefit. Craig would know all about trade shows for shoes. After her factory tour that day, Julia did feel more knowledgeable about shoe fabrication, but her dinner companions were all still miles ahead of her on that topic. That was fine. She smiled. At least she was an expert at choosing and wearing them.

After listening a few moments longer to the ongoing conversation, Valentina leaned back to Julia and Craig and added, "The older couple thinks that the political situation in Italy may affect the economy for the second year in a row. Signora Benetti is worried about the sale of shoes in general. Chinese imports are always a problem because they cost less to make and to buy than ours do."

Craig and Julia nodded politely after her explanations. Though it was interesting to be brought up to speed on the shoe industry conversation, Julia preferred talking to Craig.

When Valentina herself again became absorbed into the shoe discussion, no more explanations were forthcoming. Craig looked at Julia. "I think I know why we were seated together. The two mono-lingual Americans."

Julia grinned at him. "I think it's compassionate on their part, in that case. Might have been hard for us if we'd been stuck between people we couldn't talk to at all, getting a headache from trying to understand. Or maybe I'm just speaking for myself."

He leaned one elbow on the table. "So, Julia. Since we are left to our own English conversation, tell me more about yourself."

Her face warmed. Not only had he directed his warm green gaze to her, she was unaccustomed to talking about herself. "Um, I'm not sure what you want to know. My mother, Gianna De Luca, is Emilia and Giuseppe's older sister. She moved to the U.S. almost fifty years ago while she was in her twenties and raised me there." Julia paused. "She passed away about two weeks ago." She swallowed and a hollow wave filled her. It was still hard to say the words.

Craig's brow furrowed. "I'm so sorry. That's not very long ago."

"Thank you. She'd lost touch with the family years ago so I had no way to let them know about her passing." She stopped and waved the air. "Oh, it's a long story." He hadn't known what he was getting into when he'd so kindly asked.

"No, please continue." He hitched his head toward the noisy group of De Lucas. "I think we'll have plenty of time this evening."

She smiled at him. "Okay, you asked. There was some kind of falling out between my mother and the family. She stopped bringing me here to visit when I was about ten. I don't really know what it was about, but I hadn't seen the family since then. I'm forty-eight now, so it's been thirty-eight years. I didn't know how I'd be received after all that time."

"Seems to have gone well." His gaze roved to the small crowd at the opposite end of the table.

Not completely. She glanced at Emilia, whose features had softened with laughter and animated conversation, making her beautiful. If only she smiled more often. "I reached out to Valentina on Facebook and she was wonderful. She paved the way for me to get in touch with the whole family."

"So, you decided to come."

"Yes, very suddenly. I had taken a couple weeks off from my company to attend to my mother's affairs, so I had some time available. Valentina convinced me to come right away."

He grinned. "And here you are."

"Here I am. In Italy." She grinned and shook her head. "Go figure." Still hard to believe, even after a couple of days.

Craig reached for his wine glass and took a sip. "I like that intrepid spirit."

Intrepid, she was not. Well, not usually. Intrepid in her business, maybe. "I felt a loss, of course, when my mother passed. But it reminded me of the previous connection I'd had with the family here. I'm so glad it worked for me to come and reunite with them after almost four decades."

"I'm glad the risk you took paid off. It's also fortunate that my trip coincided with yours so we could cross paths."

Julia didn't know how to respond to that. Was he flirting with her? The possibility brought an unfamiliar well of warmth inside her. But then again, he might just be acting friendly and welcoming. Probably.

She gave him a small smile. "Yes, that's true. We can commiserate on our lack of Italian." A lame thing to say, but his intense gaze knocked her off balance.

He looked up to the doorway. "Here's another course. Hope you're ready." There was amusement in his voice.

When Amara came to them with a steaming platter, she quietly announced, "*Agnello arrosto al rosmarino.*"

"*Grazie.*" Julia and Craig spoke at the same time.

"Roasted lamb with rosemary. I've mastered the food vocabulary, you see." He lifted his eyebrows playfully.

"I see, I see." Julia grinned. The platter came by and she served herself a piece of lamb and small potatoes. "I'm so glad I saved room for this. There are vegetables coming, too.".

After she'd savored a bite or two, she turned to Craig. "Where do you live in the States? You said you were the east coast rep."

"Yes. I was happy to leave Chicago and move to Philadelphia. Can't say the winters are a whole lot better. Well, maybe a little bit. It's easier to get up and down the east coast and also fly to Florence from Philadelphia. It's also great, because my kids live in New York and New Jersey."

"How nice for you. How old are they?" Of course, he was married. He had to be. Julia ignored the slight deflation inside, then reprimanded herself severely.

"I have a nineteen-year-old at Princeton and a twenty-three-year-old newly-married daughter who lives in New York. After my divorce, their mother had custody most of the time due to my travel schedule. So, I actually get to see them more often now." He wiped his mouth on a cloth napkin.

"Oh, that's great." Was that a small wave of relief coursing through her? An image of him hanging out with adult children, like a friend as well as a father, flashed into her mind. She ignored the hollow yearning that whispered inside.

"Kids?" he asked her.

She shook her head. "I wish I had at least one. I married late, divorced even later, and it just didn't work out to have a family. I guess we should have started sooner."

Craig gestured to the table. "Looks like you have a family now."

Had he read her mind, seen her moments of longing in the storage unit back home? Of course, it wasn't the same as having children. That question no longer caused a pang inside her. She and Nick had started trying too late, but he'd never been motivated, since he was much older than Julia and had his own kids from his previous marriage. She sighed.

"I'm sorry if I brought up a sore subject." Craig's voice had softened as he watched her face. Kindness emanated from his eyes.

She hadn't realized her regret was so obvious. She smiled and shook her head, feeling exposed. "No, it's fine, really. I've adjusted to it. You can't have everything, right?" She waved at the air dismissively.

"Usually not. Whatever comes, it's God's blessing. I've learned to question less and less, since sometimes it's good not to get what you want."

She looked at him and blinked. It was true and she'd forgotten. His reminder touched a dry place inside her, spreading warmth there. Her mind went to Marissa, Sydney, and Eden, who were a family of sorts. "I believe that, too, even if I sometimes forget. I don't complain because he's given me so much. Well, I don't complain very often."

They laughed.

She leaned one elbow on the table. "I used to complain to my mother that I wanted a father and siblings and that she should get married." She stopped as her hand went to her mouth. "Oh, I forgot to tell you the rest of my story. My mother fell in love with a man she was dating then got pregnant with me, but my bio father was killed before they were able to marry. She never did get married, but I always wanted a bigger family."

"Big families are not always what they're cracked up to be. They have their problems. Hidden or not."

Julia tilted her head toward the De Lucas. Despite the festive ambiance and playful bantering, the family likely had its share of dark waters underneath. Broken bridges. Heartaches. Secrets.

She fingered the stem of her wine glass. "Do you have experience with that? I mean, with big families?" Her face grew hot. Now he'd think she was being nosy about his past.

He nodded, his face turning serious, though he smiled quickly, almost by will. "Middle child of five kids. Well, I won't bore you with the details, but it's not always a big party."

"I'm sure that's true." Julia's voice softened. She must have walked onto a wound without realizing it and was sorry to have closed him down. Surely, a big family with siblings didn't often resemble the Norman Rockwell photos she'd held in her mind for so long as some kind of ideal. Relatives and siblings were all humans, after all. Humans with conflicts, deep wounds and their own individual desires.

Her mind searched for something to lighten the moment when Craig said, "What's great about coming here is I don't live here. I enjoy family without the daily hassles." He laughed and lifted his glass to her. She wouldn't ask what hassles he was referring to.

Julia smiled back at him and lifted her glass.

Chapter Nine

Julia was accustomed now to waiting at the bus stop planted in the rolling Tuscan hills around her, but today was different. Instead of Valentina, she waited for Sergio to come pick her up. He'd surprised her the previous evening with a phone call. He told her to come the following day right after lunch because he had a special treat for her. She'd find out what it was when she arrived.

She smiled. A special treat. Whatever it would be, it was thoughtful of him. He wasn't so wrapped up in running his company that he forgot about her and the short length of her presence with them. Maybe he'd take her on another tour of the factory and explain the finer points of shoe fabrication. Though that would be mildly interesting, she'd cherish the chance to get to know the man better. He had welcomed her. That was significant, since he was the patriarch of the family.

Sergio arrived right on time. Julia slipped into the car. *"Buongiorno,* Sergio."

"You almost sound *Italiana,* Julia. Have you learned some Italian?" Sergio grinned at her. He wore dark sun-glasses and was dressed casually. Maybe he was working from home that day or taking the afternoon off. Despite his relaxed appearance, he still had a regal bearing, like a distinguished and successful businessman.

Julia laughed. "Only some words and phrases. I'm trying to perfect the ones I say a lot, like hello, goodbye, and I don't speak Italian." She thought of Craig's example. Good advice.

He chuckled at her comment. "Language is made up of words and phrases. Continue learning more words and more phrases and you'll speak Italian."

She leaned back in the passenger seat and let the breeze from the open window caress her face. It felt good to be having a relaxed conversation alone with Sergio, without Emilia hovering, or other crowds of people around. Like a friend. She smiled at him. "I'm motivated now. I've already enrolled in a class that'll start late September, once I'm back home." If her trip went well, she anticipated returning regularly to Florence, as Craig already did.

"*Bene*. It's a good decision." Sergio pulled into the circular drive in front of the villa. She followed him through the gated courtyard and the breezy tiled hallway out to the veranda. He gestured for her to sit down at the glass table and sat down across from her. Seemed like he was in no hurry to tell her about the special treat. He leaned back and linked his fingers across his stomach.

Amara came out of the house carrying a tray of tall glasses. It looked like black coffee in glass mugs. "This drink is called *shakerato*," Sergio said. "It's like iced coffee. I thought you would enjoy tasting it. It is sweetened already, but you may add one of these liqueurs for flavor, if you want." He flicked his fingers toward three small glass bottles of amber liquid.

"Thank you. This looks interesting. And of course, I'll try just about anything in Italy." Julia reached for the glass and tasted the dark beverage. She squinted as the bitter liquid went down her throat. "It's a bit strong for me."

He gestured to Amara, who still stood near the doorway. "*Del latte per favore.*" Minutes later, the young woman placed a small pitcher of milk in front of Julia.

When Amara left, Sergio sipped his beverage and leaned back in his chair. "I didn't know your mother personally. I heard about her and what happened from Emilia."

His direct statement about Gianna surprised Julia but she was glad he'd brought up the subject. "Do you know why she fell out with the rest of the family? I never could convince my mother to tell me what happened." A thread of hope rose up inside her. Valentina hadn't known the cause of the conflict, but she hadn't been born yet. Maybe Sergio would know, even though Emilia had been a child then. Surely, they would have discussed it.

Sergio shook his head and Julia's hopes fell. "Emilia didn't want to talk about it. Once Gianna had made it clear she wasn't coming anymore, it was as though, for Emilia, she had died. It's not my way to press her to explain, so I've left it alone all of these years."

Julia leaned back and laid her hands on her lap. "It's so sad, anything that breaks a family apart. There should always be some kind of resolution." Her eyes caught his and she thought she saw regret there.

"Maybe *you* are the resolution, Julia." He smiled at her.

"Me? How—what can I do to repair what went on forty years ago? I don't even know what happened."

"You came to us." His voice was calm, soothing. "You closed the circle that had hung open for so long." Though his gaze remained serious, a half-smile appeared. "I'm glad you found us."

His words touched a bruised and confused part of her. Tears welled up in her eyes. She blinked. "Thank you, Sergio. That means so much to me, especially coming from you. I hope it's true. I hope I can bring some kind of healing to this situation. I don't know how, but maybe just being here and staying involved. That is—" she shrugged, "if everyone wants me to." Her face grew warm. She hoped she hadn't overstepped her welcome into the family.

Sergio nodded as he looked back at her, eyes squinted with what seemed to be understanding, compassion. "You're thinking of my wife. I believe she is glad you are here. She doesn't show this because, when she looks at you, she is reminded of her sister. They were ten years apart, but I think she looked up to Gianna in many ways. The family was troubled—especially Lucia, your grandmother, by Gianna's desire to stay in America and raise you by herself. It's not our way to do this. If she had married, she could live wherever she wanted to. But because she was alone, it made sense to us for her to return to Italy and have the family give her support in raising her child. Instead, she chose to do this on her own."

Julia nodded. Alone to the end. Gianna's choice to raise her by herself in a foreign country had affected more people than just her. And the waves of regret and pain had continued to this day. Yet, it had been her choice. Her life and Julia's.

She took another sip. The strong brew was growing on her. The milk had definitely softened the bite. "I wonder why Emilia would be upset up to now. Seems to me she's still angry."

"More sad than angry. She has gone on and put it behind her, but I think when you came, it raised those questions again. I think in time she will accept you on your own merit and not connect you with her bad memories."

"I hope so." Maybe that was Julia's mission before leaving Italy. To convince Emilia that she was her own person and could be a part of the family without the past casting long shadows over present relationships.

Sergio's tone changed. "So, you are an interior designer, you told us the other day. This sounds interesting. Maybe you can help us with some of our outdated stores in Florence."

Julia smiled at him as a wave of pleasure and gratitude coursed through her. Another seal of approval, an invitation to participate in her unique way. "I'd love to, Sergio. That would make me so happy to help the De Luca brand and family, especially since I'm a De Luca. After all, I can't contribute anything in the creation of shoes, but the showrooms, that is something I can definitely help with."

He laughed. "No, we don't need your skills in the factory. I will talk to Emilia and Giuseppe about this and give you the address of our flagship store in Florence. You can go visit and see what you think. Then you can come back with some ideas for us, *vero*?"

"*Vero*! Gladly."

"This may help us become more modern, as the younger members of the family are always saying to us." Sergio waved the air with one hand. "There is a kind of generational fight that is always going on in the family and in the company. We have certain things we do that have always been done in the same way for generations. That is how we built our reputation and how we retain loyal customers. But you know that times change. Some of our practices have to change, too, but we don't know what to change and what to keep the same. The younger family members seem to want to change everything." He smiled but tension shadowed his eyes.

Was there a rumbling undercurrent in the De Luca empire? The other day Valentina had grumbled about the outdated practices of the company. Julia made a mental note to ask Valentina more questions about it. Competing with that thought was her curiosity about Sergio's surprise.

A commotion in the hallway echoed out toward the veranda. Julia recognized Craig's voice as he greeted someone then appeared in the doorway. He was dressed casually in cargo pants, sandals, and a pale turquoise polo shirt, even more attractive than he'd been in a business suit the previous evening. "There you are, enjoying a morning treat under the summer Tuscan sunshine." He pulled out a chair next to Sergio. "Good morning, Julia, Sergio. *Scusa sono in ritardo.*"

"*Buongiorno*, Stefano." Julia grinned. A tingling wave of pleasure flowed through her. "I have the feeling you say that Italian phrase a lot, because it sounds so fluent."

His eyes, crinkling with amusement, met hers. "I'm afraid I'm often late for one reason or another, so I have the chance to apologize frequently in Italian. My apologies are very fluent."

They all laughed. Amara appeared as if conjured by magic incantation and placed a *shakerato* on the table in front of Craig. "My, but she's efficient," Julia marveled. "You've only been here a nanosecond."

Craig chuckled. "By this time, Amara knows my preferences. I don't even need to tell her I'm addicted to this stuff. I came in the door and she knew what she had to do. It's our silent understanding. Amara *is* pretty amazing, the way she knows how to serve people. She's the only person on earth that makes me feel like I'm the king of something."

When their laughter subsided, Sergio cleared his throat. "Since you are here, Stefano, I can tell you both about my special errand I have for you. I think you will enjoy it, especially since you are visiting from America." He turned his attention to Julia. "You in particular, Julia, since you have not visited Italy in many years. I want you to take a very good impression with you. That way, you'll return and visit."

His words caused a warm flush inside Julia, the answer to a heart hope she'd held since her arrival. She breathed deeply in contentment then she and Craig gave Sergio their full attention, waiting for him to continue. The older man seemed to be enjoying the suspense he was creating. With a rare wide grin, he looked from Julia to Craig. "You will do me a great service if you will take the jugs that are in the front hallway and have them filled with Chianti from the domain, the vineyard, and bring them back here. We like to have jugs of local wine for daily meals but we keep them in our cellar with the better bottles we reserve for guests and special occasions. Aside from doing this service for me, you can and should do as you like. However, I recommend that you take the rest of the day to explore Greve and the region between here and there. Near Greve is a lovely hilltop village called Montefioralle. This will certainly occupy some hours if you want to take photos and explore the region. I suggest this because the views are stunning. On your way back to the villa, you may wish to stop by the town of San Casciano in Val di Peso." He turned his gaze to Julia. "Stefano has already seen some of these places, so he will be your tour guide, Julia. I want to make sure you have a very pleasant impression of Tuscany before returning to America. Come back to the villa with the wine whenever you like. We will not expect you for dinner. Just don't forget the Chianti."

"Wouldn't dream of it." Craig grinned at him then his eyes caught Julia's. "What a pleasant chore you're giving us, Sergio."

Anticipation at spending the day experiencing the Tuscan countryside with Craig simmered and rose up inside Julia. And so thoughtful that Sergio would arrange to give his American visitors a day to themselves to be tourists. It would be more practical for Craig to show her around since he had no obligations at the shoe factory and he was already familiar with the area. Might just be practical, though the thought crossed Julia's mind that maybe Sergio was attempting to get the two of them together. The thought wasn't unpleasant, she had to admit. Best not to run too fast, though. Definitely not her style to be impulsive or quickly swept away by a man.

Sergio helped them load several five-liter glass jugs into Craig's rental car. He handed Craig a sheet of paper. "This is what I need. Two jugs of Classico and three of Riserva. I know you can remember this, but I wrote it for you, just in case. And here is the address of the vineyard. I took you there once before, remember? We had a nice tasting of the Riserva."

"A little too much, as I recall." Craig chuckled then pulled a serious face and cleared his throat. "We will accomplish the mission, General," he said gravely. "You can count on us. We'll drink none of it on the way home. You have our word."

Once they were in the car and zipping over sun-drenched hills toward the southern town of Greve, Craig turned to Julia. "Do you think there's a reason Sergio wanted to get rid of his American tourists for the day? They must have some important business secrets to discuss."

Julia leaned back, relaxed and content. "All they'd have to do is start jabbering in Italian and that's enough secrecy for us, don't you think? They could be planning a takeover of the Italian shoe industry and we'd never know. It's so sweet of Sergio to give us a nice tourist outing like this."

"He's a great guy. Like a brother. For all the gruffness and high-class bearing, he's got a soft heart and lots of sensitivity to people."

She smiled. "I'm seeing that in him more and more. Before you arrived, we had a chat about my mother and I understood the situation a little better. Of course, no one seems to know why my mother stopped coming to Italy, but he's tuned into the pain it's caused. He thought my being here might be helpful in healing the wounds. That surprised me, because I thought my presence *opened* the wounds after forty years."

He glanced over at her. "Maybe the wounds need to be reopened before they're healed."

She opened her mouth to respond then paused. That was likely true, whether Emilia would believe it or not. "How'd you get so wise, Stefano?"

Craig grinned back at her. "Lots of life experience and a few hard bumps. I'm deeper than I probably appear."

"Yes, for sure." Julia hadn't meant it the way it sounded. They both laughed, the hearty music filling the car. He wasn't just a very pretty face, apparently. But he *was* that, especially his white-toothed ready smile and cropped dark curls threaded with gray. She wanted to say or ask something that would continue the serious vein of their conversation, eager to dip beneath the superficial joking at which he seemed so adept. His ability to put people at ease, even in Italy, was likely a huge asset in his work in both countries.

Previously, he'd seemed as gregarious and fun-loving as she was reserved and reflective. But here was a hint of a deeper side of him that stoked her thirst to know more. Her mind groped for insightful questions but came up empty, so she said, "I look forward to hearing more of your wisdom and witnessing your skills as a tour guide."

"It's been a year or so since I've gone down into Chianti country, so we'll discover it together." The serious moment had passed, but she didn't mind. She'd enjoy whatever occurred that day during her first visit to the hills of Tuscany.

Sun-swept hills and vineyards tumbled out in all directions. Dotting the peaks of each rugged slope were red and yellow stucco villas with orange tile roofs. The sky overhead stretched out velvet blue for infinity. Julia was breathless with the beauty in front of her, and they hadn't even arrived yet at the town of Greve. She had to stop herself several times from saying, "Oh, how beautiful! Look at that!" or she'd be saying it all day. Where had her introversion gone? Didn't matter now. Delight coursed through her and gushed out of her and she couldn't stop it. She was in Tuscany, one of the most beautiful spots on earth. And she'd found the De Lucas.

Thirty minutes later the town of Greve came into view. "Is this our stop where we pick up the wine?"

"No, that will be outside of town, about halfway back toward the villa. We'll be tourists first, wine porters second. I hope you brought a camera or have a good one on your phone."

"That, I do." She held up her cell phone.

The slight breeze that came in through the window did little to freshen the mid-afternoon Tuscan sun beating down on the small car without air conditioning. Instinct had guided Julia that morning to wear appropriate tourist clothing, even before knowing what Sergio's surprise involved. She wore linen capris and a red cotton tank top along with her most comfortable sandals. She hoped she was ready for the August heat.

They drove slowly into the town and after several minutes, squeezed into a parking spot. Rows of white awnings filled the main square along with clusters of shoppers milling around with shopping carts on wheels or woven baskets. Pale yellow buildings atop the arched loggia surrounded the square. "Must be market day." Craig gazed around the square and back to Julia. "Ready?"

She grinned at him and nodded, again filled with a rush of anticipation. "I'm so grateful to Valentina for her persuasion in getting me to Italy," she said as they left the parking area and walked toward the humming crowds of the Piazza Matteotti. "I rarely do things impulsively."

"Haven't you begun to see the merits of a nice impulsive choice once in a while?" There was humor in his eyes as he gestured toward the thrumming Piazza.

"I'm definitely revising my opinion. Impulsivity is not a personality trait I have, but I guess I should try to cultivate it once in a while. If I hadn't pushed through my hesitations, I wouldn't be here now. And I wouldn't trade this experience for anything."

"Good, Julia is expanding her borders. *Molto bene.* See that statue over there? That's Giovanni da Verrazzano, who was the first explorer to reach New York."

"Those Italian explorers got around, didn't they? How about Columbus? And Amerigo Vespucci?"

"Speaking of Amerigo, up there on that hillside is the village of Montefioralle, which is the birthplace of Mr. Vespucci, who gave us the name of our country."

"*Vero.*" Julia looked up to the ancient-looking village bathed in coral, yellow, and beige perched like a crown on the steep hillside.

"We can wander around the market a bit if you want, then there are some shops under those arches over there." Craig gestured toward the loggia on the ground floor of the earth-tone row of buildings.

They wandered down an aisle of produce, flowers, and olives of several shades of green, brown, and black. Merchants called out their specials over the rumble of conversations from shoppers and tourists. It felt good to be walking next to Craig, in a man's company for the first time in so long. And not just any man, but one she found attractive and attentive. That was a rare combination she hadn't found in, well, *ever.* Maybe that's why she'd stayed alone since her divorce from Nick. It hadn't been worth the emotional effort to search for compatibility, a task which seemed more futile with the passing years.

They approached another aisle of melons, tomatoes, onions, eggplants, and carrots on stands that snaked out beyond Julia's vision. Behind her, she smelled the tang of the cheese booth before she saw it. "Before we leave, maybe I'll buy a chunk of Italian cheese. I need to begin my food education, or at least extend it beyond croissants, coffee, and pasta. And of course, gelato."

"*Naturalmente.* In Italy, gelato is one of the foods on the pyramid of essentials."

Julia resisted the urge to buy samples of the rainbow of produce, tasty-looking cheeses, and salamis for picnics later in the week. She would weigh herself down too early in the excursion.

"Would you like to visit some shops? I know women like shops. I was married long enough to develop patience." Craig grinned affably. "And I like some of them every once in a while."

She laughed. "Remember, I'm a designer. All this visual stimulation is creating art in my mind even as we speak. The more sights I can drink in, the better." She turned her head toward the loggia that surrounded the square. "In fact, maybe I can incorporate those lovely arches into a home or office design one day. I'd bring a Tuscan flair back to the U.S."

"I'd love to see that when it's done." He grinned at her then motioned her to follow him toward the shops under the arches. They wandered away from the square and headed toward the shops under the arched loggia. The first shop sold pottery and several displays of colorful pitchers and bowls filled the shaded walkway. Julia stopped at a table covered with pitchers.

"So, back to your decision to come to Italy. What set off that desire?" Craig stood beside her and glanced over the display.

"This one's pretty, look." Julia held up a small pitcher that would be perfect for a small quantity of wine or milk, or even fresh flowers. Much nicer than the inexpensive glass one she'd purchased the other day at the florist shop in Florence. "When I was going through my mother's things in her storage unit, I happened upon some items from Italy. It triggered thoughts of my long-lost family here. My initial desire was simply to get reconnected to them, since they were the only living family I had left. I have some great friends, but don't have any siblings, kids, or anyone in the States related by blood. My mom's passing and the realization that I *did* actually have family somewhere created a desire to see them again. And of course, I also felt the need to let them know about my mother's death. I found Valentina on Facebook and fortunately, she responded right away." Julia smiled at the memory of her first exchange with Valentina. "She seems glad to have a new cousin."

"Valentina's great. She's like a really sweet little sister. So, Valentina convinced you to come at that time?"

"She told me I should come soon. Since I had already taken off time for my mom, it was a perfect opportunity to come. I made all the arrangements in about a day."

"That's pretty good for someone who is non-impulsive." He held up another pitcher. "Do you like this one?"

"Oh, that's even prettier than the one I have here."

"Let me get it for you. My souvenir for you in Tuscany." His eyes met hers and clung for a second.

Warmth rose in her neck and his words touched a tender spot inside. "That's sweet, Craig. You don't have to do that."

He waved off her words and approached the merchant, who hovered in the doorway of his shop. Craig spoke to the man in Italian and paid for the pitcher. Despite his claims of butchering the language, he sounded fluent to her.

They continued strolling through the shaded hallway of the loggia and stopped at a vendor of straw hats. "I need one of these for the August sun, aside from the fact that I simply *like* them." Julia tried a few, peering at herself in the small mirror the vendor had provided, then bought one. She put it on and showed Craig.

He nodded appreciatively. "Very nice. It suits you. You could wear it on an angle like this, if you want." He stepped toward her and reached down to tilt the hat to one side, standing close enough that she could smell his cologne and notice a slight shadow of stubble on his chin. Her pulse quickened. He stepped back and nodded then added in a softer voice, "Very chic for a beautiful woman."

His words surprised her as the hum of attraction inside her grew louder. At a loss for words, she simply smiled.

They returned to the Piazza, took a closer look at the Verazzanno statue, then headed toward the Santa Croce church which stood at the other end of the square. "There's a church by the same name in Florence, which I'm sure you've seen." Craig mounted the steps of the church.

"No, I haven't seen it yet. I've been squeezing Florence visits between my visits to the family."

"Are you staying in Florence proper?"

She nodded. "In Oltrarno, across the river."

"I always stay in Florence when I come. I love it. We'll be able to meet up for a meal or coffee, since we're both in the city."

"That would be great." *Wonderful.* The trip was getting better with every passing minute, but she'd try not to sound too excited.

Once inside the church, the cool air that emanated from centuries-old stone surrounded her. A welcome relief after the sizzling temperatures outside. The church was fairly plain, but clearly still in use for the residents of Greve. Scattered in straight-back chairs were several people seated in contemplation.

"You shouldn't miss the Santa Croce church in Florence." Craig stood close to her as he whispered in the hush of the cathedral. "The frescoes are magnificent. Michelangelo and Galileo are buried there."

"It's now on my list. Are you—are you involved in a church where you live in Philadelphia?" She hoped her question wasn't too abrupt. It seemed fair enough, since he himself had spoken of God the other day.

Craig let out a heavy sigh. "I wouldn't say 'involved'. I attend a church there, you could say, but more often than not, I check in online."

She looked up at him. "You too?"

"I gather you do the same?"

"Unfortunately, lately I do. One that I did attend was so big, I felt lost. I didn't know anyone. Online seemed the best solution."

"It's better than nothing when you travel as much as I do. I try to attend a small group, as long as they're understanding about how often I'm absent."

Julia shook her head and frowned. "I have no excuse. I've just gotten into bad habits. A small group sounds like a good idea, especially in a bigger church." She felt an inner uplift from his response. "I'll look for one when I get back to the States." There, she'd said it aloud, which meant she had to follow through. *Finally*, she'd follow through.

Once outside again, Craig turned to Julia. "If you're game, we can drive or even hike up there to Montefioralle. It's about a mile."

Perspiration trickled down Julia's back. She didn't want Craig to think she was a wimp, but climbing up the imposing Via del Castello for a mile might be a lot for her. She'd be drenched and exhausted by the time they reached the top.

When she hesitated, Craig said, "On second thought, we'll drive. Hiking might take us too long and we have a lot more to see. And don't forget about our mission for Sergio."

She smiled gratefully and minutes later, they parked along the street approaching the medieval village below the city walls. During their stroll around the village, Craig waited patiently for Julia to take photos from every angle of the picturesque cobbled streets, window boxes, and ancient buildings. An old man led a small group of goats through the square. One of them took a liking to Julia, nudging her thigh as if waiting for a treat. She and Craig laughed and she took pictures of the goat and Craig with the goat. The old man said something to them in Italian and erupted in a toothless laugh.

On the crest of the hill, Julia's mouth dropped open at the view of the valley below, golden vineyards bathed in the late-afternoon sun, clusters of trees, hills of green to infinity. They stood still, silent for a few moments, drinking in the sight. Then Julia retrieved her phone for more photos. She took another one of Craig and a selfie of the two of them, hoping he didn't read anything into that.

"Send that to me? I'll give you my number." His tone was nonchalant, but his eyes caught hers.

She nodded. "Sure." *Of course.*

They returned to the car. The glow of the sky told her it was late afternoon. The day was passing too quickly. She willed time to stand still. Too soon, her day in Tuscany with Craig would be only a memory.

"Time for our next adventure." Craig started the car and lowered the sunglasses that perched on top of his head. "We'll get Sergio's wine now." They pulled away from the lively town and back to the main road. He glanced over at Julia. "Tell me more about your past life in the States. Where did you grow up?"

Once Julia's window was rolled fully down, a breeze flowed in and began to cool the inside of the car. They sped past one vineyard after another, with neat rows of leafy green up and down hills as far as the eye could see. "Most of my life was spent in New York. When I was about eleven, my mom moved us to Long Island, which is mostly where I stayed until I left for college. She'd gotten a job at a nearby hospital."

"How'd you end up in D. C.?"

Julia didn't relish talking about herself, her past. Craig' seemed genuinely interested, which made it easier. "I'd gone to college in North Carolina. U.N.C. Then I went back to New York, this time to the city for design school. After a few years working in the city, I met my husband and he later got a job in D.C. I started my business during those early years there."

"How long ago did you guys split up?"

Though he wore sunglasses, Julia could see his brow furrow and heard his voice lower a notch.

"Eight years, roughly."

He looked over at her and pushed up his sunglasses. "Similar to mine. It just didn't work out, eh?"

Julia frowned as her eyes strayed toward the windshield. Her divorce had always felt like a failure to her, even though Nick was the one who'd wanted out. She'd married the wrong person, maybe had sought a father figure, but she'd been willing to make it work. "My ex-husband was about ten years older than I am and had been married before. He had his own kids, so he didn't really want any more." She sighed then looked over at him. "We were both really busy in our careers. During the last three years of our marriage, he became more and more emotionally absent. Physically absent, too. He took up golfing and was always gone in his free time. I tried different things, suggested we see a counselor. He just didn't seem interested in making the effort. I think he had someone else, but he never admitted it. Finally, one night after dinner as we sat at the table, he told me he wanted a divorce." Julia swallowed against the knot that had formed in her throat at the memory of that moment. She always remembered the dirty plates in front of her, since she'd stared at them for several moments after Nick's pronouncement, fighting tears, gathering her thoughts. "I shouldn't have been surprised. But I was."

"I'm sorry. That sounds hard. And that was it?"

She nodded. "I didn't see any point in trying to change his mind. I'd already made all kinds of efforts to get our marriage back on track but at the end of the day, he didn't want to be married to me anymore. I wasn't about to try to force him. It wouldn't have worked for very long."

"I think you're right about that. Sounds like you did all you could and he didn't respond when he had the chance."

"He'd allowed so much distance to creep in. I'm thinking he might have even planned it that way. For a while, I didn't notice, since we were so busy. Then, when I realized how little time we spent together and had become like roommates, that's when I started bringing it up to him. He minimized it. We parted amicably, I guess." Meaning they hadn't screamed and thrown dishes, but they no longer had contact. Though she hadn't shed many tears, she carried around a cold, empty cavity inside whenever she thought of Nick and her marriage.

Craig looked over at her. His lips were tight. She saw sympathy, understanding in his eyes. "Sometimes it happens, despite your best efforts. We shouldn't beat ourselves up." He swallowed and took a heavy breath. "My situation was similar, plus my wife had an affair."

"She admitted it?"

"My travel schedule led to her loneliness, she claimed. I don't know how long it went on. Likely longer than she said. But she did marry the guy." Suddenly, as if waking up from a trance, he lifted his brows and grinned. "Ancient history. Let's talk about the present, shall we?"

Julia nodded. "Yes. I don't usually talk about this. You're easy to talk to." If she weren't careful, she'd tell him everything in her heart and mind.

She thought she detected a shadow behind his eyes that belied the smile stretching across his face. There had to be hurt, even after eight years. The discussion had left a heavy coating in her stomach.

"Tell me more about your design business."

"Well, that's a better topic for me." Julia rested one elbow on the edge of the car window, reveling in the caress of the breeze. "I have a shop, De Luca Interiors. Not too original a name, I guess. I developed a simplified system where customers can find combinations and styles they like. Lots of people don't really know what they like until they see it. When I first started out, that was a problem, because they weren't able to describe the styles they loved. Books helped, you know, they'd pick out photos that they liked. But creating a system to get them more hands-on with their own design was fun and I think more useful for them."

Craig grinned. "I think I know how to get you talking. Ask a question about your business. Seriously, that sounds brilliant, getting people involved in the design themselves. It doesn't take away the need for your service, does it?"

"No, it just enables them to better describe what they like, which actually makes my job easier. Sergio wants me to look at the De Luca store in Florence and give them some design ideas."

"That's great. He'd be crazy to let you leave Italy without benefitting from your talent."

"And I'm totally willing to help. I felt honored that he asked me."

"Here we are, Castello Carnolla."

During their conversation, Julia hadn't noticed that they'd approached a long driveway that led to a one-story stone villa. Behind it were larger buildings, perhaps where the family made the wine. Craig parked in front of an imposing stone building behind the house and got out. Immediately, a middle-aged bearded man wearing overalls came out to greet them. He shook Craig's hand and said something in Italian to him. Though Craig's Italian was slower than the man's, the man seemed to understand him perfectly. Craig introduced Julia to the man and he gave a small bow. "*Piacere, Julia.*"

"*Piacere mio*, Signore Carnolla."

"*Parla Italiano?*"

She shook her head and brought out her almost-perfected apology. "*Mi dispiace, non parlo molto Italiano.*" Not yet, anyway. Soon, she'd be speaking Italian. In fact, before her next trip to Tuscany.

Craig leaned toward Julia and said in a low voice, "He said Sergio called in advance to let him know we'd be arriving this afternoon. He's going to let us taste his new varietal."

He rested one hand lightly on Julia's lower back as the man led them into the building where enormous wooden barrels were stacked up against the walls. Julia's eyes roved around the large, airy room as they followed Signore Carnolla to another room.

"Here we taste the wine." That might be the only English the man spoke, and likely said the same phrase for visitors many times per day. He pulled a bottle off of the shelf, quickly opened it and poured a small glass for each of them.

"*Molto bene.*" Julia smiled at him and he refilled her glass.

After several re-pours, Craig held up one hand and laughingly said something in Italian to the man.

Signore Carnolla led them back through the large room where Sergio's bottles were already filled and waiting for them. Two young men picked up the jugs they had filled and carried them back to Craig's rental car.

Once the jugs were firmly placed in Craig's back seat and trunk, they both waved at Signora Carnolla and pulled away from the villa. "We've completed our mission."

"Does that mean we have to go home? Can't we stay outside and play?" Julia asked in a playful child's voice.

"We'll certainly not go home yet, my child." He grinned back at her. "We have another adorable Italian village to visit. Remember, Sergio said they wouldn't expect us for dinner. No one is waiting for us. Except for the wine, of course."

Relief coursed through her. More hours to savor. "Yes, of course."

The rest of the afternoon passed like a dream for Julia. The town of San Casciano completed her perfect day with Craig. The Tuscan warmth of the stone and yellow-toned buildings, narrow passageways, and lively town center spoke to her senses, filling them completely. As if that weren't enough, having Craig beside her to share the experience imprinted the whole day indelibly in her mind. He listened attentively and occasionally touched her shoulder or her low back as they walked along. It didn't necessarily mean anything. But she liked it, despite her reflex of quickly putting up a wall. It hadn't occurred to her to do that with Craig.

In the early evening as the sun spilled mellow orange light across the sky, the trattoria, bars, and restaurants lit up and cast a golden glimmer on the stone square. Craig and Julia needed no more invitation than that to choose one and have a leisurely dinner under the setting Tuscan sun. Their conversation flowed as if they were old friends. The ease of communicating with him didn't escape her notice, though she sent herself several silent warnings to rein in her thoughts.

Finally, after nine-thirty, they arrived back at the De Luca villa. Julia couldn't regret that the day was ending, so sated was she with pleasure. It filled her to overflowing to the point that whatever happened with Craig or the De Lucas afterward, she'd keep the memory forever as a private treasure.

Craig planned to drop off the wine before driving them back to Florence. Giuseppe emerged from the front of the house and came out to the driveway. Lifting one arm, he directed Craig to drive to the side of the villa. There, they found an entrance to the wine cellar. Julia stood next to the car and waited while the men carried the full jugs downstairs to the cellar.

When they were finished, Giuseppe said to Craig, "Isabelle and Mia arrived this evening. Isabelle was hoping to see you, but she got too tired after her trip. She said she'd see you tomorrow, but she wants you to call her."

Craig nodded but said nothing.

Isabelle. The cousin she hadn't yet met, but would soon. Julia hoped to meet Luca and his family, too, before her departure. She wondered if her two other cousins were aware of her visit to Italy. She lifted her eyes toward the upstairs windows and saw a woman staring down at them. Possibly Isabelle. The woman didn't wave, but jerked the curtain back into place, as if afraid of being seen. Maybe it was Mia.

Julia was sleepy during the drive back to Florence but didn't want to miss a moment of that day. She might have nodded off once or twice, because it seemed only minutes before they sat in front of her lodging in Oltracorno in Florence.

"You're talking less, Julia, but that's okay. I think I've worn you out today."

She smiled at him. "It was fabulous. I mean it. You are a great tour guide, Stefano. I had a wonderful day." She paused as they locked eyes. "Thank you."

Craig stared back at her, his eyes visible despite the nightfall that shadowed his face. "Thank *you*. It was wonderful to spend the day with you, Julia. You were an unexpected treat for my trip to Italy."

He reached out and squeezed her hand. Held it for a moment. An electric warmth moved up her arm and sparked between them in the darkness of the car.

"It was the same for me, Craig."

She opened the car door and stepped down. Craig rounded the car to accompany her to Signora Vecchietti.'s door. An awkward moment passed as they stood still, facing each other in the darkened street. He took her hand and lifted it to his lips, where he pressed a kiss. "*Buona notte*, Julia."

"*Buona notte*, Stefano," she said softly.

He waited for her to push open the massive wooden door and give him a final wave, then pulled away into the quiet street.

Chapter Ten

Julia sped down the wide, wooden staircase, like a teenager about to go to a party. A bubble of contentment floated inside her, despite her internal admonishment to tamp it down. At the foot of the stairs, she came to an abrupt halt as Signora Vecchietti emerged from her ground-floor apartment.

"*Buongiorno, Signora. Comme sta?*" Practice of the daily greeting had improved her accent, though she still knew only a few phrases.

The older woman smiled at her. "*Molto bene, Julia, et Lei?*" She tightened the belt of her colorful dressing gown and turned toward a row of metal mailboxes.

"*Bene, grazie. Buona giournata, Signora.*" The woman waved goodbye as Julia pushed the heavy door and exited onto the street. Early morning sunshine poured down, warming her shoulders.

She took her time at the café, savoring a second cup of coffee as well as the feeling of being a local, after just one week. She could always pretend. The coffee here was addictive, much smoother than the American brand she usually bought. Maybe she'd tuck a few packages of it into her suitcase.

As she watched the morning foot traffic through the open window of the café, her mind returned frequently to her day with Craig. A tingle of warmth filled her. She'd never been very fortunate in male relationships. Besides that, he seemed a bit too good to be true. For her, anyway. But she couldn't stop herself from enjoying the memory of spending the whole day with him, sharing parts of herself, her thoughts, her life, and having it all feel so natural, so automatic. Aside from that, she had to admit, he was so darned attractive. Meeting someone like him was as novel an experience for her as hopping on a plane with under twenty-four hours' notice and flying to Florence.

The previous evening after he dropped her off at her hotel, she'd texted him the photos of the two of them in a selfie and the goats from Montefioralle. There was no response yet from him, but it wasn't yet ten in the morning. Aside from that, he probably had work obligations, though he'd said little about the work he had to do while he was in Italy.

Julia shook her head and grimaced in warning to herself. She couldn't deny the pull she felt toward him. It had grown steadily throughout the course of the day they'd spent together. Maybe the magical scenery of lush vineyards and picture-quaint Tuscan towns gave everything about that day a rosy glow in her mind. Including Craig. She'd be wise to protect herself, pay attention to the alarms going off inside of her head. Her mother hadn't fully done that and ended up with a heartache.

Yet, she remembered with razor-sharp clarity how he looked at her with his steady, green eyes while she spoke, the kinds of questions he asked, as if he truly cared, even though he'd met her only the day before. Did he do this with every woman he met? Had he broken hearts all over Europe and the east coast of the United States? Or was he simply a decent guy who'd been nice to her and showed her around Chianti? End of story? Maybe.

The giddy joy she'd felt since last evening had to be reined in and subject to discipline. Hope could be messy. Despite her best efforts, Julia felt genuinely happy and optimistic. *Also* a new experience for her. She wasn't necessarily a pessimist, but liked to think of herself as a pragmatist, stable in her emotions, not given to any extremes, either positive or negative. She decided to enjoy her buoyant attitude but keep in the back of her mind that it could lead to nothing, like a morning mist burning off in the rays of summer sun.

After checking in with Crystal, she was satisfied that things were still running smoothly in her business. Her clients had been understanding about the slower pace of their design deadlines. It was August, after all. Many of them were on vacation, too. She felt a stab of guilt for the little thought she'd given to her business since arriving in Italy. A year ago, that would never have happened.

Julia stood up and smoothed down her cotton short-sleeve blouse. She scooped her journal and notepad from the table then slipped them into her purse. A day in Florence awaited her so she began walking, heading as in a trance to the river. The sound and sight of flowing river currents invited and soothed her.

She savored a new day to spend in the enchanted city. Nothing had been scheduled with the family and that made her slightly uneasy. Would she see them again, or had they had enough of her? She hoped she'd at least have closure with them before she returned home.

Of course, she was being silly. A full week of her trip remained. Aside from that, she *had* established something with them as a family. She could always just phone them if she wanted to see them again or say goodbye.

Maybe someone from the villa or Valentina had texted her. Or maybe Craig had. She stopped along the wrought iron railing next to the river and pulled her phone from her purse. She looked at the screen. Nothing. *Relax, Julia. Don't make a problem out of nothing.* She really should stop doing that. Her thoughts went to her renewed spiritual commitment. *Lord, please help me to let go and simply enjoy your blessings in the now. I'm in the world's most beautiful city and I somehow find something to be tense about. Thank you, thank you for bringing me here.*

Well, she wouldn't go down the negative road of what-ifs. She was determined to change the habit that started when she was young as she waited for the other shoe to drop. Where had that expression come from anyway? Though she didn't know its origin, she certainly understood its meaning.

Her phone vibrated in her hand. Craig. Her pulse quickened and she couldn't suppress a smile. "Hi, Craig. Or are you going by Stefano today?" A spot of humor would mask her nerves.

"Hi, Julia. I hope you are rested after yesterday. Thanks for the photos you sent. They'll be great souvenirs." He paused. She heard traffic noise in the background. "I wondered if you'd like to go for a walk or meet for coffee later, maybe at two, if you're free."

Let's see, am I free? Julia grinned but kept her voice calm. "Sure, that would be great. Two is good. Where do you want to meet?"

"Let's meet at the Ponte Vecchio on the Florence side, where the bridge meets the riverbank. Then we'll find a place to sit or maybe just walk."

"Okay, I'll see you then."

Julia glanced at her watch. She still had over three hours before meeting him, so she'd stick with her original idea to visit the Bargello Museum. She'd wanted to find a museum that was smaller or at least less crowded than the Uffizi. Bargello wasn't far from Ponte Vecchio, either.

She located it with no difficulty, a thirteenth-century fortress with a straight, brooding tower which had been converted into a museum of Renaissance art. The first floor led to a courtyard so impressive, she wondered what the rest of it would be like. She wandered through the rooms and up to the second floor, admiring the paintings and sculptures of European masters as well as the stunning frescos on the vaulted ceilings. As she did, her mind went again and again to Craig, like a bird lighting repeatedly on a forgotten delicacy. Why had he wanted to see her again? She'd sensed but downplayed her suspicion that he was as attracted to her as she was to him. Maybe he simply enjoyed her company. Was a foreigner in Florence and sought some companionship?

She shook her head with a grimace to herself and turned her attention back to the spectacularly detailed sculptures and timeless masterpieces around her. They would certainly help take her mind off her two o'clock appointment.

Many of the Renaissance art pieces followed a religious theme. Julia imagined believers in an age where everyone had at least an outward form of faith. Was it difficult to live out a true relationship with God when the government dictated peoples' spiritual devotion? Many people in contemporary western society lived secular lives, which made believers stand out in some way, whether positively, negatively, or simply differently. She wondered if any of her employees or neighbors knew of her faith. Likely not. The hamster wheel was spinning too fast for them to see anything besides her devotion to her business and her precise work ethic.

She stopped in front of a sculpture by della Robbia and stared at it for several minutes. In a medieval artistic style, it depicted mourners taking Christ down from the cross after his death. She sensed their grief as they did the unimaginable, handled the dead body of the one they'd so loved and trusted to give them a better way. Fingers of emotion thrummed in her chest creating an ache. Then a voice beside her said something in Italian. She turned her head and a kind-faced woman, fiftyish, with wispy blond hair was directing a comment to her. Julia smiled and shook her head. "*Mi dispiace, non parlo molto italiano.*"

The woman smiled back. "You said that very well. I was just saying we weren't there when this happened, but this sculpture gives us an image of what it must have been like. The sadness and hopelessness of Christ's death." She turned again to stare at the sculpture. She, too, seemed deeply moved by the portrayal in the sculpture.

"Yes, that's true," Julia said softly. "At that point, the people wouldn't yet know he would rise from the dead." She had no idea if the woman believed that, but it was worth mentioning. Might plant a seed. "We don't often see art like this created in our day, but back then no one was shocked. They found it normal."

"And yet, here are the crowds in Florence's museums looking at them. Paying to look at them, even." Humor laced the woman's voice then she turned back to Julia. "Have you seen the naked Christ portrayal in the other room? It's quite remarkable, since most depictions I've seen have a little cloth."

Julia furrowed her brow. "No, I haven't seen it. It's hard to imagine such humiliation added to what he already suffered." Her throat tightened at the thought.

"I don't know if it was really like that, but it probably was. His enemies weren't interested in preserving his dignity." She frowned then her eyes found Julia's. "You are a believer?" Her question, posed in a serious yet level tone, surprised Julia. The woman's eyes were eager and bright.

Julia nodded. "Yes, I am. Since my college days. And you?" The woman had given Julia an easy way to ask.

"I knew you were by your statement. I am, too. He is my Savior. And my friend." The features of her face softened with her words, as if she spoke of a deeply beloved family member.

My friend. A sudden gush of emotion filled the cavity inside Julia with longing, almost a physical force that made her breath hitch. Her eyes filled. She blinked and smiled, attempting to rebalance herself. "Yes. He is." He always was. She was the one who'd drifted away. How deeply she thirsted for his friendship just now.

A man with a neatly cropped gray beard appeared beside the woman. She turned and murmured to him in Italian. To Julia, she said, "It was nice speaking with you."

Julia responded with a smile as the couple moved on to the next room. The encounter stayed with her as she strolled through the other rooms and climbed to the third floor, almost distracting her from her meeting with Craig. It was as though God himself had arranged for her to meet another believer, right here in Italy. His children were everywhere on the planet. She was warmed by the thought of that, and of Jesus as her friend.

By two o'clock, she'd managed to leave the museum and scurry to the Ponte Vecchio. She didn't see Craig. After a few minutes of people-watching, or rather, watching people look at jewelry displays in shop windows, she spied him walking briskly toward her. A small flutter began inside. He wore off-white casual pants, a dark blue polo, and sandals. Sunglasses sat on his head. He didn't look like he was coming from a business meeting.

He closed the distance between them as his eyes found hers. "Have you been waiting for long?"

"No, not at all. But you arrived just in time. I was about to make a jewelry purchase." She jerked her head toward the jewelry vendors on the bridge.

He laughed. "So, you should thank me for saving you some money." He stood for a moment. A smile stretched across his face. As if catching himself staring, he averted his eyes then looked back at her. "Are you ready to walk? Or would you rather have a coffee or cold drink?"

"Walking is always good with me. I haven't been able to get enough of it since I arrived here. And I *have* had my coffee and gelato for the day. Which I'll need to walk off."

"If you're ready for a somewhat long but scenic walk, we can head west along the right bank to the *Parco delle Cascine*. It's a huge city park along the river. You could say it's the locals' park." He gestured up the river with one hand.

"Sounds great. I think I'll just call it the *Parco*." She fell into step beside him and they left the throng of tourists at Ponte Vecchio. Walking along the river suited her perfectly, since she could keep it in her view as she was soothed by the sound of flowing water. "I figured there had to be a park for the residents, since some of the others charge admission for the sake of tourism."

After dodging clusters of tourists for another two blocks, the crowds mostly fell away. Craig said, "You'll see that the park is pretty amazing. First, it's huge, the biggest park in the city. It has loads of space for picnics, biking, walking, things like that, but there is also a bike track *and* a horse track inside it."

"Sounds enormous. And fun. Do you go there often when you visit Florence?" She longed to move away from small talk, but had long lacked skills in conversation. Usually, she felt at ease with Craig. That day, it seemed they were both dodging the subject of the previous day in Chianti.

"It depends on how long a particular trip is and how many early meetings I have. I try to go for a run there as many days as I can manage."

Made sense that he was a runner or did some other kind of athletic activity, since there didn't seem to be any fat on him, statistically unusual for a man his age. She hoped by the time she returned home, that would be the case for her, too, if she could balance excessive walking with excessive gelato-eating. "Do you do any other sports?"

"Walking, basketball on occasion. I like to ski, too. All of that depends on my travel and work schedule, unfortunately. I try to keep up with it enough to stay fit. I'm fifty, you know. Gotta be diligent."

"A mere child." She grinned at him. "I wanted to thank you for a wonderful day yesterday. You're a great tour guide." There, she'd broken the ice. Or maybe the ice was only in her mind.

No, judging by the look on his face. It softened and something changed in his eyes. "Thanks, but it was totally my pleasure. It was a great day for me, too." He paused and added with a slight hitch of his head, "Unforgettable."

Unforgettable. Her mind repeated the word, hoping it wasn't an exaggeration for him. It certainly wasn't for her. But she wouldn't read anything into it. A wave of pleasure flowed through her, all the same. "I think Chianti is my new favorite place, after Florence."

"You'll probably say the same thing with each new Italian town or village you see."

"True."

The further they walked from the city center, the more open the landscape, with free-standing buildings in beige and ochre instead of entire blocks crammed with apartments and stores stacked upon each other. The tourist crowds had thinned and the area resembled an average Italian city of residents scurrying as they did their daily errands. During their walk to the *Parco*, Craig talked more about his work in Italy and in the States, as well as some of his favorite towns in Tuscany.

On the next block ahead, the street opened up to a large square dominated by a towering statue. Julia stopped to take a photo with her phone of the piazza and surrounding buildings.

"That's a statue of Carlo Goldoni. He was an Italian playwright." Craig stood next to her as they observed the square where the statue cast a long shadow on the pavement. "That's about all I know, but I'm still trying to be a good tour guide."

Julia grinned. "You've already proven yourself, Stefano. You're off duty now. You could tell me it's a statue of somebody important in the past and that would be fine with me. That's exactly the type of tour guide *I* would be." She mimicked the voice of a tour guide. "On your left is a building that's well-known for something at some point in history."

Craig laughed. "You're pretty funny, Julia de Luca."

They shared a laugh as his eyes caught hers. Her face warmed and the hum inside grew louder.

His comment had taken her off guard. Her humor normally only surfaced when she was with her girlfriends or other people with whom she felt entirely at ease. She found it was natural to let down her barriers with Craig. To be completely herself, despite the jitters of attraction that came and went.

Ten minutes later, Julia spied a wall of trees in the distance. "That must be it, the *Parco*." She'd welcome some shade, since the afternoon August sun beat down on them as they walked.

"Yep, that's it. You could spend the entire day in the *Parco* and never get bored. You'd lounge by the riverfront, ride a bike, take pictures. On Tuesdays they have a great open market. Then sometimes in summer there are festivals and things like that. It's mostly big spaces, trees, paths. You'll see. Not like Boboli with all the fountains and statues, or even like Bardini next to it, which is also really nice."

As soon as they entered the park, a fresh layer of peace descended on Julia as a hush surrounded them. Being away from the city was calming, as were the towering trees in all directions and the wide, grassy fields in front of her. They strolled down a shaded path then Craig led her through the trees to a sloping terraced embankment that hugged the river as far as she could see.

"Mmm. This is perfect. My happy place. The grass is so green and thick, I'm tempted to roll around in it." Julia's eyes followed the line of the embankment. All over the grassy slopes clusters of people sat reading or picnicking. Their faraway voices and laughter laced the calm of the setting like musical notes. A slight breeze coated the hot sun, a caress after the heat. If Julia had been a cat, she'd be purring.

"Thought you'd like it. Want to sit here for a while? We've done our athletics."

They sat on the lush grass close to the river under the shade offered by a row of birches behind them. Julia stretched out her legs and leaned back on her arms. She and Craig stared out at the river for a moment in companionable silence.

She turned her head toward him. "Please tell me more about your life. Your family, childhood, stuff like that." She wanted to learn about him at a deeper level. He'd hinted at a large family. When she saw his jaw tighten, she regretted her request. "Only if you're comfortable, that is."

He swatted the air dismissively, though his lips pressed together. "No, it's fine. I know you value the merits of family, but families aren't always what they ought to be. I think I've hinted at that." He stared out at the greenish water of the Arno and sighed.

"Yes, I picked that up," she said softly. "I'm not trying to dig where I don't belong, Craig. I just want to get to know you better. Please feel free to change the subject."

He turned back to her with a half-smile and reached out to gently squeeze her hand. He held it for a few seconds, rubbing it with his thumb. The core of heat that had begun inside her when she first saw him at the bridge blossomed into a bonfire at his affectionate gesture. Quietly, he said, "No, Julia. I want you to know these things about me. I shouldn't hide them just because some of them were painful. I no longer hide them from myself, either."

She cocked her head to a listening angle, hoping her face spoke acceptance and compassion. He released her hand and circled his arms around bent knees. "I was the middle child of five. We know that middle kids sometimes feel overlooked, but it was a little worse than that for me. There was that, but my two older siblings were close in age. Sisters. Then there was a gap of a few years, then me. Another gap for a few years, then two more siblings, boy and girl, again close in age. You see where I'm going, don't you?"

"Like an only child, but not."

"Exactly. So, my sisters were a pair and my younger siblings were a pair and I couldn't seem to find my place with either group. I never felt like I belonged in my own family. To make matters worse, my parents both worked a lot. A doctor and a lawyer, both wrapped up in their careers. Why they chose to have five of us, I'll never understand, because they didn't have the emotional resources to deal with all of us plus maintain those kinds of careers."

"So, you were lonely in your own family." Her heart ached for him. She never imagined that could be possible. Five children, two parents, and still lonely.

"I was always an extrovert, so I coped by making loads of friends. My friends were everything, and they filled the void to some degree. Since people outside of my family were so important to me, I learned very well what it took to get along with everyone, to impress everyone, be the life of the party, be popular. I had it down to a science. And it worked for me. I *was* popular. Had friends, girlfriends. I thought I had it all figured out."

"But?"

"I suppose I could have gone my whole life like that, except for the occasional moments of self-doubt, questions like, do people know the real me, would they like me if they did, things like that. Those questions didn't surface very often, so it didn't bother me much. I got married in my mid-twenties. Had my children a few years later. Standard timeline, you know. Instead of friendships, my identity was wrapped up in my family. Of course, I still had friends. But I had an additional identity that further distanced me from my real self. Life was busy. I traveled a lot. I didn't see things unraveling in my family and by the time I did, it was too late."

He looked down at his hands and was silent for a long moment. Julia didn't know if she should say something, and stayed silent. A dog barked in the distance. Laughter erupted somewhere, and spurts of muffled conversation pierced the silence.

Craig swallowed and took a deep breath. His gaze drifted to the river as he spoke. His voice was quiet. "My son, Jason, had a drug problem for a couple of years as a teen. He's okay now, but that was the first wake-up call. My daughter, Rebecca, never got into too much trouble. She modeled her dad's high achieving ways then got married fairly young. But my wife—she had her affair, which apparently went on for a couple years, and things got much worse. Following our separation, I lost my job and was unemployed for almost a year. I lost my family and professional identity all at once." He shrugged and met her eyes. "I spent months wondering who I was."

"That sounds hard." Julia had always thought her lot was the hardest, being an only child of a single mom, but everyone seemed to have something difficult to overcome. It was a question of type and degree. And it was a revelation for her. They'd both felt lonely as children.

"It *was* hard, but it was a defining year for me." His voice took on a lilt of passion.

"Really? How so?" Julia sat up straighter.

His tense features relaxed. "One positive thing that came out of being stripped of all of my habits that worked for so long is that I became less dependent on them. I guess you could say I was set free from them, and I grew as a person. I *needed* to because I'd become a shell. A successful, popular shell with nothing much on the inside. That year made me look at myself pretty hard and decide what was important." He looked at her and smiled. "It was also through that experience that I met the Lord. He gave me pretty much everything I was lacking all those years."

Julia allowed the burgeoning smile that had begun inside to spread across her face, despite the tears that had gathered in her eyes. "Wow. That's huge. And it inspires me." The tears spilled down and she flicked them away. "Meeting the Lord changes everything already. But the personal growth you experienced through that trial—it was like you met yourself for the first time."

He smiled then and their eyes locked. His green eyes were filled with emotion. "I couldn't have said it better myself. And now looking back, I don't regret it. I'm *thankful* for it. Someone looking from the outside would probably think my circumstances aren't better than before, but worse. I'm a single guy living in a two-bedroom apartment. But I know I'm better off. On the inside I'm better off."

"Where it counts." Julia blinked a few more times. Why was she so emotional today? She'd been stirred after her encounter with the woman at the museum. Now this. Where was the focused business woman from D.C., the one respected by the design community, known to be level-headed?

Yet, it felt clean, healthy, to reach places in her heart she'd forgotten were there. She didn't want to stop going there. On the contrary, she longed for an experience like Craig's, so she could get to know herself better and discover what coping mechanisms she still had that were blocking her from something better. From knowing God better, loving others more. Accepting herself and her life more.

"You're quiet, Julia. What are you thinking about? Did I disturb you with what I shared?"

His voice was gentle, his face concerned. Julia felt a gush of tenderness for him and a sudden desire to throw her arms around him. She held back and smiled. "Not at all. I'm deeply touched by what you said. Thank you for your trust in me. I feel closer to you and happy for you . . ." She struggled for words. "I'm drawn, like the Lord is calling me to something more. Inviting me to go deeper. He's been saying little things all during my trip, like he's calling me back. Back to him, first. But it's not only about him, it's also my own life I'm thinking about. The way I always responded to things."

"What kinds of things? What responses?"

Oh boy. She'd turned the light onto her past and now she had to follow through. But he'd talked about his and she wanted to tell him, to be transparent. "You know some things already. I grew up with a single mom, never knew my father, and always wanted a bigger family. I saw my mom working hard every day, sacrificing for my sake. In spite of all she did for me, but I still felt deprived. Then that attitude made me feel guilty." She took a deep breath as her memories slid backward into the past. "When I was around eight—I can't remember exactly what age—my mom started dating a doctor from the hospital where she worked. I called him Doctor Sam.

Before that, I used to encourage her to date, since I wanted a dad and siblings. When she finally started dating Doctor Sam, I was thrilled. *Finally*. I liked him. He used to come to our apartment for dinner once in a while. Occasionally he stayed over. My mom was happier than I'd ever seen her. After a few months, the relationship was going so well that she and I both allowed ourselves to dream a little. We'd talk about whether she thought he'd propose, what our life might be like afterward. I was overtaken with fantasies about it, picturing myself with siblings, going on family vacations, living in a nice house. My mom probably wouldn't have to work anymore, since he was a doctor and probably rich. For almost a year she and I both lived on the joy of that prospect. Then it all ended. Suddenly."

"What happened?" Craig's brows furrowed.

"She learned that Doctor Sam was married. No intention of leaving his wife to marry my mother. He'd never told her until she started to hint about their future together and marriage."

"Oh, I'm so sorry. How devastating. And what a jerk he was."

Julia looked down at the grass. Amazing that telling the story still created a hollow ache in the cavern of her gut. She'd grieved for herself, but also her mother. "It devastated both of us. The dreams we'd been weaving for months crashed and burned. But here's the worst thing about it. After that, neither of us dared to hope anymore. We stopped risking our hearts. I say "we" because I watched her do it and recently, I've become aware that I do it, too." Her voice fell as she felt the tears pushing hotly against her eyes then tumbling down her cheeks. How was she still raw about Doctor Sam after all these years?

She looked up at Craig as words stuck in her throat. She swallowed painfully. He reached up and gently, tenderly wiped her tears.

A sheepish chuckle escaped her throat. "I feel kind of stupid. It was so long ago and I'm still crying about it." She shook her head and stared down at her hands. "There's more. When I got married—this is the first time I'm telling this to anyone, because I'm only just realizing it now—I married a man I liked and got along well with, but I wasn't in love with him. I didn't want it to hurt too badly when it ended, so I didn't wait for the real thing. I didn't realize the difference between true love and what I'd settled for until we'd been married for about three years."

Craig watched her silently, as if considering what to say. "I'm guessing that the fallout of the Doctor Sam experience had invaded other relationships ever since. Maybe it still hurts under the surface, unless, of course, you stay too busy to hope *or* hurt."

Silently, she nodded, feeling x-rayed by his insight. "I have to admit that my work has been an anesthesia, because I love it and can easily pour myself into it. I'm afraid to let myself simply *be*, though I've started learning to do that only since being here in Italy. It's such an unexpected gift and such a sensory overload. God has answered in so many ways. I'm unable to even describe it."

In the silence that followed, Craig said with mock seriousness, "And then you met me."

Julia laughed. "Yes, to top it off, I met you!" Her smile remained but softened as she held his eyes. "You really are a blessing, you know." Her statement warmed her face with embarrassment. Maybe she'd said too much too soon, but it had slipped out. But it was okay.

"I'm glad. And you are to me." He held her gaze then his eyes roved around her face. For a moment, she thought he'd kiss her, and the prospect overwhelmed her with craving. Instead, he leaned back on his arms. "Learning to *be* is a good goal. Living in the moment. Maybe . . ." He shrugged and gestured with one hand. ". . . we can work on that together. We'll plan some things and your assignment is to enjoy the moment. How does that sound?"

Relieved and deflated at the same time, she said, "Sounds great. I still have a week in Italy. Looking forward to things is good, but finding joy in the present is important, too."

"It's sort of related to thankfulness."

"Joy in the moment *is* tied to thankfulness, isn't it? Whether we name it or not."

Julia marveled. She'd only had conversations like this with Marissa, Sydney, and Eden. It was wonderful and unsettling at the same time to be so transparent with Craig. In one way, she'd forged a new bond with him because of the things they'd shared about themselves. The fear of losing him after such a risky investment cast shadows of dread inside her. Yet, she also needed to respond better to disappointments and losses, without letting them shut her down, because they, too, would surely come.

Her return to the States was a full week away, but already she sensed she wouldn't, shouldn't return to the exact same life of hamster-wheel avoidance. How could she? Another week before returning to her world. Maybe God would make it stick by then.

Chapter Eleven

Julia sipped down the last drops of cappuccino, glanced at her watch, and stood up to leave. For the last hour she'd been sitting near the window at the coffee shop on the corner of her street in Oltrarno, reading the news and emails from home on her phone as she waited for the De Luca flagship store to open at ten. At least she had something constructive to do that day, instead of being endlessly preoccupied with thoughts of Craig. Valentina had called the previous evening to invite her to the villa for dinner, for which she was grateful.

The sun flooded into the café and Julia closed her eyes, allowing the warmth to seep into her skin. Since the previous day with Craig, she'd decided to take his suggestion and practice thankfulness. In Florence, she found this easy. Maybe she could develop the habit before returning home. Being thankful led her to prayer, then back to thankfulness. A gratifying circle, given her goal of restoring her relationship with God.

"*A domani,*" she called to the smiling, round-faced woman behind the counter. Carmella. Julia already knew her by name, since she went to the same café each day for luscious Italian coffee and a cornetto or some other kind of pastry. Coming to the same café every day made her feel like part of the neighborhood, like a normal resident, surrounded by other Italians. With her Italian looks, she likely blended in, that is, until she opened her mouth. But her practiced phrases were sounding better each day. She didn't know if that was a good thing or not, since she was unable to go any further in a conversation. Frustrating. Yet, that frustration would serve as fuel for learning the language.

She walked down the Via Maggio toward the river, crossed the Ponte Santa Trinita and followed her city map to the address Sergio had given her. She turned onto a broad, pedestrian shopping street and joined the flow of people hurrying, shopping, and strolling. An electric energy filled the air and Julia fully partook of it. Another visual scan up and down the row of shops and she saw it, *De Luca Scarpe*. A medium-sized storefront of plate glass stretched out to display dozens of pairs of shoes. She stopped to observe the many styles, some similar to what she'd seen in the factory. She backed up a few paces and took a photo of the storefront with her phone. It seemed warm and inviting, but rather traditional.

Julia pushed open the door and went inside. Several customers were talking softly with salespeople, surrounded by open boxes with various styles of shoes spilling out. She pretended to browse the rows of shoes. A few immediate ideas flooded her mind, ways to transform the shop into a modern-looking attraction for savvy shoppers. She jotted down some of her initial ideas on a small notepad she kept in her purse. While everyone seemed busy helping customers, she snapped a couple more photos of the boutique.

"Posso aiutare?" A female voice from behind startled her. Julia turned to see a shop employee asking to help her.

"Non, grazie." Julia smiled at the woman, youngish with a tight ponytail pulled back. Her gaze was severe, distrustful. She must have seen Julia taking photos. Maybe the woman needed more explanation. Julia would have to revert to English, having fully exhausted her Italian vocabulary.

"I'm visiting Florence and was interested in seeing the design of stores here. You see, I'm an interior designer." Should she tell the woman she was a De Luca and had been asked to come up with some ideas for the showroom? She didn't know. "I've spoken with Signore Regio about this."

At the mention of Sergio's name, the woman's eyes widened. "Ah, *capisco*. I understand. You are welcome to look at the shoes and the store. Tell me if you need any help."

"Thank you. The shoes are lovely."

This met with a smug nod from the woman. "Yes, they are."

Julia smiled at the woman. She might just need to buy a pair as a completely appropriate souvenir from Italy. Not just any shoes, De Luca shoes.

She took a curving staircase to the second floor and found another equally traditional space filled with men's shoes. She took several photos then returned downstairs. After taking three more photos of the main part of the store, Julia was drawn by a pair of colorful sling-back flats. She tried them on in her size and bought a pair. Pleased with her purchase, she left the store and continued strolling through the crowded street. She stopped for lunch followed by a gelato. While she ate, she scanned her phone.

As Craig had suggested the day of their Chianti visit, she found the Santa Croce church, created from the same colored marble as the Duomo. She mounted the steps and went inside. Once her eyes adjusted to the dim light, she caught her breath. He hadn't exaggerated. The beauty of the frescos drew her gaze for more than a few minutes. She stood still, drinking it in. Then Julia took her time as she strolled past the sixteen small chapels, gazed at the altar and the stained glass.

The air was cool and damp. Muted voices occasionally pierced through the hovering silence. Julia pushed aside thoughts of Craig and tried to focus on the present moment, on the calm all around her, on the gold-tone crucifix before her. *My friend.* The words of the woman from the Bargello museum came back to her. Jesus, her friend. He was speaking to her still, calling her back. *I'm sorry, Lord. I'm on my way back.* She murmured softly, feeling small in the cavernous space as tendrils of faith and awe began to unfurl inside her. In her fast-paced life so far removed from quiet reflection, it was easy, too easy, to jump into the lane of life and miss so much that was vital.

Again, she recalled the year when she came to know Him, to be adopted by Almighty God. Her fatherless void had been filled to overflowing. Yet, in the subsequent years, He was not the one who had drifted away. *My Father.* She was still his daughter. *I'm still here, Father. I want to feel what I felt before, close to You.* She paused as her eyes stung. *I want to be filled instead of empty.* Yet, that change had begun, she knew it, felt it. God had to take her all the way to Italy to speak to her, call her back.

Following her visit to the church, Julia walked. She walked for an hour, covering the main parts of the city. She had wanted to see everything with her own feet and eyes. *Bring me back, guide the way, Lord. Help me be open to joy*, she kept praying as she walked. The beauty of Florence filled her eyes, but the burgeoning desire fueled by her prayers filled her entirely.

As she returned toward Oltrarno, she looked at her watch and gasped. She'd lost track of time. It was four o'clock and she was expected that evening at the villa for dinner. Maybe she'd finally meet her cousin Isabelle, who had arrived the day before yesterday. Two cousins down, one to go. She didn't know if Luca would be there at the dinner, but she doubted it. Valentina had told her he kept to himself.

She hadn't seen Valentina in a few days and she missed her cousin. Maybe she could ask her for a ride that evening so she could see her again. In addition to that pleasure, she'd also be on time for dinner. Or she could call Craig and ask him if he were attending the dinner. She should, though he hadn't mentioned it the previous day. After their intimate conversation, he might fear she was now assuming something about their relationship, so she called Valentina instead.

"*Buongiorno*. I've missed you, Cousin."

"I have missed you, too, Julia. I traveled to Milan for work but just got back this morning. I hope you're enjoying your time in Florence."

"Oh, yes. Very much. I was able to see some of Tuscany and had a proper visit of Florence, including the Santa Croce, Bargello, and Parco delle Cascine. I hope I pronounced those right." She held back mentioning Craig, as if it would somehow jinx her. She *must* get rid of those thought habits. Yet, she didn't want Valentina jumping to conclusions before Julia herself knew what her status was with Craig.

"*Si, perfetto*! You've seen many beautiful things. I'm so glad it's a good visit for you."

"Are you going to the villa for dinner tonight? And can you take me with you?"

When Valentina said, "Yes, of course," Julia sighed with relief. She didn't relish the idea of the train and the bus then waiting in the field until someone picked her up. "I will come by your flat at five-thirty to pick you up."

"Fabulous. Thanks so much, Valentina."

That way, she'd have time to clean up and dress for dinner.

At five-forty, Julia stood in front of the big, wooden door waiting on the street for Valentina. She wore a loose-fitting red dress, its light fabric perfect for a summer evening, and red sandals with small heels. Valentina's sporty red Fiat pulled around the corner and stopped. Julia slipped into the passenger seat.

On the way to the villa, Valentina chatted about her trip, who she saw, where she went. "Milan is a very cosmopolitan place, and not so far from Firenze. It's the Italian capital of the fashion industry, so what Milan wants, Milan gets. We listen to them. But there's a lot of culture, too. And a gorgeous cathedral. You can plan to go on your next trip to Italy, *non?*"

Julia grinned. "Maybe. I'm just trying to enjoy this visit first."

They arrived at the villa before dinner. Giuseppe, Sergio, and Emilia were sitting in the living room talking in Italian. With them was another woman whose back faced the doorway as she talked to Sergio and Emilia. The woman's head turned toward the doorway when Valentina and Julia entered. Her jet-black hair, full, pouty lips and dark eyes, gave her a dramatic, stunning beauty.

Emilia stood when they entered. "Julia, this is your cousin Isabelle."

Isabelle rose, gave Julia a cordial but reserved smile. She extended her hand and shook Julia's. "I heard that I had a new cousin. Well, I guess not a new one, but one I hadn't met." Her English was nearly flawless, edged with a slight accent.

Emilia sat down. "Yes, you met Julia and her mother when they were here years ago, but you were too young to remember."

"I remember the stories, though." Isabelle still smiled but her eyes were frosty.

A cool shudder rippled through Julia. Was Isabelle another Emilia, clinging to Gianna's mistakes? A picture of a two-headed dragon flashed into Julia's mind and she flinched. Emilia may have inculcated Isabelle with her anger toward Gianna and anyone born to her, or else Isabelle had absorbed it over the years through the silent anger. When would this craziness stop?

"What did you see today in Florence, Julia?" Emilia asked her, warming up slightly.

No one had asked her to sit, so Julia remained standing near the doorway, feeling like she'd interrupted their conversation. Valentina had left the room. "I did a lot of walking around the city, which I do nearly every day. It's nice to get the overview that way. I also visited Santa Croce."

"Ah, I'm sure you found it beautiful, inside and outside. And did you enjoy Chianti the other day?"

"Very much." That was easy to answer. "What a stunning region." A warm glow rose up inside her at the memory. Intuition told her not to mention the day at the *Parco*.

"You were gone all day. Was Stefano a good tour guide?" At Emilia's question, Julia thought she saw Isabelle stiffen.

"Yes, he knows the area very well. He actually speaks more Italian than he leads everyone to believe."

Emilia let out a polite laugh and slid a quick glance toward Isabelle. Something was going on, but Julia didn't have a clue what it was. Her spine prickled.

"Dinner is ready," Sergio announced.

Just then, voices rose in the marble hall. Julia recognized Craig talking to someone. A smile slid across her face. When Isabelle impaled her with a stare, she let it fade.

Craig appeared in the doorway and began, "*Scuzi—*" but was met by laughter.

"You always say this, Stefano." Giuseppe spoke more English than he let on. Craig had indeed perfected his apology for lateness. He glanced at Julia and smiled warmly, then looked toward

Isabelle. Julia couldn't read the expression on his face when he looked at her striking cousin.

Isabelle rose and went to Craig. Her facial expression had completely changed, softened, making her even more beautiful. They gave each other a kiss on each cheek. "*Buona sera*, Isabelle. How was your trip with Mia?"

Isabelle waved the air and rolled her eyes, but followed with a smile only for him. "You can imagine shopping every day in Rome with a young lady, preparing for her coming year. Not so much fun, but we did see some interesting sights."

"And where is the young lady in question? Will she be joining us tonight?" Craig's eyebrows lifted. He turned to Julia. "Isabelle's daughter can be quite entertaining, in her condescending teenage way."

"Unfortunately, she is with her friends tonight, since she leaves for university next week. You will see her tomorrow."

"*Bene.*"

Sergio waited at the door and everyone seemed to remember that he'd called them to dinner. Craig and Isabelle went through the door first. As they passed in front of Julia, Isabelle placed her hand on Craig's arm. Julia froze as a cold wave coursed inside her. They were together? Why hadn't he said something? Maybe it meant nothing except that they were good friends. He'd said nothing about her in the two days they'd spent together.

Everyone sat down around the glass table on the veranda, Isabelle next to Craig and Julia across from them. Beyond awkward. She just wanted to claim a headache or anything at all then excuse herself. She'd been stupid about Craig's intentions. She'd allowed her mind to run away with her without clear evidence. Craig had been kind, attentive, a bit flirtatious, if she were honest. He could have been that way with anyone. He'd said himself that he'd learned what it took to get along with everyone, both male and female. Maybe especially female. She'd read too much into their two days together.

To his credit, he looked uncomfortable and tried to engage her and otherwise include her in the conversations. Not wanting him to guess that she'd assumed too much, Julia tried to respond in a friendly way that would leave no clues to how exposed and humiliated she felt.

"Isabelle, do you work for the De Luca shoe company, too?" she asked her cousin, striving for an open, enthusiastic tone. She already knew the answer, but groped for a conversation opener.

Isabelle turned a cool gaze to Julia as if she'd distracted her from a more important discussion. With a wan smile, she said, "Yes, we're all destined to work at De Luca. It's our family business and we all want to support it with our efforts."

As if she didn't know. Julia kept her eyes on Isabelle's, though she bristled inside. She strove for a tone of naïve innocence, accompanied by a smile. "Well, I'm sure you could work elsewhere if you wanted to. I'm sure the family would want you to follow your *own* dreams. I hope that's true, anyway."

"You can do that in America where everyone can start a business or run for president. It's not like that in Italy." Isabelle's eyes held a challenge.

"I'm sure it's different here, but most individuals can carve their way if they're determined enough. They don't have to blindly follow what everyone else wants them to do." Maybe she'd said too much, was too blunt, but she truly believed in what she said. It might make Isabelle reflect, if she was one who felt conscripted to work in the family business despite her own desires.

Isabelle shot her a bored look and shrugged. She leaned toward Craig in an intimate posture and murmured something to him that

Julia couldn't hear. Maybe she was commenting on the idealistic American.

Craig spoke up, directing his comment to Isabelle, but including Julia. "Julia's an interior designer in the States and has her own company. So, she's not just spouting theory."

Julia sent him a grateful smile. Isabelle didn't respond. It didn't matter. Valentina was a wonderful, sweet cousin. One was enough for her. Julia glanced at Valentina, but her cousin couldn't come to her defense. She'd missed the exchange while she bantered with Giuseppe.

During the rest of the meal, Isabelle did her best to monopolize Craig's attention. Julia had lost her interest in conversing and simply observed. Valentina, who was seated next to her, leaned toward her for the first time and whispered, "Is everything okay, Julia? You seem a bit sad."

Julia smiled. "Just a little tired." Not so much that, but she didn't have anyone to talk to, since everyone seemed involved in their own conversations. She decided that she'd leave the family alone for a few days over the coming weekend. Maybe she was there too often and they were tired of her, or just needed some family time without guests, though she hadn't dined there in the past three days.

During dessert, a creamy panettone with raspberry preserves on top, there was a commotion in the hall, the unfamiliar voice of a man shouting in Italian. Julia heard the conciliatory voice of Amara as she guided the man to the terrace. Fabrizio, the shoe designer Julia had met the day of her tour, stepped down onto the terrace. "*Scuzi, tutti,*" he murmured with a slight bow of his head, which did nothing to soften the aggravation painted on his face. Sergio rose and the two of them went into the house. Their heated voices echoed back to the terrace.

After a few minutes, the sound of their discussion stopped and the front door slammed. Sergio returned to the terrace, a drawn look on his face. He sighed as he sank down into his chair. "Fabrizio has just returned from an early trade show and saw his own designs in someone else's store. He thinks there is a spy at De Luca or else someone on the outside who had access to his work." He gave this news to everyone at the table. Gasps and surprised expressions erupted from several of them.

"A spy? We have never had this problem." Emilia's brow furrowed. "Do we have any new employees that could have come on for that purpose?"

"No one new, except in the warehouse. The boxes are sealed in there, so the chance of spying is low." Sergio reached for his wine glass and downed the last sip.

"The only new person I know of," Isabelle said slowly in English, "is Julia." She leveled a glare at Julia. "The spying seems to have begun when you arrived." She turned to Sergio. "She had a tour of the factory, apparently, and has visited our store in Florence."

Julia stared at Isabelle as a staccato laugh escaped her throat. "You've got to be kidding, Isabelle. That's completely ridiculous."

She shrugged. "A coincidence then?"

"Stop, Isabelle. Julia is your cousin." Despite her defense, Emilia's voice was weak and her face lacked warmth.

Giuseppe said, "*E pazzesco.*" It's crazy. No one else refuted Isabelle directly. Julia hoped no one in the De Luca family gave credence to her insane statement. A heated conversation erupted in Italian at the end of the table, supposedly about the identity of the spy. Julia glanced back at Isabelle who slid back a cool stare. Craig said nothing and seemed to avoid her eyes. The easy connection they'd had the previous two days might as well never have happened. It certainly didn't appear as though he would defend her.

Julia wished she could leave immediately. She'd had enough emotional stimulation for one evening. Her positive feelings about her time with Craig, her acceptance from the family, her peaceful contentment—all evaporated in an instant.

As if sensing her misery, Valentina turned to her and said, "I'm quite tired, Julia. If you're ready to go, I will take you in my car back to Firenze."

Julia nodded and smiled gratefully to her cousin. She rose from her seat at the same time as Valentina, who called out to the group, "I'm sure it's a very interesting conversation to discover who the De Luca spy is, but we won't learn this in one evening, *vero*? We must leave now. *Buona notte, tutti.*"

"*Buona notte.*" Julia said to everyone at the table, though her gaze avoided Isabelle and Craig. She followed Valentina back into the house and out to her car on the circular driveway.

When they got into the car, Valentina started the ignition and turned to Julia. "Don't worry about Isabelle. She's been a mean girl since she was young. She's ten years older than I am and she has never been a nice person, despite how beautiful she is."

They pulled away from the house and after they'd driven several kilometers, the tightness in Julia's chest lessened slightly. "She seems very possessive of Craig." She stared out the window as the darkened landscape flew by. The same landscape that had charmed her the day before as she reveled in its beauty. Was it only yesterday she'd felt attraction for Craig and sensed he'd felt something for her too?

"She's possessive of every man who has any potential. She's on the hunt for her next husband. Isabelle has been divorced for I forget how many years and hasn't found the right victim—I mean man." Valentina laughed aloud at her own statement. "Don't get me wrong, I love my sister. Except when I don't. But I'm nicer than she is. I try to help everyone and be a good person. You shouldn't worry about what she said."

"So—are she and Craig together?" Julia hated to ask the question and tried to sound simply curious.

"Honestly, I don't know. Clearly, she is in love with him, but I don't know how he feels. Mamma—Emilia—hopes it won't go anywhere because she doesn't want to lose her daughter to the States, just like she lost her sister."

Julia leaned back against her seat, more confused than reassured about Craig and Isabelle. She had already put up a small barrier around her heart. It was better that way, wasn't it? Despite what she'd told Craig the day before.

It was all so confusing. Her new cousin despised her and now there was a spy in the company. And Craig? She couldn't even think about him.

When Valentina dropped her off and the taillights of her car vanished around the next corner, Julia stood for a moment in the empty streets, feeling just as empty inside.

Chapter Twelve

Cool drops of water splashed onto the surface of the Del Carciofo Fountain and sprayed Julia's arms. She fanned herself against the mid-morning sun with an area map. Earlier that day following breakfast, she'd wandered the streets in her Oltrarno neighborhood then headed toward the Palazzo Pitti to look at the famed "artichoke" fountain. Most of the adornment of the fountain consisted of cherubs, but near the top sat a large, bronze artichoke. She made a mental note to ask Valentina if artichokes had a special significance in Italy or in Italian history.

During her walk, her mind churned over what had occurred the previous day. The hostile start to her relationship with her cousin Isabelle had thrown her off balance, just when she thought she was settling into the family. Maybe Isabelle would get over it soon if she understood that Julia wasn't after Craig. She'd never been involved in a cat fight over a man and didn't intend to start now.

Soothed by the musical waters, her mind rested. In the coolness of the fountain spray, she relaxed her tense shoulders and unwound her thoughts. She'd have to have a talk with herself. And an even longer talk with God.

Before she could figure out where to start, her phone rang. It was Eden, who had texted once, but hadn't called since Julia's arrival in Italy. "Hi, Eden. What a nice surprise! Is everything okay?"

"Everything's fine. I was thinking about you and decided to call. Is this a good time for you? I figure, it's morning. Am I right, is it morning?"

Julia chuckled. "Don't worry, it's morning and I've been up for a while. But it's two or three in the morning for you. That's not typical for you, is it?"

"No, it's not. I'm usually in bed by eleven, but couldn't sleep. I haven't been on a hot date or partying with friends, even though I just sold my restaurant."

"You did? That's great. Congratulations! Are you happy about it?" Julia wasn't sure by the tone in Eden's voice or the late hour of her call.

"I *am* happy about it. It's like a burden off my back. There's only one problem, though."

"What's that?"

"I'm an independently rich woman with no direction whatsoever."

Julia laughed. "Is that a bad thing? I'm sure you'll come up with some interesting life directions very soon. If you don't, plenty of people will have all kinds of plans for you."

"I guess that's true. At least I didn't win the lottery. Then everyone would be lined up at my door with requests. No, I guess I'm not used to having this void, this sudden lack of purpose. Maybe I should follow your example and visit a foreign country I've always wanted to see." Eden sighed audibly into the phone. "You know, the restaurant was never my idea or my passion. It was Gerry's. When he died, I just took it over without thinking about what *I* wanted. So, for ten years I've somehow helped it grow through good ole common sense but along the way, I've forgotten what I wanted and who I was." Her voice quieted. "Who I *am*."

Julia smiled. Seemed to be a common problem among the adults she knew, including herself. "I think it's a perfect time to figure that out, don't you? Who you are and what you want *now*. Just take your time and try different things. Don't be pressured to jump into the next thing, Eden."

"I think I need to give myself that permission." Eden's voice took on a quieter reflective tone.

"You owe it to yourself. You've invested long years in the restaurant to make it what it is. Now, you can reap the rewards of that investment. I think it's an exciting time for you."

"Thank you, Julia. You encourage me." She paused. "Now, enough about my angst. Tell me you're having a blast in Florence."

"I'm having a good trip so far." Julia wouldn't mention the fiasco of the previous evening. She had to look at the whole trip, not just one incident, and so far, it *was* good. "I'm sitting on the edge of a four-hundred-year-old fountain surrounded by cherubs. It's a fabulous city."

"Sounds so beautiful. Have you met any interesting Italian men?"

"There are plenty of naked men everywhere, but they're made of marble." Julia couldn't resist. She grinned when she heard Eden howl with laughter. She didn't want to mention Craig, since there was nothing more to say. Her disappointment still felt heavy in her stomach.

"And the family members you wanted to meet up with? Have you seen them?"

"Yes, I met my cousin Valentina first and she was my passport into the rest of the family. I've been there frequently, to the villa, I mean, since my arrival. This weekend, though, I'm going to hang out in the city by myself. I don't want to be the guest that won't leave, even if I'm family. I'm still new to them. And there's a lot here I haven't seen yet. I don't just want to be a tourist. I want to absorb *everything.* I want to drink it in so I can take it with me when I leave." Valentina was spending the weekend with Marco, so Julia would *really* be alone. But that was fine. "I've been to a couple of museums and the art is exquisite, really. Goes back for centuries, too. And churches. Then just out on the streets among all the people—it's just amazing." Julia laughed at herself and the way she'd just babbled without stopping. So unlike her.

"Oh, I understand." Eden's voice took a tone of awe. "I'm not even there but I can feel the experience you're having. You're becoming more talkative than I remember you, and that's a good sign!" Eden laughed. "I want to hear much more and see pictures, of course, when we're together again at Thanksgiving. Though you could certainly text or Instagram a couple in the meantime."

The women chatted a few more minutes then hung up. Julia sat for a moment and thought about Eden, free from the responsibilities of a busy restaurant. Free and empty and in need of rediscovering herself. Julia herself wasn't free from her work and didn't want or plan to be. But she did sometimes feel empty, even that day, despite the beauty surrounding her. Despite the encouragement she'd just given to Eden. She, too, needed to rediscover her heart.

Nick used to tell her that she always looked at a glass as half-empty. "Where's the joy, Julia?" he would ask in exasperation. "Why are you always looking for something else? Don't you have enough right here?" Truthfully, that may have been why he decided to leave the marriage. He felt he hadn't been enough for her and she'd never be happy, no matter what he did or didn't do. He couldn't win, so he gave up.

She'd developed that habit early in life as she pined for siblings and a father. Growing up, she'd had a few close friends, but it was siblings and family she'd wanted. As Craig attested, having siblings didn't always provide a loving bond and a forever friendship. Some of her childhood girlfriends would have sold off their annoying siblings in favor of a few good friends. She *had* those, then like now, and they were a huge blessing she wouldn't trade.

She had so *much*. So, what was missing? It was as though her hands weren't open wide enough to receive everything that was already there, as well as all God might have for her, afraid of disappointment, as she'd shared with Craig. At the memory of their day together and the depth of their emotional bond, she winced. Just a memory now, tempting her to say she was right to fear, that she'd been wise to dodge hope.

No more. She wouldn't do that anymore, let fear smother her hope, no matter how it might expose her to hurt. In doing that, she'd also shielded herself from joy. Why was she sitting here thinking of how sad it was that Cousin Isabelle didn't like her? Why did she even care? The others in the family seemed to like her fine. Even Emilia was thawing out ever so slowly.

If she were honest, nothing had changed since yesterday. Now she had a clearer view of things. She was in Florence and had met her family. Wonderful. She thought there had been something with Craig and there wasn't. Fine. She hadn't known him long enough to be broken-hearted. She'd get over it. He was with Isabelle, who disliked her because of jealousy. She could handle all of this and it wasn't going to ruin her trip. No, it wouldn't.

Besides that, God seemed to be calling to her in a soft voice. She wanted to discover what he was saying. Maybe calling her toward the joy and abundance he promised, toward what she *had* instead of what she didn't have. And what she needed, instead of what she thought she wanted. Maybe that was the answer to the hollowness inside.

Julia stood up from the fountain and rounded the Pitti Palace, a military-looking structure containing priceless art treasures. She continued on to stroll through the immense Boboli Gardens that stretched out behind the Palace. The green spaces and the sounds of fountains were like a salve to her prickly feelings. *Thank you for this and for everything I have. I will look for you and be grateful for what I have instead of what I don't have. You are enough.*

Her phone rang amidst her heartfelt words. She found a nearby bench under the shade of a burly branch. "Julia, it's Craig. How are you today?" She sensed concern in his voice. A bit too late. No. His distance yesterday meant nothing.

"I'm enjoying the Boboli Gardens. How are you, Craig?" Her voice came out cool, cordial.

"I'd like to see you today. Do you have time to meet for lunch or a drink?"

A small flutter began inside, like a butterfly batting its wings. She pushed it down. Was he courting her and Isabelle both? Or was he merely friends with Isabelle? *Remember, Julia, you don't care.* "Sure, I have time. I'm on vacation, remember?" She followed with a chuckle to let him know that the scene at the table the night before hadn't bothered her at all. Even though the memory of his silence still stung.

"Can you meet at about one-thirty on the Via Roma corner of the Piazza della Repubblica? There's a place I know of near there where we can eat."

"I'm familiar with the Piazza. I'll see you at one-thirty."

"Great. I'm—I'll see you then."

What had he been about to say? She looked at her watch. She'd see Craig in an hour.

For the next hour, Julia wandered up the riverfront, taking photos as she went, then crossed the Ponte Amerigo Vespucci to the north bank. A bit more exploring among the labyrinth of streets and she arrived at the Piazza della Repubblica.

Her breath caught when she saw Craig on the opposite corner. He turned and saw her, watching her as she crossed the Piazza.

"You're right on time, Stefano." She slid her sunglasses up on her head. "You can't use your well-worn phrase today."

He laughed and his face lit up. She pushed down the intense wave of attraction that flooded her. He wore a white cotton shirt open at the neck, revealing a suntan which extended up to his face.

"No, not this time. I wanted to be *sure* I was on time today."

She fell into step beside him on Via Roma. "Why is that?"

A shadow crossed his face then he brightened. "For one, because it's the right thing to do, and I need to work on being more prompt. But mainly, I was looking forward to seeing you."

A pool of warmth surged inside, though his statement told her nothing. She would simply receive it and enjoy his company. And not expect anything. At all.

"Here it is." He led her to a cozy brick establishment with a terrace on one side. Craig spoke to the maître d' who seated them outside under a spacious yellow awning. Baskets of red geraniums hung from each corner of the awning. A musical murmur of Italian conversations from nearby tables blended with city sounds of the pedestrian street beside them. A sharp but appealing scent of Italian cheese floated in the air.

"This looks perfect. It's the first time I'm having a meal at a restaurant in Florence *with* someone instead of alone." She definitely preferred eating with someone. Especially with Craig, despite everything.

"Well, it's about time, then." He smiled, but his eyes looked tense, vigilant. Something had changed.

They looked at the menu and he ordered in Italian for them. When the waiter left, Julia crossed her arms against the table and looked at him. "I don't believe you anymore. You *do* speak Italian."

Craig grinned. "I've had more practice on this trip, so I've seen faster progress. Still, my context is restaurants, stores, bus drivers. Nothing too deep."

"That's more than I can say. And the rest will come for you easily, since you have a base. As Sergio says, you know a lot of phrases, but language is made up of phrases, so you're well on your way."

"I hope so." He paused and looked at her intently. "Julia, about last night." He sighed heavily. "I felt like I sort of abandoned you and I'm sorry."

She leaned back in the wicker chair. Relief coursed through her. "Thanks for saying that. I felt abandoned by everyone, except Valentina. Isabelle's behavior was clearly a case of jealousy. Before you arrived, Emilia said something about you being my tour guide in Tuscany, and Isabelle—" *thinks she owns you. Don't say it, Julia, you'll sound jealous yourself.* She sighed.

"She *is* jealous." He finished her statement. "I know her."

"Look, if you're with Isabelle, that's your business. You don't owe me anything."

"But I should have stood by you when she made that crazy accusation." He thrust one hand through his curly hair. "And we're not really *together*."

Julia lifted her eyebrows. Not *really*. Partially? "Does she know that?"

"This is complicated." He paused and she said nothing. "So—well, I met Isabelle during one of my trips about four years ago. She was still married then. I think she liked me, but knowing she was married, I kept my distance."

"But you were interested in her."

He threw up one hand. "I wasn't against the idea at first, once she was divorced. She's very beautiful, as you've seen. I was open to getting to know her better. That's all, just open. The De Lucas are like family to me. They welcomed me in. I think Isabelle and maybe even family thought I was a good match for her. Especially since we're both over forty and she was interested in me."

"So, they betrothed you to Isabelle?" Julia laughed but her insides were heavy. "Do people still do that?"

Craig looked uncomfortable. The Craig she remembered from their day in Tuscany and at the *Parco* might have laughed at her statement and had a come-back. The Craig in front of her was weighed down by something.

The waiter arrived with plates of salad and a basket of bread. He placed them on the table. "*Grazie.*" Craig nodded to the waiter and looked back at Julia. "It's not like that. I wanted to get to know her at first, as I said, but unfortunately, that gave Isabelle too much encouragement. Each time I came, she wanted us to spend time together. In a short time, I knew she wasn't the woman for me, despite her allure. Her behavior last night is just one example. I didn't like how childish she was or self-centered. But it was hard for me to backpedal with her, since by that time, she had assumptions." He paused then and added, "Especially hard, given my relationship with the family and the fact that I don't come here but a few times a year."

"So, you never told her."

He shook his head.

"Do you talk on the phone when you're back in the States, or give her other indications that you are interested in her?"

"Mostly, when I was home, she texted me. Or emailed. I texted back, but felt more and more cornered, unable to tell her. I guess, for fear that the family would think I'd led her on. The longer it goes on, the more trapped I feel."

He leaned back in his chair and stared, frowning, out at the street. Julia saw clearly how he'd gotten into this bind. Would his job be on the line because of Isabelle? Or just the inclusion and acceptance by the family that he seemed to value so much? Just like she did.

"Couldn't you simply tell her once for all? Take her to dinner and tell her she's not the woman for you? Or do you think that would create waves in the family?"

Craig shook his head. His shoulders drooped. "The fact that I didn't nip it in the bud might be a problem. In the States, we go out, get to know someone, and if it doesn't feel right, we break it off. Here, it's more serious from the get-go. Then, being a part of this family makes it very complex." He poured water for both of them from a carafe on the table and took a swig. "I don't want to hurt her."

"I don't think she'll be hurt. Her heart seems too hard for that. But she *might* blow up your car." It was quite possible, given the look on Isabelle's face last evening.

He laughed, despite the heaviness that emanated from his usually cheerful face. "You're right about that. Revenge may be what I'm most afraid of." He shook his head again. "I can't believe I let this illusion go so long."

Julia cocked her head. "She must know you aren't 'into' her, as they say. A woman can feel it. Unless you put on a good show, and then, you don't come often. But where would that kind of pretending lead? It would have to lead to something sooner or later. Either you marry her or you break up."

"It's getting harder because my heart—or, rather, the Lord, is confronting me on my hypocrisy. I'm playing a role, like I used to when I was young. Trying to stay in everyone's good graces, even though that's weak. It's not what God wants for me. I'm not being true to myself or to her. It's eating me up. In fact, I told myself before coming on this trip that I was going to talk to her this time."

"Well, you have time. How long are you staying in Italy?" She looked up as steaming plates of pasta and chicken were placed down before them.

Craig hadn't moved. His eyes caught hers and his voice softened. "But now, I've met you."

She opened her mouth then shut it. Her pulse began to pound in her ears. She didn't shift her gaze from his. *And I've met you.* She thought of several possible responses but stayed quiet.

He swallowed. "If I break it off with Isabelle now, she'll say it's because of you. It isn't because of you, because I should have broken it off long ago, with or without meeting you. Otherwise, it *would be* because of you. Do you see what I'm saying?" He leaned in over the edge of the table toward her.

Julia moistened her lips. "Um—go on. I want to be sure of what you're saying." Before she walked into an embarrassing trap.

"I would say I'm attracted to you, and I am, but it's much deeper than that, even after just a couple of days. I've traveled the world, dated lots of women since my divorce. Don't get me wrong, I've been a good boy. Mostly." They laughed. "But I'm looking for a soul-mate. There has to be a soul connection in order for that to happen. I felt connected to your soul the other day. I know it's only been a few days, but I don't want to let you go until we know if this can go somewhere."

Tiny waves of joy surged higher and filled her. She couldn't stop a small smile from creeping up her face. The aromas that rose from her plate peripherally reminded her that her meal was getting cold, but she didn't drop her gaze. "I felt the same about you." Timidly, she slid her hand out to the center of the table and he clasped it. "Connected." Their hands mirrored her phrase. It was true for her but he'd felt it too. When had *that* alignment ever happened in her life?

He swallowed and his eyes roved around her face. "You're so beautiful, Julia. But your spirit is beautiful and sensitive, too. I can tell." He looked down at the food and back up at her. "We should eat. Otherwise, I've bragged about this restaurant for nothing."

She grinned. "*D'accordo* already."

He sliced off a forkful of meat and tasted it. "Mmm, do you like the chicken? Was I right?"

Julia tasted a bite and nodded. "Delicious."

Once they'd sampled their meals, Craig's face once again took a serious expression. "Do you see why this is complicated for both of us? For me because the family might be expecting me to marry her or at least stay with her because I've carried on this charade for about a year. If I back away, I'm not sure how they'll take it."

"They won't expect you to marry her. This is the twenty-first century, Craig. People break up all the time." She paused and blinked but he didn't respond. "You could tell Isabelle you don't want to continue with her but not mention me, since you said yourself that I wasn't the cause. Would that work?"

"She'd know. Because she wouldn't know that I'd had doubts about her a long time ago. She'd assume it was because of you, and I'm afraid she may try to ruin what you've been building with the family. I know that's important to you."

Julia sighed. "Either way, you can't continue with her for fear of the family or your job. You know that." She'd have to consider her own level of risk when she was alone and had head space. When he wasn't staring at her with those gray-green eyes rimmed in dark lashes, eyes that made her feel she was falling into them.

"Of course. It's just the timing that's not good. I don't want you dragged into it."

"I'm already in it because I'm interested in you." At her words, Craig's scowl lightened. "But no one has to know just now. We'll be friendly but otherwise not let on. Though, maybe you'll want to back off a bit with Isabelle, don't you think?"

"Yes, but how? Never mind, I'll figure this out. I made the mess and it's up to me to get out of it. Now, we should talk about something else."

She reached out again and took his hand. He covered her hand with both of his, enveloping it with warmth.

"Julia, Julia." His whisper swept over her like a caress. "Wish I'd met you a year ago."

Julia smiled back at him. "You wouldn't have. Circumstances would never have lined up while I still had my mother. Everything happens for a reason. But I think things with Isabelle will work out."

If only her emotions were as peaceful and optimistic as her words.

Chapter Thirteen

"I'll never forget what it's like eating gelato in Italy. It just tastes different here." Julia savored the treat that had become almost a daily indulgence. For sure, she'd gained three pounds from gelato alone. She stood with Craig under the awning of the gelateria facing the Duomo. The piazza encircling the mammoth edifice overflowed with clusters of tourists.

Julia had spent a glorious afternoon walking with Craig through the streets of Florence, passing hours as they talked, seemingly unable to stop. The gelato soothed her dry throat. She was unaccustomed to sharing so many thoughts, memories, and facts about herself. Apparently, she'd ceased being an introvert, as Eden had observed during their phone call. Might have something—or everything—to do with Craig. He had an uncanny ability to bring her right out of her shell. In fact, she was becoming less fond of that shell of reserved protection she'd maintained for so many years.

"You would know." Craig's mouth twitched with humor. "You claim to have sampled gelato from the entire city of Florence." He finished his cup of chocolate gelato and licked his lips. "And of course, it's always better in Italy."

She simply smiled at him. "*Certo.*" Certainly.

He lifted his brows. "Of course, you must have also sampled the crema which is only available in Florence, right?"

"*Certo.*" She said again, her smile stretching to a grin. "*Molto certo.*" Her Italian words were likely redundant at that point, but well merited when describing gelato.

Since the other day when he'd told her of his feelings for her, she wondered if she was dreaming, if all of this was real. The moment she met him on the terrace at the De Luca villa, she sensed the connection she'd voiced. Was God leading in this? Or was it too early to tell? So many relationships hadn't worked out over the years, the few times she even tried, that she'd stopped expecting anything in the romantic realm. It felt fragile to her. She should enjoy it while she could, though it would be wise to hold back. Meeting Craig would likely be a treasured secret memory of her trip to Tuscany, but nothing more.

He held her gaze for a moment then reached up and touched her chin. "You have a little drop there." He was close enough that she saw the sun cast a streak of light on the stubble of his jaw. The hum that had begun earlier when they met on the steps of the Uffizi Museum increased its tempo. He left his hand on her face for a moment then pulled it away, his touch leaving a tingle on her cheek. He grinned and said softly, "You might be saving it for later, but you should keep your appetite for the party tonight."

Her smile fell. "What party?"

Craig gave her a quizzical look. "Giuseppe's birthday. You didn't know?"

She shook her head. "Maybe I'm not invited."

"Of course, you're invited. It was an oversight. If not, you can come as my guest."

She let out a short laugh but shook her head. "No way. I'm not going if I'm not invited. And imagine what Cousin Isabelle would do if I came as your guest. She'd put something in my food."

"Now, now. It's not that bad. You two got off on the wrong foot, but she'll likely warm up sometime." He paused. "Okay, not too realistic, given our current, uh, entanglement, but we can always hope for the best."

"Or just avoid her. It's one thing that makes me glad I don't live here. Otherwise, I'd wish I did." Julia sighed. Being overlooked for Giuseppe's birthday cut into her previous buoyancy.

Her phone rang. Valentina. "Hi, Valentina. Are you and Marco enjoying your romantic weekend?"

Valentina giggled. "Oh, yes. We didn't do any work this weekend. It was lovely just being together." Her voice was soft. She was in love. Julia hoped it worked both ways. "I'm calling you because I did a bad thing. I forgot to tell you about Uncle Giuseppe's birthday party tonight. I'm so sorry, it's my fault. It's such short notice, but I hope you will come."

Julia laughed at her previous petulance. "I wouldn't miss it. Thanks, Valentina. What time is it?"

"Show up at around seven. Maybe Craig can bring you in his car?"

"Yes, I'll ask him." She caught Craig's eye and he winked. "See you later on."

She hung up, feeling foolish. "Okay, my near tantrum of tears is over. That was Valentina, who forgot to tell me about the party. She suggested you could give me a ride."

"That, I will." He laughed softly, probably at her. She wouldn't ask.

Julia crossed her arms. "Only problem now is that it's Sunday, so nothing will be open for me to get him a gift." Not that she had any clue what to get for an older uncle she barely knew.

Craig's face lit up and he held up one finger. "I have an idea. I bet the Ponte Vecchio leather merchants are still open today. We can go over there and see."

"Buon' idea."

Several hours later they drove in Craig's rental car toward the villa. Julia had been able to find a small leather wallet for Giuseppe. He likely had a nice one already, but it was the thought that counted. She hoped so. Craig had bought a bottle of upscale whisky, which was sure to make the older man happy.

Craig slowed the car as they emerged onto a smaller road leading to the valley outside of Florence. As they left the city behind, the sky darkened and the hills rose up like purple mounds in the distance. He reached over and briefly squeezed her hand. "You look beautiful, by the way. My brain was well aware of that, but I neglected to tell you."

She'd worn a turquoise sundress with a slightly full skirt. A silver necklace of turquoise gems and matching earrings dressed it up. "Thanks. You're not so tacky yourself."

"Are you ready for lots of Italian relatives and more Italian language than your head can absorb?"

Julia swallowed. "I sure hope so. I'd like to ask you to stick close by me, but I know you probably can't, so you're exempt."

"You know I'd love to. In fact, I kind of wish we could skip the whole thing."

She smiled. "Me too."

But here they were. De-facto members of the family attending the patriarch's birthday party. Craig pulled into the driveway where a dozen cars were already parked. He wedged the car onto the lawn between two other cars. Julia braced herself to face the crowd. At least they weren't there for *her* sake. Once she'd been introduced, she could fade into the woodwork and observe. Except for in her business, that was a role she was often comfortable with.

Before entering the villa, she heard voices raised in Italian bantering, laughter, and conversation. Most of the people Julia saw in the hallway and in the living room were strangers to her. She spotted Isabelle across the living room. She wore a deep red two-piece dress with a string of pearls that did nothing to hide her ample cleavage. She'd twisted her hair into a thick loop on her neck, making her resemble a stunning, dark-eyed flamenco dancer. She was engaged in conversation with a man who leaned toward her attentively, but when Julia and Craig entered the room her eyes swept toward them, lighting on Craig.

"Julia, Stefano, you are here." Sergio's voice boomed over the din. "Come, you must meet our friends." He looked handsome in a crisp Armani suit and neatly-trimmed hair, though for the first time since Julia had known him, his eyes showed a strain, evident despite his jovial hospitality.

He led them to a small cluster of men and women, glittering and colorful, dressed for a party. They smiled and greeted them in Italian and broken English. After the introductions, they lapsed into a discussion with Sergio about shoes. Julia surveyed the room, noting the elegant clothing and shoes. This was, after all, a fashion capital, and the De Lucas were kingpins in the shoe world. Though she looked rather humble next to all of them, Julia was glad to have brought one nicer dress. She always traveled with one or two, just in case. Otherwise, it was capris, sandals or espadrilles, and tunics or tanks, depending on the season.

In the corner sat the guest of honor, Giuseppe, the center of attention, with Paola next to him. King and queen of the evening. He laughed and thanked the people who passed by to express their wishes and kiss his cheek or his hand. His Stalin mustache was neatly trimmed and wispy white hair formed a fluffy halo over eyes that sparkled with life, more so than she'd ever seen.

"I'm going to go wish Giuseppe a happy birthday," she told Craig. He smiled at her and turned back to listen to the conversation. She slipped away from the group and approached Giuseppe. Once the older couple was alone, she said, *"Buona sera, Paola. Buon compleanno, Zio."* Happy birthday, Uncle. She had left her small gift on a table in the hallway with the others.

"Grazie, ma bella," he called back. To her surprise, he rose with a grunt and kissed each of her cheeks, a gesture which nearly brought tears to her eyes. Dear Giuseppe.

Several people waited to speak with him, so she nodded a greeting to those waiting behind her and to Giuseppe and Paola. When she left them, she scanned the room for Craig and saw that he had quickly been absorbed by Isabelle. Good thing he didn't have intentions toward her. She'd gobble him up in no time flat and want to control his every move.

A twinge stung inside. That was nasty and unbecoming, even if no one heard her thoughts. This would be an opportunity to take the high road, and she would do it, including in her thoughts. Nevertheless, it would be difficult to pretend she liked Isabelle. Before she could consider how to do that, she felt a nudge from behind.

Sergio again. "Your cousin Luca and his family are here. You may wish to meet them as well as more of your relatives who are arriving."

His phrase *your relatives* stirred contentment inside her, like a long-awaited bud that had just flowered. Julia gladly followed him to meet the elusive Luca, who stood near the doorway in the living room surrounded by what she guessed was his family. He was shorter than Sergio, with dark hair, but had the same strong nose and black eyes. He wasn't handsome, but pleasant-looking when he smiled, which he did when he made eye contact with her. "*Buona sera.* I am happy to finally meet you, Cousin Julia." He extended his hand to shake hers.

Next to him a pretty blond woman smiled and shook her hand as well. "My name is Sofia. This is my son, Diego, and this is Alessandra." Sofia spoke carefully, possibly conjuring up her high-school English. Two wide-eyed children stood near their mother and stared at Julia. Diego squirmed, likely wanting to do something more active. They looked to be around ten and eight.

"How long you are—are you in Italy?"

Julia relaxed in response to Sofia's gentle smile and expression. "I'm in Italy for two weeks, and I have been here more than a week already. I'll leave next Saturday." She swallowed, pained by her words. It was going by too fast.

"This is not very long after so many years." Luca reached out and placed a hand on Diego's shoulder to stop his fidgeting. "Next time you should come for the entire summer."

An appealing idea. Could she run her business from Italy? Julia smiled. "I might not be able to stop working that long, but it's a tempting idea."

Under Sergio's guiding hand, Julia ambled toward another small group of adults and young adults who had just entered the noisy room. To them, he said, "This is your cousin, Julia, from America. She is here in Italy visiting." He turned toward Julia and continued, "This is Edouardo and his wife, Angelica. He and Martina are the children of Giuseppe and Paola. Edouardo's wife, Carmina, died years ago, sadly."

Julia shook hands with them. "*Piacerre,*" she said to each of them. They smiled and responded, but didn't seem to speak much English. That, or they were letting the introductions take place without initiating further discussion, since Sergio was speaking on their behalf.

"Edouardo doesn't work at De Luca nor even live in Florence. He had three children with Carmina. Jacopo, who is here, and his sisters, Livia and Luciana. Livia cannot come tonight. She is studying in Switzerland." Two young adults in their early twenties shook her hand and repeated, "*Piacerre*" to her. Maybe the younger ones spoke some English. Before she could ask them a question, Sergio guided her away. "Here is your cousin Martina and her husband." He nodded to Edouardo's family as they moved on and lifted a hand to catch the attention of another couple standing near the door.

When they reached the new cluster of newcomers, Sergio said, "This is your cousin Martina and her husband, Francisco, and their sons, Cosimo and Federico." Although Julia's head was spinning already with of all of their names, she was encouraged to realize that she had two more cousins. Edoardo and Martina. Now she'd met all five of them.

To Julia's relief, Martina and Francisco spoke some English and asked the usual polite questions. Moments later, Sergio tapped a wine glass with a spoon. "*Attenzione, tutti,*" he called. He addressed everyone in Italian, Julia guessed, about Giuseppe and the meal. Everyone looked at Giuseppe and everyone applauded or called out to him. Then the guests began to move en masse toward the dining room. Nearby was Valentina, who had joined Luciana and was locked in a giggly exchange with her. Julia remembered Valentina saying she and her cousin were close.

Her eyes combed the room for Craig and she saw him talking with a couple she didn't know. Isabelle hovered close by his side. Just like a couple. He hadn't had a chance to break off with her and this certainly wasn't the moment.

Julia averted her eyes and followed the group down the hall, doubting that there would be enough seating for everyone on the terrace. Emilia appeared at her elbow. "Hello, Julia. I haven't seen you in a few days."

Julia didn't know how to interpret Emilia's comment. Maybe her aunt had missed her, or had expected her to come every day? *Who knows?* She wouldn't bother herself with the question anymore.

Emilia raised her voice slightly over the increasing noise of the group. "We are using both the dining room and the terrace for dinner because we have so many guests. We have designated seating, so I have you on the terrace. You will see your name on a small card at your place."

Julia nodded. "Thanks, Emilia. It's a lovely party so far."

Emilia gave her a slight smile. "Tonight, we have almost everyone in the family who lives in the region and a few from other cities. A few family members who live too far away were unable to come. Then we have many associates and friends here tonight as well."

"The De Lucas have been here in Tuscany for so many years and have an established reputation. It's nice that your associates and all the family can come and help Giuseppe celebrate his birthday." Julia's statement seemed formal to her ears, but hopefully expressed approval. Anything to hold out an olive branch to her aunt. She shuffled through the hallway toward the terrace behind a couple she'd just met whose names had quickly dispersed from her mind.

Her comment seemed to please Emilia, whose smile broadened somewhat. She nodded as her eyes scanned the group. "Yes."

Julia was relieved to see that she'd been seated between Valentina and Sofia, with their men next to them. Marco was already there talking loudly with the man to his left. The man guffawed in response. Craig sat at the other end of the table, but Isabelle was several seats away across from him. At least they hadn't been placed side by side. If Emilia had planned the seating arrangement, was she attempting, as Valentina had suggested, to keep Isabelle and Craig apart for fear Isabelle would move to the States?

Craig looked up just in time to catch her gaze. His face warmed and a subtle smile appeared. That look would be enough to pull her through the noisy dinner party. Her relationship with Craig still felt like thin ice to her, but once in a while throughout the evening, his eyes caught hers and he smiled. Their silent communication told her that he, too, felt a bit helpless just then. She'd leave her hands open in faith. It was all she could do.

Valentina turned to Julia. "Julia, have you met Marco?"

"We met briefly when you gave me the factory tour the other day." She leaned slightly past Valentina to speak to him. "*Buona sera*, Marco. I'm glad you were able to join the party this evening."

He turned to Julia and his eyes engaged hers. "Thank you, Julia. It's a great party. Giuseppe looks happy." He looked around the table then back at Julia. "It's wonderful that you can come to Italy to visit your family. Valentina tells me you haven't come in many years." Marco grinned and deep dimples formed on his dark cheeks. She could see why Valentina was so taken with him, at least on a physical level. It was doubtful she'd get to know him much better that evening with so much noise and so many guests.

"Yes, nearly forty. A long time." Almost her lifetime.

At that, his eyes widened. "You should come back more often." Everyone told her the same thing, then the conversation would die. It was normal, since they didn't know her and weren't sure what to say afterward. *Relax, Julia. Getting to know a whole group of people who forgot you existed is going to be a marathon, not a sprint.*

That thought helped her relax and truly enjoy conversing with Sofia, Luca, and Valentina through the meal, a delicious risotto with porcini mushrooms followed by lamb chops in white wine. Time slipped by as wine and laughter flowed. Dessert would follow later, a special birthday cake for Giuseppe. In the meantime, many of the guests rose to return inside while others lingered around the terrace table. Craig was embroiled in a debate about shoes with an older guest who'd had too much to drink. Julia found herself between two conversations, so it seemed an ideal moment to get some much-needed silence in the garden.

As she strolled, putting space between herself and the terrace, voices became diluted with the hush of the dusk, which fell like a soft blanket. Regular intervals of faraway insect sounds studded the silence. It had been a good evening getting to know Luca and Sofia and joking with Valentina and Marco. Their friendliness put her at ease. It was as though she'd been able to jump over some of those missing years and catch up with them like old friends.

Julia found a bench, the same one where she'd sat with Valentina a few days earlier. She didn't even know when. The days were blending together like a runny watercolor. Before she knew it, she'd have to leave. Just when she was getting to know everyone and feeling some acceptance as a family member.

And Craig? Everything was so loose-ended. He didn't seem close to taking a stand with Isabelle, so again, she let go. Whatever was supposed to happen would happen. She'd keep telling herself and hopefully peace would keep returning to her.

She breathed deeply of the wild primrose growing around the villa, its sweet tang wafting around her on a balmy breeze. Closing her eyes, Julia leaned back on the bench. She felt it shift under her as someone sat down. She opened her eyes and saw Craig beside her, smiling as if he had a secret.

"Looks like you needed to escape, too. The noise, the crowd. Feels perfect out here." He took a deep breath and briefly closed his eyes.

"It's been a nice evening, but I reached my noise limit," she confessed with a wry smile. "Have you enjoyed yourself?"

He shrugged. "I guess so. I get energized talking to people I know, talking shop, meeting new people. But then it gets to a tipping point and I need to run away." He grinned at her. "I think your tipping point comes about two hours before mine."

Julia chuckled. "Yes, we're different that way. But it's a nice balance, I think."

Craig crossed his arms over his chest and leaned back. "Very nice. I like the way you're different from me. For example, you're artistic and creative. I'm not. So, I can appreciate that about you." He caught her eyes. "You're also more reserved, maybe a bit closed at times. Am I right?"

She nodded. "I'm more open with you than most people, except my group of girlfriends. I learned to be closed when I was a child because I spent a lot of time alone or with adults. I was like a small adult." She let out a nervous laugh, but knew it wasn't funny. "But I—I'm learning."

"Learning to trust?" His tone was gentle like a caress.

In the dusky light his tan looked deeper and his teeth glinted when he smiled. A warm pool bubbled inside her and spread. "I guess you could say that. Learning to let go and receive from life and from God. Like I told you the other day, I get fearful of good things."

"Are you afraid they'll disappear, like Doctor Sam?"

"I guess so." She looked up at him. "But you're here and I met you. That's a good thing." *Though I don't want to assume anything.*

Don't want to count on you. Her face grew hot. Even after what he'd said the day before, she couldn't allow herself to let go and believe it would last. It could all splinter into dust any moment.

He didn't answer but stared intently through the darkness into her eyes. He lifted a finger and traced it lightly down her cheekbone. A shiver rippled through her. "I'm sorry that happened, the Doctor Sam incident. It's a double wound because not only was he the source of your disappointment, but he was a man."

Was he trying to tell her something? Julia said, "I think I do distrust men sometimes. I distrust happiness, too." She shrugged. "After losing Joe then losing the doctor, my mom didn't think her heart could stand another disappointment so she protected herself from then on." She looked up at Craig in the murky light. "I don't want to be like that. But in some ways, I already am."

"It's not too late, Julia. You can choose not to protect yourself from people who are safe." He grinned. "People like me."

She laughed. "I'm not too protective of myself when I'm with you, am I? You already know my whole life story and all my quirks. Even though I've only known you a few days. Normally, I'd never do that, and it wouldn't even be a good idea."

"True." He leaned his head toward hers. "But I'm not just anyone." His smile fell and his voice became husky. "I meant what I said to you the other day. I have almost never said that to a woman. I know it's early, maybe premature. I probably should have kept my mouth shut a little longer. That might have given you time to test me out and build your trust. But what I feel for you is rare. It's special. And it's real."

As she drank in his words, her gaze didn't move from his eyes, darkened in the shadows of evening. With one hand he tipped her chin up then leaned in and kissed her, slowly, tenderly. He slid toward her on the bench and circled his other arm around her back.

He drew her closer and deepened his kiss. At that moment, she didn't care about her doubts. She'd allow his warmth, the softness of his lips and the scrape of his evening stubble to fill her senses, fill the void inside.

"Stefano?" A woman's voice called.

They pulled apart. Julia sat up straighter and slid a couple inches away from him on the bench just as Isabelle rounded the hedge. "I thought that might happen." Her lips still tingled from Craig's kiss. She craved more of his kisses, but the moment had passed.

"There you are." Isabelle's glare brushed over Julia then her eyes locked on Craig. "We are about to serve the cake. I was afraid you had left, Stefano."

"No, we're just getting some calm and quiet," he said. "It was noisy in there."

Julia wondered if his word choice was deliberate, speaking for both of them instead of just himself. He didn't move from the bench, though Isabelle's stance suggested she thought he should jump up immediately.

"Cake sounds good, don't you think?" Julia asked Craig, hoping to break the awkward silence. She made a point to speak with him directly instead of responding to Isabelle. As long as the moment with Craig was broken, they may as well go in to rejoin the festivities.

"We'll come in for the cake," he responded to Isabelle then turned to Julia. "You're ready to go in now?"

"Sure, let's go join everyone. We'll need to sing to Giuseppe. Oh, do they do that in Italy?"

Craig shrugged and looked up just as Isabelle huffed and turned to walk back to the house. He waited until she was out of sight and chuckled. "I didn't want her to think her wish was my command. And I don't want to end this moment with you, Julia."

"Me, either. But I think we should go to Giuseppe."

"You're right." They stood up. He put his hands on the sides of her face and stepped forward for a fast but firm kiss before leading her back into the house.

They slipped into the only available corner of the crowded dining room. All of the guests gathered around the table. Giuseppe and Paola were seated near the middle. Amara and two other apron-clad young women came in and placed small plates and a large, colorful cake in the center in front of Giuseppe. There were no candles, but rather the number '76' painted with bright red icing. Julia hovered behind Craig and covertly scanned the room for Isabelle. Her cousin scowled from where she stood in the doorway at the opposite end of the room.

Giuseppe's jovial spirits continued throughout the cutting and serving of the cake as he made frequent comments in Italian which drew laughter and noise from the gathered crowd. Following the cake, champagne was served. Sergio made a toast, and the guests raised their classes, Julia supposed, to Giuseppe's health and happiness.

After the party, Craig drove Julia back to Florence. It was close to ten-thirty and the city streets dwelt under a blanket of darkness, with few residents and tourists in evidence. He pulled up in front of her hotel, cut the motor, and rounded the car to accompany her to her door. They stood together for a moment in the empty street, standing just inches apart.

Darkness cast shadows over his face. Quietly, he stared at her, his eyes roving her face. Then he leaned forward to kiss her, gently, but taking his time, as if completing what had been begun earlier in the evening. She reached around his neck and drew close as his arms tightened around her waist. Now there was no deadline, no crowd awaiting a slice of birthday cake or a sip of champagne. *This* was the dessert Julia had awaited, the moment where she felt herself falling, getting lost, wonderfully lost.

Craig kissed her as though she meant something to him.

She shouldn't get carried away. *She shouldn't.* Though, it might be too late.

Chapter Fourteen

Julia quickened her step and dodged a baby carriage pushed by a tired-looking mother. The pedestrian street overflowed with shoppers and tourists. She had only five minutes to walk two more blocks and locate the restaurant where Valentina waited for her for lunch.

Rather than jogging the rest of the way, she punched Valentina's number into her phone. "I'm almost there."

"Don't worry, Julia. I have a table for us on the terrace."

Anticipation welled up inside at the thought of seeing Valentina, since several days had passed since they'd talked one-on-one. Not only did Julia enjoy her perky and optimistic cousin's company, but she'd be able to summarize the events of the previous evening for her, since most of it had transpired in Italian.

As she slowed her pace, the thought that hovered in her mind, or rather, had taken up residence there, was Craig. That first kiss in the De Luca garden, both a culmination of the increasing closeness she felt with him and a promise of what might come, and even more, the second one by the door last night. It had taken her time to fall asleep that night.

The Matriciana Ristorante came into view and broke into Julia's dreamy thoughts about Craig. She shook her head as if to snap herself back into the present just as she spied Valentina, who was seated at a small table staring down at her phone, swiping and reading. Julia walked through the attractive restaurant to access the terrace. Valentina looked up as Julia sat down. Her eyes were heavier than usual, her smile forced.

"*Ciao, Bella,*" Julia offered with a smile.

"*Ciao,* Julia. Did you get enough sleep after the party last night?"

"Yes, I did. But I'm on vacation, so I didn't have to get up too early. Did you sleep well?" Her cousin's face, usually bright and smooth, didn't look that way, unless something else was bothering Valentina.

Valentina smiled, her eyes slightly hooded. "No, not really. Normally we'd have a party like that on a Saturday, but some important friends of my parents weren't able to come that day. I was glad we had so many friends and most of the family."

"It was a good opportunity for me to meet Luca, Edouardo, and Martina." Her other cousins.

"Yes, they're all very sweet. They will make up for Isabelle." She laughed and Julia joined her. "My sister didn't seem happy last evening."

Did Valentina know something? What would she think about Julia's relationship with Craig? "No, she's never seemed happy the few times I've seen her."

"That's because Stefano doesn't fall at her feet. She's used to this, you see. Men are very attracted to her."

"Why hasn't she remarried yet? Seems she would have lots of choices. I wonder why she's so drawn to Craig when he lives in the States and is from another culture."

Valentina shrugged. "Maybe that's exactly why she's interested in him. He lives far away, so maybe that's exotic for her. Maybe she wants to leave Italy. I don't know. Maybe the fact that he likes her less makes her like him more, like a challenge she has to conquer."

"You and Isabelle never talk about this?" She who had no sisters had always imagined that sisters would be like best friends, confiding in one another about the men they liked.

Valentina shook her head. "No, we've never been like this. Maybe it's the age difference. I'm closer to Sofia, Luca's wife. And my cousin Luciana—she's Edouardo's daughter—she and I are close but she lives in Bergamo, north of here."

Julia nodded and wondered if she should talk about her relationship with Craig. Valentina was like an ally. "Maybe Craig likes someone else."

Valentina's eyes glinted as they met Julia's and she grinned. "And I know who that is."

Julia felt a hot flush rise to her cheeks. "How did you know?"

She pointed two manicured fingers toward her own face. "I have eyes, my cousin. His face is easy to read. I think he loves you. Do you remember when I told you I know someone who is perfect for you?"

Julia shook her head. "I must have forgotten, since I didn't know who you were talking about then. You think he's perfect for me?"

"Oh, yes. Not just because he's American, of course. That would be silly. He is a nice, honest man, but very funny and laughs a lot. He can be serious as well. And he's quite handsome, don't you think?" Valentina seemed to be enjoying herself, having learned Julia's secret. "You two look very good together."

Suddenly, Julia felt self-conscious. So, their secret was out. But she was glad Valentina knew. "Yes, of course. I'm attracted to him, not just physically. He's easy to talk to. I'm kind of shy and he brings me out of my shell." It was true. It wasn't her style to talk about men she liked, except with very close friends. Not that she'd had much opportunity in the last few years. But lately, uncharacteristically, she caught herself wanting to say things to Valentina that she would have ordinarily kept under wraps.

A waiter came to the table to take their orders. Valentina looked up at him with a coy expression and said something to him in fast Italian. He gave a slight bow and grinned, seeming charmed by her, then left them.

She leaned forward. "We should be ready to order the next time he comes."

Julia decided on a pizza, since she hadn't yet had one in Italy. Once the waiter took their orders and left, she looked up at Valentina. "You said before that you didn't know if Craig and Isabelle were together. He told me they aren't together, but Isabelle still has expectations of him, as if they are. That's confusing to me." His explanations had been vague. "He might have just been friendly and she took it the wrong way."

"That may have been what happened. I don't have a close relationship with her, or I would ask her for you."

"If Craig and I, um, get together, do you think Isabelle will be angry?" And how angry would she be?

"Probably." Valentina's voice was cheerful, despite her prediction. "But soon you'll be back in the States and it won't matter."

"But I'll still come back from time to time. I hope so, anyway, if everyone wants me to come back." And she didn't want a problem with Isabelle during her trips to see the family.

Valentina reached out and squeezed Julia's hand. "Yes, everyone wants you to come back to us. Maybe not Isabelle, but she's just one person. She'll probably meet someone else once she knows there's no hope with Craig."

Julia smiled and squeezed Valentina's hand in return. "You're right, she's just one person." And she could deal with Isabelle's scowl as long as the rest of the family accepted her. Even Emilia had shown a few signs of coming along, albeit very slowly. "Is there any progress with Marco?"

Valentina sighed and her grin became more of a pout. "We had a wonderful weekend, and he was very attentive to me at the party. He seems to be content with the way things are, but I want progress, as you said."

"Is that why you seem less cheerful today, Valentina?"

"Not only that. There are some troubles in the company."

"Oh. Really? What kind, or are you able to say?" A sudden weight fell inside her stomach. That was unwelcome news, though not completely surprising, given Sergio's comments the other day.

Valentina leaned back. A grimace marred her otherwise smooth face. Just then, their drinks arrived. She waited until the waiter left the table and lowered her voice. "Well, there's the spy, which you know about. Everyone is worried about that and many security measures have been implemented in the company. My father has gotten quite tense and irritable about it, and of course, Fabrizio is *very* dramatic about protecting his creative genius." She laughed and waved at the air, then her smile fell. "But there's another thing. My parents run the company, but they're older. I know that many older people have young ideas, but my parents are traditional Italians. They have run the company in the same way for years. They don't give any top positions to younger people, as if we're all kids and don't know what to do. And what do they think will happen when they get too old or sick to run everything? Luca and I have talked of this and we are both angry. We feel cast aside in some ways."

"Have you talked to your parents about this?"

"Not exactly. I have encouraged them to research some younger ideas, to hire some new—how do you say this, 'new blood', or to look at what other people are doing, you know, their competitors. They have this custom shoe division where they hand-make shoes for rich customers, and sometimes famous ones. It takes tons of time and they have limited production. They refuse to cut that out, since it's one thing they are well-known for. Also, they need a bigger factory, or else they should outsource some things. All of this will give them more volume, but they don't want to listen." She paused and stared down at her salad without touching it. "I'm getting tired of feeling like a piece of a big machine. The De Luca machine. I just help keep the machine running, but I don't feel interested in this anymore."

Julia sliced the thin crust of the pizza. A tangy aroma of tomatoes and cheese rose like a cloud from the pizza. "Have you thought about what you'd like to do instead?"

Her head snapped up and her eyes engaged Julia's. "Marry Marco and start a family."

Julia laughed. "Okay, that's specific. I think he's nuts not to marry you now, but maybe there is a reason he's waiting. Maybe he's saving up for a nice ring or something." Her comments didn't erase the frown from Valentina's face. Softly, she added, "Have you talked together about marriage?"

Valentina shook her head. "It seems like to me it should come from him, and after almost a year, he should have brought it up. Even to tell me he isn't comfortable with the idea right now. I'd like to know, before I waste a lot of time with him. I'm thirty-two and I don't have a lot of time to have children."

"If you two are close, you can ask him if he's thought about it. I know you don't want to be the one to bring it up, but at least you'll know. If he isn't of the same mindset as you are, you can meet someone else who you'll love as much or more."

Valentina shrugged. "That's hard. But there is a man at the factory who has paid a lot of attention to me. He's in management. His name is Andre." She colored slightly as she spoke of him. "I thought his interest might make Marco jealous, but so far it hasn't. I talk to him sometimes. I like him, he's nice."

"Well? Maybe there's potential with Andre. Just remember there are more fish in the sea." At Valentina's look of confusion, Julia added, "I mean there are more men in the world to get to know."

She nodded slowly but the faraway look in her eyes made Julia guess her mind was still on Marco.

After lunch, Julia waved to Valentina before she disappeared in the pedestrian crowd to return to work. She allowed herself to join the flow of the crowd, like a slow-moving stream. Her thoughts were far away from that moment as the complications that had arisen in just a few days swirled like asteroids in her mind. De Luca Shoes hid cracks of dissent under its successful surface. There was a spy in the factory, a mole yet undiscovered. How much damage would be done before then?

Then there were Craig and Isabelle. What was the nature of their relationship? Craig had said they weren't *really* together, and that it was complicated. She sensed there was something he wasn't telling her. And despite the depth of feeling she had developed for him in a short time, she didn't truly know how much she could trust him. Could she trust his declaration of attraction for her, of finding his soul connection? Or was he just as attracted to Isabelle and holding both of them on a string? What was the real reason he hadn't broken off with Isabelle?

A tangle of conflicting emotions wrestled inside her. The bare sincerity of his kiss the previous evening led her to want to trust him. The desire in his eyes, the blunt honesty of his words to her. Yet, there was more she needed to know about his history with Isabelle. The other option was that he was simply afraid of the consequences in the De Luca family, consistent with his longing for family after his own lonely childhood. Kind of ironic that they both craved a family connection despite different backgrounds.

Julia reached the end of the pedestrian street and turned the corner toward the river. The sight of water immediately soothed her. Back home in the States, her house wasn't far from a small river with a walking path alongside. The thought of home jarred her, as though it had been months, not days, since she'd left. Yet, she'd return there in just a few more days. Back to her normal life and her business. And her solitude. She frowned and flicked the thought aside. Maybe she should touch base with her employees today, in fact, though they knew she was on vacation. No, she wouldn't. They'd reach out to her if they needed to. There were enough loose ends to think about right here in Italy.

One loose end was her design project for Sergio. Since the day they spoke about it, he hadn't mentioned it again. She wondered how serious his desire was for a redecoration of the store, or if he'd mentioned it simply to give her something to do while she was there. Maybe the new pressures with the spy were taking his mind away from less important priorities. Next time she saw him, she'd bring it up in a gentle way and see if it was still on his radar. Or simply phone him.

She reached into her bag for her phone and saw a text from Craig. She smiled and a warm flow puddled inside. *Want to get some supper tonight? I'd love to see you.* He'd read her mind. She'd love to see him, too. As soon as possible. She could ask him plainly about Isabelle and not build up suspicions without cause. Hopefully, he'd tell her the truth.

Julia reigned back her thoughts. He'd seemed frank and authentic so far. And Valentina had said he was honest. That didn't mean he wasn't a player acting honest. People sometimes had differing standards for different areas of their lives. But she'd choose to give him the benefit of the doubt and let him speak for himself.

She typed back, *Would love to see you as well. Let me know time and place.* Within a few minutes, he'd responded with the information and closed with, *Can't wait to see you.* She couldn't have said it better herself. Doubts or not.

At seven o'clock Julia stood outside an elegant-looking two-story restaurant with glass walls on every side. The evening breathed a balmy breeze over her bare shoulders and stroked her hair. Well-dressed customers passed by her and entered the restaurant. She was probably underdressed, in her roomy red dress, but she'd pulled her wavy hair into a wide barrette and added dangly gold earrings.

She felt a presence behind her and a low voice by her ear. "Julia De Luca, your presence is requested for a dinner with a fascinating man."

She turned around and laughed. Craig stood close to her, wearing a crisp, white shirt open at the neck. "I accept, Stefano—what's your last name? I was going to respond in kind, but I can't." He held out one arm and she curled her fingers around it.

"No need, just say you'll have dinner with me, Ms. De Luca. Name's McAllister."

"Finally, we're properly introduced, Craig McAllister." She walked close beside him, enjoying the feel of his arm under hers. He held the door open for her. As they waited to be seated by the hostess, she asked, "Are you Irish, by any chance?"

"Scottish, they tell me. Several generations ago. Anything against the Irish?"

"Of course not, but my father was Irish. So, I'm half Irish. I think for a while I didn't like Irish men because of that. Silly, isn't it? It wasn't his fault he was killed, and I was fatherless."

"No, I think he would have preferred to be a loving dad to you. I bet you were adorable when you were little."

She wasn't sure how to respond to that. She'd never seen her life through Joe's eyes. He might have been a good dad to her, and certainly would have rather been that than dead at age thirty. Something soft opened up inside her at that realization and her long-term frustration at Joe Connelly unlocked and began to fall away.

"You're always a tad bit dressier than I am. You look very nice." She noticed the perfect tailoring of his clothes and wondered if they all came from Italian designers. She should do an afternoon of clothes shopping herself before returning home. Aside from her De Luca sandals and a truckload of gelato, she hadn't bought very much.

"I'm supposed to say that to you. You always look classy, even if you're casual, which you are supposed to be when you're on vacation. That just comes from inside you. I had some meetings today with Sergio, so I was a working dude."

Julia took mental notes of the décor, colors, and lighting of the main dining room as they waited to be seated. The hostess led them up a winding staircase toward a second-floor terrace to a small table that overlooked the city of Florence. Julia caught her breath at the sight beneath her. The sky bled purple and pink down to the tops of the buildings. Lights glowed out from their windows. When they'd had lunch together a few days earlier, the ristorante had been cute and cozy. This one out-ranked it by kilometers.

Craig held out her chair, but her eyes were still riveted on the sprawling city below. "The view is stunning." She sat down and looked at him. "I won't forget this place ever." *Or you.* Regardless of what happened between them.

"I discovered this restaurant the last time I was in Florence. I was alone then, but I told myself, one day I'd love to bring a very special woman here. So, this is the day, and you are that woman." He caught her eyes and almost looked shy for a moment.

She put a hand to her chest as the warmth fanned up through her neck. "I feel honored." If Craig McAllister wasn't for real, he made an excellent show. "I keep forgetting that you're in Italy for work. Seems a foreign concept to me, after only ten days of vacation." Julia laughed and Craig joined her.

"I can't say I'm on a full-time schedule. I have a few meetings but a fair amount of free time."

Julia wondered what he did in his free time. She could always ask him, couldn't she? He'd already spent a lot of time with her. How much did he see Isabelle? She couldn't ask *that* question, or she'd look possessive. "You said you had meetings with Sergio. How did you find him? Valentina told me he was tense because of the company spy."

Craig shrugged. "He's always very controlled, very professional. He did tell me that they had all the departments on high alert, but he knows it may come from outside the company as well. I think everyone assumes it's from the inside."

"That would be logical. Did they put Fabrizio under lock and key?"

He laughed. "They should. He creates some of the panic all by himself. But it's necessary to protect his work even more, of course. They'll figure it out."

"Have you ever sensed tension in the family, like generational tension between the older De Lucas and the younger ones?" Julia didn't want to break Valentina's confidence, but had wondered since that afternoon how deep the fault lines went in the company.

Craig looked thoughtful for a moment. "I'm not here enough to see that aspect. I know several younger family members work for De Luca. I always assumed they were happy to have secure family jobs, but maybe that was naïve on my part."

A waiter came to their table and presented menus, opening each one and placing it in their hands. He looked at Craig and asked a question, maybe about wine. Julia caught the words *vino* and *bottiglia*. Again, Craig's Italian, though slower than Valentina's, sounded smooth and unhesitating.

When the waiter had left, she shook her head, smiling.

"What?" Craig's brows lifted.

"I'm consistently amazed by your Italian. You may claim to be a hack, but I'll be happy when I can hack as well as you do."

"Thanks for the compliment. You didn't see me floundering at a department store this afternoon. You encourage me to keep going."

Throughout the delicious meal, their conversation flowed. Julia found herself caught up in it like a strong current in a river, despite her earlier questions about Craig, Isabelle, and the company. Every layer of his life she learned about intrigued her. She enjoyed hearing about the current lives of his siblings and the activities he pursued as a teenager. Of course, there were positives in his background, which he acknowledged along with the difficulties. She, too, had positive memories that she ought to bring to mind as a decision.

Finally, as one dessert and two spoons sat between them on the table, she summoned her courage to ask about Isabelle. Before she could formulate her thoughts, Craig said, "I've been putting off talking to you about Isabelle."

Relief flooded through her like a balloon releasing air. She didn't have any right to be jealous or possessive. She'd just met Craig. But she *was* curious. No, more than curious, after his claims of his feelings for her. She set her forearms on the table and waited, with what she hoped was a patient, non-demanding smile on her lips. "Why is that?"

"I need to give you some background so you'll understand."

He sighed heavily. Julia braced herself.

"A little over a year ago during one of my trips, I got a call from Isabelle. I was staying at a hotel in Florence. She told me that she was in town doing some errands and asked me if I wanted to have dinner. I wanted to decline because her intentions were clear to me and had become bolder during that particular visit, but I didn't know how to say no without looking like a jerk. She's my boss' daughter, after all. I felt stuck, so I said yes and we met for dinner." He refilled their water goblets from the glass carafe and took a long swig. "During dinner she opened up about a lot of things, her marriage, her dissatisfaction with her job in the company. She even told me some very personal things I shouldn't have heard. And we drank a bottle of wine between us, which I'm not used to doing. Afterward, we walked a bit in the city and ended up on one of the bridges to look out at the lights. Not sure how it happened, but I ended up kissing her. To this day, I regret that, just because it gave her a green light I hadn't intended. To be fair, I was attracted to her. I probably sent signals that invited her. But in my heart, I knew mixing romance with a family business was a bad idea. Along with that, I was pretty sure she wasn't my type and wasn't likely a believer."

Julia tilted her head. "I can easily see how that happened. That was a year ago, you said?" What had happened since then?

He nodded, his lips pressed together. "It—it gets worse, but I want you to know this." He hesitated and took another sip of water, then another. "I'm stalling." He let out an awkward chuckle. "So, that evening ended and I hoped it would be forgotten. Don't know why I thought that. I should have manned up then. About three months after that I went back to Italy. This time, she invited me to her apartment for dinner. That would have been the time to gently let her down. I was still feeling very attracted to her and fighting within myself. You may be sitting there wondering, why didn't I just *tell* her? I know I could have easily told her I didn't believe in mixing romance with work. It was a struggle, not only because of my relationship with Sergio and Emilia and the fact that she's their daughter, but because of my attraction to her. Again, I was conflicted about the dinner because I saw no way of refusing without offending her. Part of my brain, the really stupid, naïve part, said, what harm, it's just dinner. So, I went for dinner. Again, wine flowed, conversation. Another kiss, a few kisses, and then—"

He paused and Julia cringed, knowing what he'd say next. Something heavy dropped inside her. She swallowed.

"You know what I'm going to say. I hate to admit this, because I'm really not that guy. But I slept with her. To a large extent, it was the wine. I'd just been through a hard breakup with someone, so that played a role, too. I was vulnerable. But it was also due to me not stopping a sneaky progression and a very determined woman. I underestimated her."

Craig looked up at Julia and she saw tragedy in his defeated gaze. Pleading for understanding or a rebuke, or something. Her mind scrambled for words, but what kind? "Is that the only time this happened?" Her voice was soft, but she hoped, not condemning.

"Yes. I did talk to her the following day and apologized for what happened. I told her I hadn't meant for it to happen. I think, honestly, that she intended it."

"Obviously. It seems like she set you up." Julia hoped she hadn't just been judgmental. After all, she hadn't been there in that apartment and didn't know the thoughts and intentions of either Craig or Isabelle. And she didn't want to completely excuse Craig from his own part, his decision. He'd had several points where he could have averted the situation but hadn't.

"That may be true, but as a man and as a follower of Christ, I should not have let it happen. I saw it coming and I was weak. It took me months to forgive myself and I pleaded with the Lord for months to forgive me."

At that, her heart melted and she reached out and grabbed his hand. His warm fingers curled around hers, though his expression remained haunted. "Craig, sounds like you've been beating yourself up. Yes, it's a bad thing, I'm not saying it's not. But it's clear to me that you're sorry, you regret it. God's forgiveness can cover even that, don't you think?"

A ghost of a smile hovered around his lips. He squeezed her hand hard. "I finally stopped feeling like scum, but it took a while. That incident got me back into church and into fellowship with other believers. I'm stronger now, much stronger, but the damage was done."

"What did she say when you apologized to her?"

"She was angry. For her, it was a beautiful expression of passion, or some other thing she said. Can't remember. She thought I was belittling it by saying it was wrong. I told her it was against my beliefs and I had gone against my beliefs, but it was like speaking Chinese to her, I'm pretty sure."

Julia smiled and nodded. "Yeah, I bet it was. For her, it was probably a fitting ending to a romantic evening with someone she liked. She saw it completely differently but still may have assumed it meant something. What happened after that?"

"I did tell her I didn't think we were meant for each other, but she told me she wasn't in a rush. I'd come around. I told her no, but maybe not strongly enough. And we stayed in touch. We kissed only one other time, and she initiated that."

"She isn't going to let go. Not unless you bring out your bullhorn."

"No, probably not. I even stopped coming to Italy as often. I went six months without a trip but when I finally did, she came on even stronger. That was the last time I was here. Again, I tried to let her down gently."

"Too gently, I imagine."

"Yes, too gently. That's why it's tricky now that you're here, given my feelings for you. I should never have gotten involved with her, but there you have it. My dilemma."

Julia leaned forward. "You're a good man, Stefano. I knew it from the start. We all make mistakes, and some of them are big ones. I have a few of those myself, which I'll tell you about sometime." She smiled at him and they locked eyes for a moment. His grateful smile spread warmth through her whole body.

Her mind was another matter.

Chapter Fifteen

Julia dabbed butter from her lips and chin, still savoring the decadent cornetto and creamy cappuccino, though her thoughts were far away from the familiar café where she ate breakfast every day.

The bombshell that Craig had revealed to her the previous evening brought Isabelle's behavior—and the difficulty of his situation—into perspective. Maybe their one night of intimacy meant a commitment to her, though Julia was inclined to doubt it. She knew dozens of people who wouldn't consider one night equal to any kind of commitment, only an experience of recreation or affection. The fact that, for Craig, it had been a major failing spoke of his standards for himself. Even broken ones.

He'd texted her that morning. *Good morning, Julia. I hope you are still speaking to me after my confession last evening. I've made mistakes and wanted to be honest with you about them. But I care about you and hope you see my heart. I regret that I can't see you today because I need to be in Milan for the whole day, but please reserve some time for me tomorrow evening.*

She smiled. She did see his heart and loved it, despite his failings. And she was disappointed not to be able to see him that day. He was working, after all, and she was still on vacation. She texted him back. *I value your honesty with me. We all make mistakes and your response to it says a lot about you and your heart. I'm looking forward to seeing you tomorrow. Have a good trip.* Her mind added, *I miss you already,* though she didn't write it. Even if it was true.

Only four days before she would return to the States. To her real life. She ought to put it out of her mind completely until the day right before her flight, but couldn't stop random questions about her business or her home or friends from seeping through, more frequently as the date of her departure approached. What was she going back to?

She frowned. She loved her home, her business. Yet, there was something missing. It had hit her the other day as she walked the streets of Florence. Of course, her relationship with God was the first thing she needed to work on. That part of her life had been flagging for years, and though she'd gotten passive about the vague sense of emptiness and tug of regret, her longing to get back on track had increased. It took solitary walks through a stunning European city to jar her out of her complacency and stir her thirst.

But what of her relationship with Craig? How would that play out once they were back in the States in their separate cities? He'd said himself that he worked a lot, traveled a lot. Would all the closeness they'd shared evaporate once they arrived on another shore and were immersed once again in the routine?

Julia shook her head. Not going to go there, not going to worry in advance, see the glass half-empty. She'd change that bad habit. She was determined. She'd live in the moment and not even think of the future. In fact, she had an objective that day, to return to the *De Luca Scarpe* store to continue planning the renovation.

The streets vibrated with movement. The rumble of city noises and peoples' voices hung in the air. Since the day she arrived, she'd felt pressed on every side by strangers—tourists, locals, workers. That day was no exception, even though it was nearly September and vacationers would need to go home to put their children back in school. It didn't take long to get to the store, since she remembered the path from a few days earlier when she'd gone there. She stopped a few yards in front of the store to take more photos at different angles and then entered.

The stiff young woman who had spoken to her the first time was waiting on an elderly woman. She looked up at Julia and her eyes narrowed. A mask of what seemed like hatred slid over her face. What was that about? The woman went through a doorway and returned with another box of shoes. She placed them on a stool in front of the women then turned and came toward Julia.

"Signora," she hissed as her face contorted. "You are not to come into this store again. You are not welcome here. Now, get out, please."

Julia's mouth dropped open. "Excuse me?" She gathered her shock and pushed it aside. Anger began to simmer just under the surface. "I told you the last time I was here at Signore Regio's request to create a new design for the store. You can phone him if you like."

The woman shook her head and crossed her arms over her chest. "Non, non. This is not true. It is a pretext. You must leave. We know that you are possibly a spy and are only *saying* you are a designer."

At that, Julia laughed out loud. "And you think I'm coming into a store where shoes are available to the public," she extended one arm to indicate the rows of shoes on warmly-lit shelves, "so that I can *copy* them and sell the designs?" That didn't even make sense. She shook her head, about to say more, but realized that she was wasting her time. This woman was following orders. Isabelle's orders. She mustered a remnant of dignity in her voice and told the woman, "I see you've been listening to my cousin Isabelle. Very well, then." She turned before the shopgirl could make a scene and left the store.

Although she understood exactly what had just happened, Julia still felt humiliated and her body trembled for a few moments. She stopped to breathe deeply and regain her composure. She'd never been cast out of an establishment of any kind before. On the contrary, back home, she garnered a certain level of respect and deference for the reputation she'd built over the years. She didn't feel proud or arrogant about it, but in design circles, people knew Julia De Luca. But this wasn't home. And logic and fairness were not in charge, jealousy was. She stopped herself. *No, Lord, you are in charge.*

Following her silent prayer, her heart stopped pounding. She'd planned to spend the next part of her day at the Mercato Centrale, the market she'd heard so much about, then take in a two-hour walking tour of Renaissance Florence. Her day was full enough to push dark thoughts of Isabelle from her mind. However, she'd call Sergio to ask about the design, without mentioning the incident at the store.

She called his number and left a voicemail. Sergio called back thirty minutes later while she strolled through the aisles of the noisy Mercato. She ducked out one of the doorways. "*Ciao*, Sergio. I'm sorry to bother you during the work day. I was wondering if we could make time to talk about the design of the flagship store before I leave Italy."

"*Scusi*? The store? Wait a moment." He sounded flustered as if he had no idea what she was talking about. "You can say this again, Julia?"

"Sure. A few days ago, you said you wanted me to think of some design ideas for the store in Florence. I've been twice to the store and I have some ideas, but we haven't had a chance to talk about them."

"Ah, si, si. I remember now. I am very occupied with this spy situation and some other pressures in the company. It isn't a good time for me, but why don't you meet with Emilia tomorrow afternoon and she can talk to you about it? I will tell her to expect you tomorrow afternoon. You can explain your ideas to her."

"Oh, okay, Sergio. That's fine." Julia felt deflated, but it was logical. The man was beleaguered with a spy and generational arguing and discontent in his own family. No wonder he forgot about the redesigning of the store. Emilia hadn't been in on that conversation, so Julia doubted that her aunt would be enthusiastic about the idea. She'd find out when she showed up at the villa the following day.

The noise and electric atmosphere of the covered market took her thoughts away from Sergio and the shoe store incident. She stopped frequently at counters and displays to take in the color, smells, and variety of produce, homemade ravioli and pasta, restaurants offering take-out, flowers, candy, more than she could imagine. Pungent aromas of cheese and sausage mixed with warm baked smells of bread and pastry. A noisy hum filled the air as shoppers milled around her. She'd come back the day before her departure and buy cheese and some other food souvenirs.

Julia bought a small quantity of cooked homemade ravioli and tucked the small cardboard container into her canvas bag. She could heat it up later for dinner in the microwave that Signora Vecchietti had made available. For lunch, she'd likely buy something else she was itching to try and eat it at one of the tables on the massive food court that covered the second floor.

After a satisfying lunch of grilled fish with lemon sauce, she glanced at her watch. She had thirty minutes before her afternoon tour. She'd have to walk a few blocks to arrive at the meeting place, but she'd have enough time to finish her espresso and people-watch.

Her phone rang, but she didn't recognize the Italian phone number. Only Sergio and Valentina were in the habit of calling her. And Craig. "*Buongiorno,*" she said, unsure if the phone greeting was the same as the in-person one.

"Julia," said a woman's voice. "This is your cousin Isabelle."

Julia stiffened, a layer of dread coating her stomach. What could she want that would not be unpleasant?

"Hello, Isabelle. *Come stai?*"

A chuckle on the phone. Maybe in derision of Julia's attempt at Italian courtesy. "You are practicing your Italian. That's very good. I am fine, thank you. I am calling you because we got off on the wrong foot, as you say in America. I apologize for this."

Julia's eyes rounded in surprise. Isabelle's words were contrite but her tone still had an edge. "Thank you, Isabelle. I came here in good will with a desire to meet my family after many years. I don't mean anyone any harm." *And yet you accused me and were rude to me*, she wanted to say. Julia bit her lip. Her heart pounded.

"Yes, of course that's true, you came to see the family. I was not very welcoming. It has been a bad month or two for me and it put me in bad humor. I will be in Florence this evening and I would like to meet you for a coffee or a drink at around five. Can you do that?"

Tension bolted up like a rocket. She fully understood Craig's dilemma. How to refuse someone simply because of distrust? There was no easy way to say no, especially after Isabelle's admission, be it sincere or not. Julia's gut told her Isabelle had a strategy, a trap. But if she said no, she'd create still more offense.

Julia took a deep breath. It was just coffee. Then she remembered Craig's words as he, too, stepped into Isabelle's trap. "Sure, Isabelle. I can meet you for coffee. It will be nice to get to know my new cousin." *And see what else you have up your sleeve.*

"*Bene*, very good, Julia. I will see you at the corner of Campidoglio. It's near Repubblica Square."

"Yes, I know the area. I'll see you there at five."

Julia swallowed. What could she want? To threaten her away from Craig? She pretended to want to make amends and maybe she did. But that would be a big surprise. Julia suddenly remembered her tour and hopped up, almost spilling the last dregs of her espresso. Once outside, she trotted at a brisk pace for several blocks until she could see the tour group that was already gathered.

Once she arrived, she was panting and sweaty. "*Scusi—*" She wished she could remember Craig's late arrival phrase, but noted that the people waiting were mostly tourists.

The tour guide, a college-age guy with a ponytail and wire-rim glasses, looked up and asked her name. "Okay, you're our last arrival." He checked off her name on a clipboard then looked at the group and said loudly, "Everyone's here, so we can start now." His gaze panned across the group. Julia felt mortified for the second time that day and smiled apologetically. The guide then addressed the group and instructed them to follow him.

The two-hour tour was interesting, or would have been, if Julia had been able to focus while the guide spoke in a loud, animated voice and pointed to various landmarks across the city. What could Isabelle want? Julia was glad to have the tour to distract her from concern, but somehow questions seeped through. She was fairly certain Isabelle was up to no good. If only Craig had had a chance to set Isabelle straight about their relationship, Julia would have more ammunition. Leverage, even. As it was, she felt like a sitting duck with Isabelle already in control.

At five o'clock, Julia waited on the corner of Campidoglio, tightness in her stomach as though she were delivering ransom money in exchange for her beloved. *Lord, don't let me fall into her trap. You are my shield, my deliverer*, she prayed. Wily as a serpent, innocent as a dove . . . that phrase kept coming back to her from a long-forgotten Scripture. That's what she hoped to be. She didn't want to fall naively into a trap, nor did she want to stoop to Isabelle's level.

Finally, she spotted Isabelle in the distance. She wasn't hurrying, even though she was six minutes late. She wore a clingy black dress and red stiletto pumps, likely from De Luca. Though the day was hot, a red fashion scarf draped around her neck and down her shoulder. The black sunglasses completed her elegant movie-star look. Julia looked like the cleaning lady by comparison.

"Julia, so nice to see you," Isabelle crooned and leaned forward to kiss Julia's cheeks.

Kiss of Judas? Julia's mind whispered. *Lord, help me believe the best.* "You look lovely, Isabelle. Do you live here in Florence?"

Isabelle inclined her head and Julia followed her onto a busy sidewalk. "Thank you, there's a nice café over here not far away. I live in a nearby suburb with my daughter, Mia. I don't think you have met Mia yet. She is usually away at university. My home is not far from the De Luca factory."

"What does Mia study?"

"She studies business, but she says she doesn't want to work at De Luca. She wants to go far away from De Luca." She chuckled.

When Isabelle smiled, her face lit up and seemed almost relaxed, peaceful. Maybe asking her about Mia was like extending an olive branch. She said, "Mia has a spirit of adventure and wants to live in some other countries, perhaps even in the States. Though lately, she seems interested in Asia."

They arrived at a small café with a row of outdoor tables. "Is this good for us? We'll go around that corner. It is less noisy." The women walked to the end of the row of tables and sat down.

The harsh Isabelle Julia had expected softened when she spoke of her daughter. Was she lonely when Mia was away at school? Is that why she was driven to find a man? "That might be difficult for you if she went to Asia, wouldn't it? It's so far away."

Isabelle shrugged. "She's a young woman, so she needs to find her own life. I would miss her, but be happy for her to have an interesting life."

"What about you? Do you enjoy your work at De Luca? I had the impression the first evening that we met that you didn't enjoy it. Am I right?"

Isabelle seemed taken off guard by the directness of Julia's question. She fluttered her eyes and waved the air dismissively. "It's my job, my family. I stay busy and I do my job well."

A waitress came and took their drink order. When she left, Julia asked, "Is there something you'd rather do?" She leaned back, glad to be the one asking the questions, although she was also interested in what Isabelle would say to her. She was relieved that she'd found in herself the capacity to be interested instead of only suspicious, although her distrust of her cousin still hovered just beneath the surface.

"I don't know. When I was married, I was able to work part-time. I liked that better. I don't mind my work, but I'm less free." Again, no specific answer, but that was fine. Her eyes raised suddenly to Julia's. "I've been waiting to find the right man and think I have found him."

Julia's heart pounded at the abrupt shift in subject. She got right to the point, didn't she, her wily cousin. "Oh? Someone at the factory?" Playing dumb would open things right up.

Isabelle leaned forward slightly. Her eyes narrowed and her voice increased, not in volume, but in intensity. "You might say that." A faint smile appeared on her red lips but no warmth showed in her eyes. "I think you know who I'm talking about. I don't want to act possessive, but I can tell you like him, too."

Julia swallowed but tried to appear calm and uninvolved. Her heart pounded in her chest but she kept a blank mask on her face. *Don't let Isabelle get to you.* She moistened her lips and said slowly, pointedly, "And you *shouldn't* be possessive. People aren't possessions. If you're talking about Stefano." She leaned back in her chair to give Isabelle the impression that Craig could be a friend or something more, but she wouldn't indicate which. She shook her head, feeling a surge of strength within. "You do come right to the point, don't you?" She'd known this wouldn't be just a 'let's start over again' conversation. "You came here today to talk about Stefano, as if he belongs to you. Keep in mind, cousin, that Stefano has a mind of his own and *he* will decide who he loves and who he wants to commit to. You can't force him. At this point, you aren't married or engaged to him."

Isabelle's eyes shuttered. "No, but we have a close relationship."

Julia leaned back and forced a conversational tone into her voice. "What do you like about him?"

Isabelle looked startled at the change in Julia's voice, from confrontation to curiosity. Her beautiful but hard features softened. "We have the same heart, Stefano and I. We understand each other. He sees into my soul."

At her words, Julia flinched inside. Craig had used a similar expression. Had he said the same thing to Isabelle or she to him at one time? *She can't be telling the truth, Julia.* Maybe Craig sees her soul as lost. And of course, that's not what she'd meant.

Suddenly, Isabelle's face stretched into a full smile and she was gorgeous. "It will be wonderful when Stefano moves to Italy this fall. When that happens, I will see him often."

A jolt shook Julia from inside. "What? He's moving to Italy?" Julia tried to keep the shock out of her voice, but it was too late. Was this a ruse or had she missed something? She thought she'd been prepared, but Isabelle had skillfully unbalanced her. "Why would he come to Italy when he's the rep for the east coast of the U. S.?" And if that were true, why didn't he tell her?

"Well, it's a new development. My father thought it would help Stefano connect better with our vendors here and also be better versed in Italian. And in the way we do things. With his English, he can communicate with associates from all the countries where we do business."

Julia's head was spinning. Isabelle *must* be lying. And why on earth was Julia sitting here, close to believing her? Julia stuffed her confusion and outrage and returned a bland smile to Isabelle. Her cousin's claim would be easy enough to refute. "Well, that will be a nice experience for him."

"He hasn't told you, has he?" Isabelle looked smug.

Julia didn't respond. She could easily say something to give her cousin a dangerous foothold. Saying nothing was safer. She'd simply ask Craig when she saw him the next day.

The waitress set down the steaming drinks on the table as the atmosphere froze with tension, like two tigers facing each other in a cage. Julia didn't want to be one of them. It was time to leave.

When the waitress left, Isabelle sipped her espresso. She chuckled, though her dark eyes still lacked warmth. "Stefano has his faults. He loves women, you know. He's a typical man that way, I guess. Yes, he has his feet of clay, but so do I. Maybe that's why we understand each other and complement each other. Once he settles here, this will be even better because he'll better understand the Italian culture."

Julia leveled her eyes at Isabelle. "Why did you want to meet me tonight, Isabelle? To warn me to stay away from Craig?"

"I told you, I wanted to make amends for my rude behavior. And I don't need to warn you about Stefano. It's not as though he's tempted by you. You're here visiting and you'll go back home. You have nothing to do with De Luca after this."

"*Vero*?" Julia raised her eyebrows. Her blood was beginning to boil under the surface of her skin. "What about the family? This is *my* family, just as it's yours, Cousin Isabelle. You can be sure that I'll be back on a regular basis, so we need to learn to get along. You may want to stop trying to intimidate me and lie about me."

Isabelle's dark, well-shaped eyebrows gathered. "Who is lying about you?" She'd pulled off her confused look very convincingly. A consummate actress.

"You have called me a spy, which is so crazy no one would believe you. Except the shop girl at the De Luca store, who will likely believe anything you tell her. She accused me of spying when I was there working on a design for your father. I am an interior designer and he asked if I could create a new design for the flagship store."

Isabelle waved the air. "I didn't lie about you. Anyway, Julia, I didn't wish to argue about Stefano or anything else. I wanted to get to know you better. My apologies if you misunderstood my intentions."

"I'm sure I did *not* misunderstand," Julia said quietly. "Look, Isabelle, you can attract a man by being beautiful outside. You can *keep* him by being beautiful inside. We women know that the inside is more important. Right?"

Julia didn't wait for an answer but a strange wave of compassion blended with her anger. More softly, she added, "Let go, Isabelle, and things will come to you more easily. I'm sure of it. You'll probably meet a wonderful, rich man who adores you." Julia smiled at her scowling cousin. "I'm sure you'd rather be adored than try to force the hand of someone who doesn't love you. If you let go and relax, you'll be happier." Julia stood up to leave.

"So, you're a psychologist, too."

"I have to go now, Isabelle." She'd given her cousin as much time as she needed to. Julia fished into her purse for some change to cover her drink.

Isabelle waved it away. "I'll pay, Julia."

"*Buona sera*, Isabelle." Isabelle didn't move as Julia left the table without looking back.

Chapter Sixteen

Next time she came to Italy, she'd rent a car. Standing here at the bus stop outside of Florence was getting old. This time, Amara, who worked in the kitchen, was coming to pick Julia up and take her to the villa to meet with Emilia. Julia hadn't been there since Giuseppe's party. That event seemed like weeks ago, though it had been only a few days.

The afternoon temperatures had dropped, a pleasant contrast to the heat of the previous few days. A caramel-colored glow coated the rolling hills surrounding her as the valley prepared for the day's end. Soon, a tiny black car approached and stopped in front of her. Julia slid into the passenger seat and made small talk with Amara for the ten minutes it took to arrive at the villa. They entered the cool, marble hallway and Amara led Julia to the living room where Emilia was seated at a desk. Papers covered the desk from one side to the other along with neater stacks with post-its. A computer monitor perched on one end of the space.

Emilia turned her head toward the doorway where Julia stood. "*Buongiorno*, Julia. I'll be right with you. Have a seat. Better still, wait for me on the terrace and I'll have Amara bring us something cold to drink."

Julia did as Emilia instructed and slid into a chair at the glass table, cool under her elbows. A mental photo of her first lunch at the villa floated into her mind. It, too, seemed like a long time ago. So much had happened since that first day, with the family, Isabelle, and Craig. She'd also fallen in love with Florence and, family or not, she'd come back to the enchanted city.

At first, it had seemed like Sergio was passing her off to Emilia for a task he didn't want to handle. Now, she was grateful for a few minutes alone with Emilia, which she hadn't had since the first day. And as Sergio himself had told her, his hands were full with the troubles in the company.

Amara placed two tall glasses of sparkling water on the table in front of Julia. Five more minutes passed and Emilia came out from the house. Her features weren't exactly warm, but less rigid than the day they'd first met. She wore a denim skirt and a flowing pastel blouse with silver jewelry. Always neatly dressed, but never quite relaxed or peaceful.

She sat down across from Julia and slumped her shoulders. She let out a sigh. "So much to do. I'm too old for all of this." Fatigue and possibly worry weighed on her face. Somehow, this added humanity and softness to her otherwise hard features. What was behind the protective layers Emilia had built around herself?

Julia sent her aunt a gentle smile. "Do you work full-time for the company, Emilia?"

"No, not really. I help Isabelle with the accounting and payroll and I do some billing, too. I don't like working at the factory, so I mostly stay here at my desk in the parlor. I can do most things from here."

"I don't blame you for wanting to work from home. A lot of people in the States work from home, especially if their jobs can be done on a computer." Julia took a sip of the sparkling liquid. It burned her throat slightly as she swallowed. She lowered her voice. "Is there any progress with finding the spy?"

Emilia shook her head. "Not yet, though we have cameras set up around the factory. We did this without telling the employees. We don't want anyone to be warned. Obviously, I trust you, or I wouldn't be telling you this." She gave Julia a grudging smile, which felt like a long-awaited prize.

Julia suppressed laughter. "That's a relief. I assure you, the idea of spying has never crossed my mind."

Emilia waved the air dismissively with a roll of her eyes. "No, of course, it hasn't crossed anyone's mind. Do not worry. I think we will find the spy soon. Fabrizio is retracing his movements and conversations over the last two months since we've had this problem. He is estimating the time when it started, but he cannot be sure. Fabrizio is very dramatic, but he's good at his job and he has a good memory as well. I think this will help us."

"I'm glad. Sounds like you're doing everything that can be done, except hiring detectives or plain-clothes guards."

The older woman's eyes widened and cocked her head. "Good idea, Julia. I have not thought of this. We'll do that next, if we don't have any answers soon." She sipped her sparkling water. "Sergio says you have some ideas for the store in Firenze."

"Yes. It's very respectable-looking as it is, but I had some initial ideas to give it a fresh look." Julia pulled open her purse and took out a folded piece of paper from her purse then spread it on the table between them. The store's current appearance wasn't terrible, but predictable and dated. "Here's a preliminary sketch. It's very rough, of course, because I don't have any of my tools or anything. I often do this kind of sketching on my computer, but this will give you an idea. Also, I don't have measurements of the store, so that will help if I can have those eventually. And any brand colors your company uses would be important to know."

"Yes, of course. I don't imagine it will be a quick process, but we are not in a hurry, either. We are only beginning to think about this and it is not our priority." She paused and met Julia's eyes. "I am sure we have to solve the spy problem and then get through the fall season to see where we stand financially. It's an up and down situation lately. This renovation is a less necessary expense, but we are still eager to hear your ideas."

Julia nodded. "Of course, I understand. I'm happy to help at whatever point you are ready for the project." No surprise at all, given the turmoil that seemed to be erupting everywhere. She leaned forward to point to the drawing. "This rough design will show you a bit of the traffic flow, which can be improved, I think. I noticed that there are two floors in the store, so the upstairs can have a different theme, such as being a place for more elegant or formal shoe collections for men and women. That is up to you all, but it's just an idea. Women's casual and professional footwear and kid's shoes could stay on the ground floor. Those will be the most sought-after, of course."

Julia continued explaining some of her ideas for color and lighting as well as artful arrangements of the displays, instead of predictable rows, as they currently were. Emilia nodded, paying close attention to Julia's words as she described some of the possibilities.

Emilia leaned back in her chair. "When you are back in the States, can you send me some photos of stores you have already designed? I can also look for features I like in different stores or even magazines. That would help me know what style I like."

"Absolutely. The more aspects of your own tastes and needs that you can tell me, the better. As you said, this will be a work in progress and we can stay in touch online once I go home."

Emilia paused. Something like a wistful sadness seeped through her usually stern expression. "Your visit has gone quickly. I hope it has been a good one."

"It's been wonderful. I'm sad it is ending in just a few days." Would she be invited back? Maybe she didn't have to be invited next time. "I appreciate all of the hospitality and grace with which you received me. I understand after such a long time, it wasn't easy."

Emilia's jaw tightened. "It was a shock, at first. We had so much hurt with Gianna deserting us like she did. I'm not sure of everything that happened with our mother, because afterward, no one would talk about it. I sometimes bickered with my sister, but I really missed her when she stopped communicating. She sent a couple of postcards over the years, but never came back." She shook her head, eyes pooled with sadness and regret.

As if catching herself becoming emotional, Emilia straightened up in her chair and said briskly, "I'll be the one who will be in touch with you about these designs. Sergio—well, I'll just tell you that I'm much more interested in this type of thing than Sergio, and he simply doesn't have the time."

Julia grinned. What a surprise. Emilia must have an artistic flair. "That will be a pleasure. We'll work on it together."

A faint smile and slight nod of her head was the only response.

"Can I ask you a question, Emilia?"

"Yes, of course. What is it?"

Julia hated to ask this question, but it would put her mind at ease. Emilia would immediately debunk the lies that Isabelle was trying to weave about a Craig. "Isabelle told me that Craig—Stefano is planning to move to Italy. I was surprised by this, since he is the U. S. rep." Not to mention that he never said a word. "Is it true?"

"Stefano? Yes, he should be able to arrive this fall or later and will help with the Europe-wide communication."

A cold wave flowed through Julia's stomach. So, it was true. She'd been so sure it had been Isabelle's manipulation at work. Why hadn't he told her? Why would he begin something romantic with her if he were going to be living in Italy?

Julia forced a smile, though hope fell down inside her with a crash, like a rotten tree after a storm. She should have known it was too good, too soon. Why didn't she predict that something would fall apart in her seemingly ideal discovery of Craig McAllister?

She continued talking about design ideas with Emilia, coaxing her voice and her facial expressions, trying to ignore the tempest inside. She'd ask him. He'd tell her. They'd get it straight.

One way or the other.

As their conversation ended, Emilia asked Julia, "Why don't you stay for dinner tonight, Julia?"

She had an appointment—a crucial dinner date where she'd get answers. Should she admit this to Emilia? "I have a dinner date, but thank you anyway." If she'd told Emilia simply, 'with Stefano', it could either create a needed reality check about his relationship with Isabelle or it could generate resistance. In the end, privacy won out, along with fear of consequences.

Then it struck her. Fear. She was no different than Craig in this. They both feared the family's reaction to their relationship for no reason. They were adults, after all. Adults with free will. Time to take a stand. "Actually, I'm having dinner with Stefano."

Emilia's eyes widened just slightly, then a slight smile appeared. "*Bene.* He's a good man and you seem to get along well. *And* you are both staying in Firenze during your visit, so it's convenient."

The brief seconds of comfortable silence that followed was ripped apart by shouting inside the house. Emilia's head jerked in the direction of the back door. It was Valentina's voice, then a man's, then Sergio's. Then all three at once, shouting. Valentina's voice was clear as she shouted. Was her anger directed to Sergio?

Emilia pressed her lips together. Her eyes were glued to the doorway. "This is bad. Valentina and Luca are talking with Sergio and it isn't going well. The tension has been building with them for some time, but they have never had this kind of argument that you can hear all the way outside."

She turned her gaze back to Julia and offered a slight, sad smile. "They don't see things the same way, the younger people and the older ones. That's us, I guess." She let out a short laugh that lacked humor. "My children are full of passion and wonderful ideas, but they find themselves stuck in the tradition of the company. I know we need to change some things. That was one reason Sergio wanted to change the store appearance. But we both know that is a superficial change. It won't satisfy our children if there aren't deeper changes as well." Suddenly, Valentina screamed from a room inside. Julia flinched. The front door slammed. Silence followed.

In the silence, Emilia stiffened and seemed to close down. She leaned away from the table and gathered the papers that Julia had brought. "May I keep these drawings?"

"Yes, of course. I have a copy on my phone. I'll make a proper rendition when I get home."

While Julia rode the train back to Florence, she watched the green hills speed by, villages scattered here and there. Had the De Luca family tension finally exploded? It sounded that way, but how serious it was, she had no idea. She hoped it would lead to productive discussion between the generations rather than widening the faultline.

Soon, the landscape transformed as buildings sprang up and trees fell away. Julia's train pulled with a screech into Stazione di

Santa Maria Novella. Julia got out and started walking. It was a long walk back to her room in Oltrarno, but she needed to clear her head along the Arno River, through the beloved city, across the timeless bridges.

Craig had sent a text. *Are we still on for dinner? My train from Milano should be in at 5:30 or so. Want to meet at 7:30 in Piazza Frescobaldi? It's on the Oltrarno side near the Santa Trinita bridge. I'll come to your side of the river.* A grinning emoji. Julia smiled, despite the heaviness inside.

Yes, of course, she typed back. *I'll be there. Hope your trip to Milan went well.* It wasn't overly warm, but it would do. She couldn't quell the wave of electricity that seemed to flood through her. She looked at her watch. She'd see him in two hours. Deep breath. What would that encounter reveal? Every time the relationship bumped up in closeness and possibility, it was followed by a cloud of confusion and doubt. Back and forth.

Julia opened her city map, which she still often needed despite her daily treks across the city. She located Via Santa Catarina, a small road that jutted away from the station and changed names two more times before crossing the Amerigo Vespucci bridge. It felt good to stretch her legs and move, breathe, observe everything around her while she still could. She'd had too many intense conversations lately and it wasn't over yet. But for now, she'd still her racing thoughts. *Lord, I pray you'd superintend all the craziness. With the family, Isabelle, and with Craig. I want your will for this relationship with him.*

Though her prayer diluted part of the heaviness inside, it did nothing to remove the hope stubbornly rooted, like a weed that had germinated in only a few days since meeting Craig, but now would take months to dig out. She rebuked herself for that hope as she walked along the river. By hoping, she'd given herself something she now had to recover from. A new hurt to heal. Hope was dangerous. She'd learned that plenty of times.

So, Craig was moving to Italy in the fall. It was almost fall. She'd had a friend who'd moved to Stuttgart a few years back to pursue advanced studies in something scientific. Her friend had prepared for months ahead of time, arranging shipping, getting a visa, finding a renter for her condo. Maybe Craig had already done those things and simply neglected to mention to her that he was leaving. Or maybe he'd be postponing the move, though both Isabelle and Emilia had referred to the fall. Maybe he envisioned a pen pal type relationship with her, with an occasional romantic weekend throughout the year. Philadelphia was already long-distance for them, but Florence? No. She'd tell him no.

Julia shook her head as her feet kept moving and the heaviness returned to her stomach. Combined with the fact that he hadn't told her of his move was his continued foot-dragging in setting Isabelle straight about their relationship. The woman was still plotting and planning, which had been obvious during the curtailed coffee meeting the previous day. He'd had a year to do it, and now, even in the face of a new romantic relationship—with a *soul mate*, no less— he *still* hadn't told Isabelle. What did all of this mean? Was Isabelle telling the truth when she said Craig had his faults and loved women? His failure of self-control with Isabelle added weight to her claim.

Julia had to put it out of her thoughts for now if she could, since her mind felt like a tangled ball of yarn. They'd talk. But would he tell her the truth? Had he been telling her the truth?

At seven-thirty the sun was still high enough in the sky for Julia to spot Craig on the opposite corner of the Piazza Frescobaldi. Her heart did a little flip as she drew closer. He looked classy as usual, but had changed to a casual polo shirt and dark jeans. He was scanning the crowd and when he saw her, began walking toward her. As confused as she was about him, she went into his arms, which felt warm and strong around her. He kissed her lightly and said, "I missed you. What's it been, two days?"

She simply smiled at him, though her thoughts immediately wondered what it would be like after months, if he moved to Italy. He held onto her arms for a moment, his eyes latched to hers, as if memorizing her face. Anyone—including Isabelle—who'd been watching them in the square would assume they were long-lost lovers. Looks could be deceiving. She had no idea what they were or were not, though just then, her insides were definitely not doubting. No, instead, they felt like a pool of lava filling her whole being with tingling heat and desire.

"I missed you, too." She had to admit, and his statement made it easier, though the turmoil and questions still spun around in the back of her mind. Hopefully, the power of the attraction she now felt wouldn't chase away all of her legitimate questions. For those, she still needed answers.

He smiled. "I'm glad you missed me." He pulled her close for a slower, lingering kiss. "I know a place a couple of streets from here. I think you'll love it. It's on a quieter street. More romantic and we'll be able to hear each other talk more easily."

She linked her arm through his. "So far, your taste has been impeccable."

They walked for a few minutes as he told her something humorous about his return trip on the train from Milan. Another picturesque ristorante near a lively square appeared. A gentle summer breeze caressing the awning overhead as they sat down at an intimate table. Julia wanted to savor every second, every café, every square, every breeze. Every moment with Craig. Soon, she'd leave Italy and return to her normal life. Somehow, it didn't seem like it would ever be quite the same. For better or worse.

"You looked sad just then." Craig reached across the table of the shaded terrace and pulled her hands into his.

Julia shrugged. "I—I try to avoid thinking about leaving Italy in just a few days, but I can't help it. Everything I see now—I try to capture it all in my senses."

"You're leaving Saturday, aren't you?"

She nodded. "Emilia and Sergio want to have a final dinner for me Friday night before they take me to the airport Saturday." Heaviness rose up in her stomach and produced a grimace on her face. It could even be a pout. "I shouldn't have said the word 'airport'. I think I just got indigestion, and haven't eaten anything yet."

Craig laughed. "All wonderful vacations must end, but we won't end, Julia. We'll see each other again. I'm determined."

Now would be a good moment to bring up his move to Italy with a question. *How will we see each other if you live in Florence?* She wasn't ready to throw cold water on that moment of warmth, his eyes on her as he grasped her hands. Maybe that would be their final time in Florence together. She wanted it to last.

A waiter came to the table and brought them menus. "Maybe I'll order for myself tonight. I'll prove to you how humble and vulnerable I am." She met his eyes and they shared a laugh.

They spent a moment looking at the menu then she asked, "How did your meetings in Milan go today?"

"Fine. I've met with these vendors before. I don't have too many of those meetings while I'm here. I mostly come to reconnect with the Regios. Tomorrow, I have to go to France, though. This time, to see my sister."

"Your sister?" Another surprise from nowhere shoved Julia off balance.

"My little sister is married to a Frenchman so I try to go see her when I'm in town."

"Oh." She frowned. "You talked about your family but didn't mention your sister was in France. Or I missed that."

"I might have forgotten to tell you. With so many siblings, their comings and goings are hard to keep track of." For him, maybe that was true, but she couldn't imagine overlooking a detail like that.

"How long has she been in France?"

"They've been married for about five years but lived in the States until just last year. So, it's fairly recent. Not sure I'm used to it just yet, but at least I get to see her sometimes when I'm over here."

No mention of the move. Maybe he'd changed his mind. Hope flared up in an unfounded spike.

The waiter returned to take their order. Julia smiled up at him, silently requesting patience. "*Posso avere insalata di giorno poi pesce alla grillia.*" She sighed and leaned back in her chair, as if she'd exerted herself physically. And all that for fish and a salad. The waiter smiled indulgently.

"*Comme contorno?*"

Her eyes widened for a moment. "Rice. I mean, di riso."

The man nodded and turned to Craig for his order, which of course, sounded flawless to her. When the waiter left, she muttered, "Show-off." They laughed.

He gazed at her with a lazy smile and hooked her finger with one of his. "I thought you did very well. Think of how much Italian you could speak two weeks ago compared to now."

"You have a point." Suddenly, she *did* feel proud of herself, instead of severely lacking. Even coming to Italy by herself had been out of her comfort zone, and now she'd ordered in Italian. So there.

As they ate, Craig talked more about his work and his role in Italy. Again, it would have been an easy segue to his imminent move, but as he spoke, it seemed he had no intention or idea about it. Julia told him about her meeting with Emilia that afternoon, but held off mentioning her encounter with Isabelle. That would certainly put a shadow on their romantic dinner.

"*Dolce per Loro?*" asked the waiter when he'd cleared the plates and returned to the table.

"*Non, grazie.*" No dessert for her. Not only was she full, but the butterflies had begun aerial training exercises inside her stomach.

"I, uh, had an interesting experience yesterday afternoon." She launched, but feared where they'd both end up.

Craig lifted his eyes in interest, waiting for her to continue.

"I got a call from Isabelle. She wanted me to meet her for coffee."

His eyes widened. "Did you meet her? What did she say?"

Julia breathed deeply. "Well, at first she said we'd gotten off on the wrong foot and she wanted to start over. She was going to be in Florence and would I meet her for a drink. Just like your experience with her, I felt trapped, like I couldn't refuse her without making things worse. Without offending her. There was always a small chance that she was sincere, but I think we both know Isabelle better than that. I fully expected some kind of a trap."

"Good, I'm glad you were ready for her. Tell me what happened." He leaned back in his chair. The relaxed, affable expression was gone from his face. She couldn't interpret what she saw there now.

"We talked a bit about Mia. I asked her some ice-breaker type questions. We had a bit of small talk but quickly she made her intention clear. She talked about you, saying she wanted to find the right man, but thinks she's found him. Meaning you, of course. She knows there's something between us. Or maybe she just thinks I'm after *you*. She said you see into her soul." She watched his face.

Craig let out a staccato laugh. "Whatever. I'm not sure what she means by that."

"Did you ever talk to her that way?" Julia kept her voice soft, trying to determine the truth.

He shook his head. "Nah. She's talked to me that way, wanting me to agree, which I did not. Anyway, I'm not surprised that she cornered you and warned you. It's kind of childish. I don't belong to her. I'm not her boyfriend."

"Does she know that?" Seems she had asked him this question before. She longed to ask him what was holding him back, but didn't want to look controlling.

His eyes met hers but the warmth she'd seen there minutes ago had diminished. "I—I'm sorry that happened to you. I'm going to talk to her. I promise."

Julia gave him a muted smile through tight lips, wanting to believe him. Wanting him to take a stand one way or the other. "If you are having doubts about me, Craig, just tell me. We just met. I like you a lot, but you aren't bound to me."

Craig was already shaking his head. He leaned forward and grabbed both of her hands. "Julia, none of that. I know we don't know each other well, but I don't doubt what I feel for you. My, uh, failure, I'll call it, since that's what it is, my failure to talk to Isabelle clearly has nothing to do with you. Please believe me. Partly, I've been busier than usual with meetings and honestly, I haven't seen her. Each time she tries to get together, I have a reason to decline, usually legitimate. She might be sensing me drawing back, but I do plan to talk to her. Soon. I don't want any shadows between us, Julia. Do you believe me?"

"Yes, but—"

"But?"

"She told me, quite triumphantly, in fact, that you'd be moving to Italy this fall."

His mouth dropped open slightly and he started to speak.

"And Emilia confirmed it, Craig. Emilia said you were moving to Italy. I can't imagine why you wouldn't tell me this."

"I didn't tell you because it's not going to happen." He leaned back and fell silent, his brow furrowed as if he were thinking hard about something. "I understand how this got started. First, let me tell you the background. Last spring, I was on the phone with Sergio and he suggested I spend a longer time in Italy, maybe a few months, especially during the trade shows and runway shows. I loved the idea, because the thought of living here part time, soaking in the culture—that really appealed to me. I said I'd be open to thinking about it and everyone figured it was a done thing. Isabelle jumped right on it with her assumptions, though I hadn't actually confirmed that I was coming." His eyes leveled with her and the warmth simmered there again. "If I hadn't met you, I would have been really tempted."

Julia frowned, only partially reassured. "Am I keeping you from coming to live here? Do you really want to come?" Now she was *really* confused. "Craig, if you want to come—"

"You want me to come? I thought you didn't."

She sighed in exasperation but could see the confusion on his face. "No, you're misunderstanding me, Craig. I couldn't see how you'd be pursuing a relationship with me but still planning to move to Italy. But I also don't want to be a *blockage* to you if you truly want to come. You might refuse to go because of me, but eventually resent me because of your lost opportunity."

He fell silent, as if he were considering the options. As if she had released him to move. Her insides felt like they were tearing, just small, persistent tears ripping her hope to shreds.

He shook his head. "It's a nice idea, Julia. It would be fun. That's all. Getting to know you is more important to me. I wouldn't resent you. And I'm sure I'll have other opportunities to come to Italy for a longer chunk of time."

She swallowed. "You're sure that's what you want?"

"Seems you're still doubting me. Well, I guess I can understand that." He frowned but instead of looking angry, he looked sad. Defeated.

He looked up and their eyes met for a long moment. Then his phone rang. "I'll leave it. This is important." He inclined his head toward her.

"Don't you want to see who it is? If it's Isabelle, send her to voicemail." She smiled, trying to lighten the suddenly serious mood.

He glanced at his phone and his brow furrowed. "Gotta get this. It's Sergio." He leaned away from the table to respond.

Julia couldn't guess the content of the call from Craig's responses, but it seemed serious. Her stomach felt unsettled at the conversation that still hung in mid-air, at Craig's forlorn expression. Yet, she didn't want to be a barrier to him. She couldn't, she'd known him less than two weeks. But she did want him to choose her over Isabelle. If he already had, she wanted him to take a stand.

Craig hung up and looked at her, his face drawn. "They found the identity of the spy."

"Oh, that's good, isn't it?" Her voice came out thin and uncertain because of the grim look on his face.

He shook his head, frowning, then met her eyes. "It's Marco."

Julia's hands flew to her mouth. "Oh, Valentina!"

Craig nodded. His lips were pressed together in a line. "The scumbag. After all they did for him for the last two or three years. I have to go out there now and meet with Sergio. I think he needs me." He reached out and grabbed her hands. "Our conversation isn't over, I hope. Let's not let it be."

"No, of course not. We'll have a chance to see each other when you're available. This is a crisis situation and I know you'll be a comfort to Sergio and Emilia."

Valentina was another story. She hoped her cousin was strong enough to bear the shock. And hopefully, Julia could be a comfort for her before having to leave Italy.

He stood and Julia stood with him. He stepped forward. Reached out and gently pushed a lock of hair away from her face. "I'll walk you home."

They walked in silence the short distance to her hotel. She wanted to break the tension, to restore their previous warmth, but Craig seemed preoccupied. With Sergio, with her questions, maybe both.

"I'll be in France tomorrow with my sister, but I'll stay in touch." His voice was soft, but held a finality that chilled her. Had he remembered she was leaving Saturday?

In front of the door, he pulled her close and kissed her, fast and hard. The tenderness he'd shown earlier had ebbed away. She hoped it was only because of concern for Sergio and the company.

She feared it was more.

Chapter Seventeen

A band of morning sunlight slid across the pillows, awakening Julia. She turned her head away from the brightness and groaned. Her sleep had been fitful, filled with images of Valentina, Marco, and Craig, like a disjointed movie that had no point and no conclusion.

She pulled herself up and disentangled her legs from the sheets. Valentina. Her chest hurt for her cousin. Did she know yet about Marco? Julia wanted to be a comfort to her, but didn't want to be the one to give her the shocking news. She didn't know any of the details, how they discovered that he was the spy, how they were sure. Had he been caught in the act? Captured on film?

Julia's thoughts ricocheted from Valentina to Craig. Would she see either one of them before she left on Saturday?

She showered and dressed then went down the winding wooden staircase to her coffee shop. She would miss the warmly-lit café with its small, round tables and friendly employees. She even recognized and greeted the noisy locals who came to share news, joke together, and read the daily paper.

Julia made a beeline for her table next to the window and returned to the counter to order a cappuccino and two cornettas.

She carried them back to the table, the smell of baked sugar and coffee rising to her nostrils. She settled at her table and savored a sip of the hot beverage, enjoying its warm descent down her throat. She stilled her tumultuous thoughts, relaxed her shoulders, and offered a simple, silent prayer for the uncertain day ahead. Gradually, her groggy stupor faded.

Craig was in France with his sister, though he hadn't mentioned before yesterday that his sister lived there. Maybe it was a guy thing to forget a detail like that. He hadn't told her how long he'd be away. Another guy thing? She frowned. In fact, she didn't even know the date of his return to the States. There was a lot he hadn't told her. Seemed like now the ball was entirely in his court. While she hung in mid-air.

She drained her cappuccino and ordered another one. Should she reach out to Valentina? She could always call her, pretending simply to get in touch, couldn't she? Then she'd get a pulse on how her cousin was doing and how much she knew about Marco.

Her phone rang and her hopes shot upward. Either Craig or Valentina would be a welcome caller. It was Valentina. "*Ciao*, Valentina. I haven't seen you in a few days. How—"

"Julia, have you heard about Marco?" Valentina's normally cheerful voice broke then she stifled a sob.

"Um, yes, I did hear about it. When did you hear?"

"Early this morning. My father called me to give me the news. Of course, I've been crying all morning. I must leave town today. I have to get out of Florence for a while. I'm going to Bergamo to see my cousin Luciana. I told you we're close. I don't know how long I'll be there, but I want to say goodbye to you before I go. Do you have time today?"

Julia's spirits leaped. "Yes, of course. I'm available anytime you want. Right now, I'm at the coffee shop I go to every morning. When do you want to meet?" *Thank you, Lord!* She'd see Valentina before she left Italy.

"I need to pull myself together and pack a suitcase, but I can meet you around one. I have a train at two-thirty."

"That's perfect. Do you want to have lunch?"

"I don't know if I'll be able to eat, but I can meet you at the same place as before, La Matriciana. *D'accordo*?"

"*Sì*. I'll see you at one. It's good that you're leaving town. It'll do you a lot of good. But I'm *so* glad I can see you before I leave Saturday."

"I wouldn't leave without saying goodbye, Julia."

Julia swallowed and something full and deep swelled inside. Several tears spilled onto her cheeks for her cousin's pain and the fact that they'd soon part company. "See you at one, my dear cousin."

When Valentina slipped into the seat across from Julia at the restaurant, Julia hardly recognized her. Crinkled, blue eyes without make-up stared out of a blotchy pink face. Her blond hair was pulled back into a severe ponytail, though a few wisps had escaped, making her look like a lost little girl. She must have been crying most of the morning. A small suitcase sat on the floor next to her seat.

Julia throat tightened at the sight of her and her eyes stung. She arose and stretched her arms toward Valentina, who stood and fell into her embrace. Julia held her tightly for a long moment, rocking her gently, while both women wept. Julia then released her, but held onto her upper arms. She looked into her eyes and said softly, "It's going to be okay, Valentina. Your heart is broken now, but this does not define your future. Please remember that."

Valentina nodded mutely as tears continued to slip out of her reddened eyes. The women sat down again. Valentina swallowed and moistened her lips. She reached for a napkin from the table and dabbed her eyes. "I know what you're saying, Julia, but I'm still in shock. I feel like someone has died." She bowed her head as several more tears flowed. "*Scusi*, Julia." She sniffed and blew her nose. "Marco always seemed so sincere, so loving. At least he acted that way. Who knows if it was true? He worked hard, long hours at the factory, when all the while—" She blew her nose again. "I still can't believe it. Now I know why he hasn't talked about marriage. He was using me."

Julia's heart went out to Valentina. "He might have also loved you. He may have been sincere in that."

Valentina sniffed. "I don't know. It doesn't matter now. He is fired from the company and is seen as a traitor. There's no way we can be together now, whatever his excuses are. I just can't understand what his reasons could possibly be. He had a good position in the company. A good salary. He was one of my father's trusted managers. He was my father's protégé. I think my father assumed we'd get married and one day Marco could replace him in the company." Tears came again, more slowly. "That was *my* dream. And now, nothing." She splayed manicured fingers.

Julia took her hands. "I'm so sorry, my Valentina. You deserve to be happy, and I believe you will be one day. Marco wasn't the man for you. He could have proposed long ago. You knew something was holding him back. Now you know at least part of what was blocking him. But he probably really cared for you, though his heart wasn't completely there and never would be."

Valentina's tears slowed and finally stopped, though misery was still etched on her face. "Maybe you're right. I wanted so much for it to happen, but no one can force this."

"And you wouldn't want to."

She shook her head and tightened her lips together.

"You deserve someone who is crazy about you, and you'll have that one day, I'm sure of it."

Valentina gave her a weak smile and said nothing. It would take her a while to take comfort in that thought. To believe it fully.

Julia leaned back as a waiter came to the table. She hadn't even looked at the menu, but remembered the wonderful pizza she'd had the last time she was there and ordered the same one.

Valentina ordered a coffee and a dessert. She managed a small smile. "I don't usually have dessert, but I think it will make me feel better."

Julia grinned. "Totally appropriate. In fact, when you go to Bergamo, you should go shopping and eating and visiting. Go everywhere you want and have a good time with Luciana. Try to forget about everything here for a while."

Valentina nodded. "I'll try."

Julia leaned forward. "And if you ever need to talk, you can call me anytime or text me, even after I go back to the States."

"Okay. Thanks, Julia. I'm so glad we met." Her smile was sincere and broke through the tearful misery.

"Oh, me, too, Valentina. You're a wonderful cousin and friend. Thank you so much for all you did to help me reconnect with the family. But getting to know you has been so special. I never had a sister or a cousin or anyone as I was growing up. You're like my sister, cousin, and good friend all together."

Valentina chuckled as her eyes filled up again. She blinked. "I feel the same, Julia."

"Maybe one day you can come visit me in the States. Would you want to come one day?"

She nodded vigorously. "Yes, of course! I'd love to come." Valentina fell silent as a wistful look came over her face. "Who knows what the future will hold for me. Things aren't going well in the company. Yesterday, I had a huge fight with my father. It was awful."

Julia pressed her lips together. "I—I was at the villa yesterday talking to your mother and I heard everyone shouting. I recognized your voice and could tell you were upset."

"My father, he just refuses to live in the present. Luca was there, too. He and I have told him repeatedly that he needs to modernize his process. And listen to others, believing we have some good ideas. Once in a while he seems open but other times he shuts down, like a fearful old man." She shook her head, looking stormy. "Yesterday, he was shut down. Luca and I were trying to reason with him like adults, but of course, he doesn't see us as adults. Then he accused me of being 'just a woman in love'." She sing-songed the phrase, imitating her father. "That's when I screamed at him. I wanted to hurt him when he said that. Well, not really, he's my father and I love him, but I was so angry I wanted to explode." Valentina's fingers thrummed the table faster as she spoke.

"I understand your anger, Valentina. He was invalidating your feelings and everything you'd been saying."

"He was treating me like a child. My feelings for Marco have—had nothing to do with my insight about the company and its need to change. These are separate, but he was looking for a way to dismiss me. I almost hated him at that moment. I feel guilty for that, but I did."

"I think he *has* to change things now," Julia said. "Seems he won't have a choice. I know he wants to have a better relationship with you and Luca. Maybe he'll listen now."

Finally, it was time to say goodbye. They clung to each other for a long moment. "I'll stay in touch, I promise." Valentina picked up her small suitcase. "*Arrivaderci*, Julia."

"*Arrivaderci*." Julia watched Valentina disappear through the front door of the restaurant. She sat back down, not sure what she would do next. She felt paralyzed by the events of the last twenty-four hours. Loose ends hung everywhere, with De Luca, with Craig . . . Tears pushed against her eyes again and her head pulsed with pain.

She'd gotten attached to her young cousin in just a couple of weeks' time. A wave of melancholy swept over her as she looked through the window to the busy street outside. A waiter came to her table and she ordered a cappuccino, wanting to linger a bit in the cozy restaurant. The lunch crowd was thinning and the quiet was a comfort surrounding her noisy thoughts. Problems in the De Luca family and business had surfaced during her visit, but it wasn't her job to fix anything. They would have to tackle these issues as a family, as a company. Still, she was concerned for them, especially for Valentina.

Craig was another story. At that moment, she felt far from him, as though she'd never see him again. What had happened the previous evening that led to this coldness she now felt? Was it her fault, her doing? Was she again protecting herself? Or were her questions about Isabelle valid? And what about his supposed move to Italy? His answers had been vague, his response, lacking conviction. She had no idea how to interpret this, since his previous communication had been so clear, so satisfyingly healthy and authentic. Aside from Valentina, she'd told no one, not even her girlfriends back home, about Craig. It had crossed her mind, but she'd held off in case it turned out to be nothing. As she'd expected it to be. Was she now backing away before it had a chance to become something?

Suddenly, she longed to talk about it with one of her friends. It would be eight in the morning on the east coast, but Marissa would be up. And she, too, had recently met someone while on a short-term trip. She'd been in Julia's shoes in some ways, though Marissa's relationship seemed much less complicated.

"Hello? Julia, is that you?" Marissa's cultured southern voice answered on the first ring. "I saw your name pop up on my phone and I know you're still in Italy. I hope everything's okay over there."

"Hi, Marissa. Everything's good, I'm having a great trip." Minus the drama, it *had* been a very good trip. "I was just thinking of you. I have a situation a bit similar to yours and Jarrod's."

"Oh, you've met someone in Italy? Wonderful! Wait, he's not Italian, is he? I don't want you to move so far from us."

Julia laughed. "No, it's kind of a long story. He lives in Philly." Julia related some of the details of how she'd met Craig. "We get along well. He's attractive and fun, loves God."

"But?" prompted Marissa.

"I don't know, I don't have doubts about him per se, but my cousin Isabelle is after him . . ." She hesitated. It might take another half hour to explain what was going on with Craig, the company, Valentina. "Then he had this possible move to Italy, and his sister in France—" Julia stopped. She wasn't making any sense. "I'm sorry, Marissa. I'm just feeling cold feet, I guess. But he's a great guy."

"And you haven't liked anyone in a long time."

"No. I'm thinking, it's too good. Too good for me. He's not perfect, he has some baggage. Like I do. He needs to tell Isabelle it's over between them, but he hasn't done it yet, so that gets me doubting, like, what is he waiting for?"

"Well." Marissa paused, as if she was thinking of the best thing to advise Julia. "Maybe just let him handle that on his terms while you stay open? You've just met him, so if you hold it all with open hands and let him work through that relationship . . . How does that sound? I mean, you don't want to pressure him, and you don't want to send signals that say 'I'm closed off now'. Do you?"

"No, certainly not. I need to stay open. I *want* to." Was she doing it again? Closing herself off? Maybe the tiny red flags she saw in Craig could be explained.

"To be honest, I could have done the same thing. Jarrod lives in Asheville, four hours' drive from me. I could have found some reasons, said it was too far, if I'd wanted to protect myself. But Julia, I was tired of doing that. It was exciting to meet someone who had more than a teaspoon of potential."

Julia nodded then smiled. "Craig has lots more than that." The women laughed. "I see your point. It's kind of a risk, I guess. And I need to get better at taking risks."

"You aren't marrying him this week, you're just staying open. You'll see how it unfolds. There's a freedom in being open and leaving the results to God. You don't have the pressure of controlling anything or any stake in the outcome, because you know he knows best. Trust the good plans he has for you. I'm thinking of a verse I read recently in Psalms. I'll just quote it, probably badly, from memory. 'Open wide your mouth and I will fill it with good things.' I like that, because it shows he's a loving father who loves to delight *us* by giving good gifts. We don't have to be afraid of losing it if it's from him."

Her friend's words stroked a bruise deep inside Julia's soul. She'd been afraid of blessings for most of her life. She'd watched her mother get her hopes up too high and be devastated to the point of turning away from any more opportunities. She died alone, except for Julia at her side.

She took a deep breath. "So, you're saying it's okay to hope."

Marissa chuckled. "More than okay. Do you know how many times hope is mentioned in Scripture? Tons. The God of hope. 'In you I hope all day long.' Another Psalm from memory, but you get the idea. Our hope is in *him*, not in the thing we hope for. We hold those loosely, but know he has our best in mind. *That's* what we need to remember."

"I—I feel lighter inside just hearing you say that." It was a beautiful, airy feeling that was somehow different from the soggy reserve she so often wore like a jacket. "It's like a weight is off my shoulders, in a way."

"Oh, I'm so glad. You've had a lot on you lately, with your mother's passing and all. But it sounds like the thing we're talking about now might go back even further. Am I right?"

"Yes, you always were the insightful one." Julia chuckled.

"Speak for yourself. You and your quiet wisdom. That's why everyone usually goes to *you* for advice. I'm glad if I can help you in that same way. We're friends, after all."

"Thank you, Marissa. You've given me a lot to think about. What about you, how is everything going for your writing and with Jarrod?"

"It's going well. Both, in fact. I am halfway through the first draft of my new novel, the one that takes place in Wilmington. And Jarrod came to Raleigh to visit a couple of weeks ago. I'll go to see him in Asheville once I finish my draft. Maybe next month. And we talk on the phone. A lot."

The women laughed. Julia said, "If my relationship works out, I'll follow your model of how to do a long-distance romance. Maybe you should write a novel about that one day."

"We'll both have a lot of experience to draw from."

After they hung up, Julia thought about Marissa's gentle suggestion. The word 'hope' was floating around in her mind, and for once, it didn't seem like a self-deception to her, but a joyful way to live. An open way, one that relied on the good intention of a loving God.

It was time to leave the restaurant and walk the city of Florence again, to thresh through her thoughts. Before she did, she pulled her phone back out of her cloth purse and found Craig's text address. What would she say? Her questions about Isabelle and moving to Italy had been legitimate, but her feelings had knee-jerked into fear and self-protection. She would give the relationship a chance to blossom, if it was meant to.

Hi Craig. I hope you're having a good visit with your sister. I hope I can see you before I leave Italy on Saturday. I'm sorry if I came across frustrated or closed the other night. I want to give us a chance. Julia.

Julia reread her text message and swallowed. She wasn't accustomed to such vulnerability, but there it was. Maybe she should reword that last line. It reflected a lot of—hope. She blinked and took another heavy breath, then hit 'send'.

She decided to walk down the Lungamo Corsini, an avenue that paralleled the river on the north bank, then cross over the bridge toward her temporary home. A wave of fatigue reminded her of her tumultuous night's sleep. After her walk, she'd lie down for a half hour or so. Then she'd find a way to fill her solitary hours.

The afternoon sky was coated with nubby clouds that allowed a filtered sunlight through and cooled the temperature. A faint breeze met her from the other direction, a comforting caress that carried the sweet aroma of baked gelato cones from a nearby vendor. She would miss Florence, which was feeling like home already.

She'd miss the De Lucas, too. Even Emilia. Julia smiled. Her cool and distant aunt had warmed up a bit since Julia's arrival in Italy. In a short time, she felt almost like a true member of the family. She'd more or less accomplished her goal in coming to Italy, to reconnect with her relatives. And she'd grown to truly care about them. She'd promised Emilia that she wouldn't disappear like her mother had. She meant to keep that promise.

She checked her phone. No response from Craig. But there was a small return text written in Italian. She didn't know what it said, but it seemed to be from the local phone company, maybe saying her text hadn't gone through. She frowned. Just when she'd wanted to reach out to Craig. Just when she'd been willing to put herself out there. To risk hoping. All she could do was put it out of her mind and try again later. If it wasn't too late.

She arrived at her familiar street, the one she'd leave in two days. She mounted the circular, wooden staircase and pushed open the door to her small room, where she'd spent so little time. On the dresser sat the pottery vase that Craig had bought for her in Greve. Despite her uncertainty, she smiled at the memory.

After walking for over an hour and returning to her room, some of her fatigue had lifted. She sat still on the edge of the bed. Maybe she should start organizing her clothes to get a head start on her packing.

The thought of the suitcase under the bed jarred her with a sudden force. The letters. They'd remained tucked into a pocket of her suitcase since arriving in Florence nearly two weeks ago. She hadn't thought about them since then and she'd be leaving in two days. She *had* to know the contents of the letters before she left. She had to unlock the mystery of her mother's desertion of the De Lucas.

She'd planned on asking Valentina to read them and translate for her, but her heartbroken cousin was on her way to Bergamo.

Who else could she ask to read the letters? The obvious choice was Emilia, who was the closest person to Gianna. Would she even agree to read them, or would she refuse, unwilling to open up the healed scars of so many years ago?

Julia reached for her purse and pulled out her phone.

Chapter Eighteen

Julia's fingers fumbled as she dialed Sergio's number. She only had his and Valentina's number, but he could get her through to Emilia.

"*Buona sera*, Sergio. It's Julia. Can I please speak with Emilia? It's important."

"*Certo*. I'll go get her. Is everything alright?"

"Yes, I'm fine. I—I just want to talk to her a moment about my mother."

A few moments later, she heard Emilia's voice on the phone. "Julia, what a surprise. Are you well?"

"Yes, I'm fine. Emilia, I have three letters that I brought with me to Italy. I found them in my mother's things after her death. I forgot to mention them before now. Two of the letters are from Nonna Lucia to my mother and a third one is from my mother, but that one is still sealed. She never mailed it. I brought them with me so that someone in the family can read them for me. They're in Italian and I wasn't able to understand them."

"*Si, si*. What is the date of these letters?"

"That's what I think is significant about them. They are dated just after the last visit we made to Florence. Following these dates, she and I never came back. There may be clues in these letters as to why we never came back to Italy." Julia paused as Emilia fell silent on the other end of the line. "I realize this may be a door you don't want to open, Emilia, and if so, I understand. I'll find someone to translate them for me if you don't want to know what's in them."

Emilia cleared her throat. "Thank you, Julia, for your consideration. I do wish to know what's in the letters. We've waited forty years to find out what Gianna was thinking and this is the only way we will ever know. You're coming tomorrow for your farewell dinner with us, but I want that to be a light, joyful time. Perhaps you should come tonight so we can get this out of the way first. Can you come and stay for dinner? I'll come and pick you up at your hotel."

Julia was surprised that Emilia was willing to drive into Florence. It was almost four o'clock. "That's very kind of you, Emilia. If you don't mind." It would save her a trip on the train and a wait at the bus stop.

"No, it's no problem. It will take me about thirty minutes at this time of day, but I'll text you when I'm there. I'll get your cell number from Sergio."

The priority of this task hovered like a blimp overhead for Julia, since she'd be leaving in two days. Emilia must feel a sense of urgency, too. As she'd stated on the phone, they'd waited nearly forty years for answers. At the beginning of Julia's visit, she thought Emilia preferred to leave it buried, but Emilia needed closure, too.

At four-forty, a text arrived from Emilia. Julia ran down the winding staircase, pushed the heavy, wooden door, and slipped into Emilia's waiting car. She longed to ask about the discovery of the spy, Valentina's response, the company. The three tattered letters, yellow with age and sitting in her purse, were on the forefront of their minds.

"I had a chance to say goodbye to Valentina this morning." Julia broke the silence as they drove.

Emilia glanced over at her. "She took it very hard. I understand this. She was waiting for a marriage proposal but that's what she got instead." She shook her head and made a sound in her throat.

"It'll be good for her to get away."

"Yes. I'm glad she decided to go see Luciana. This will help her. Here, we have things to deal with concerning Marco." Again, she shook her head and scowled.

Julia could tell by the firm set of Emilia's jaw and the stiffness of her posture in the driver's seat that it wasn't a good idea to continue that conversation.

They drove in silence for the rest of the trip to the villa. Julia watched the beloved hills go by, now painted with a pink haze of late afternoon. Summer was drawing to a close and the days would be shorter. When would she return to Italy? Next summer? Too early to think of that. Especially with all the crises at hand among the De Lucas.

Soon, they arrived at the villa. Julia was surprised to see Sergio, Giuseppe, and Paola assembled in the living room. Apparently, this would be a family event. Julia greeted them with a soft murmur of *buona sera* and a nod in their direction. She pulled the letters from her purse and handed them to Emilia, who settled into her chair and set the letters on her lap with a sigh. Julia took the facing armchair, perching on the edge, and watched Emilia. Fatigue was traced on her aunt's face and something else—dread?

Amara appeared in the doorway and asked a question to Emilia in Italian. She shook her head and responded to the young woman, who nodded and left the room. "We'll do this first," Emilia explained to everyone, "then she'll serve us dinner a bit later."

Emilia took the letter on top. "This appears to be the first one according to the date stamp." She pulled a single folded sheet of paper from the envelope. "This one is short. I will summarize in

Italian then in English." Everyone in the room waited in silence while she read silently. She spoke in Italian for a few moments for the benefit of Giuseppe and Paola.

Giuseppe said something back to her. Emilia nodded. "He says I should just summarize in English, because he can understand and explain to Paola later. That is fine. This is from Lucia, my mother, to Gianna. It was written shortly after Gianna's final visit to Italy. It starts out stating how much they enjoyed her visit and how good it was to see her. She mentions you, Julia, and how much you look like your mother, how tall and beautiful you had become. She states how wonderful it was to have you here, getting to know you as a young lady."

Julia felt strangely touched by these words from the grandmother she hadn't seen in four decades, who she'd never seen again, thanks to her mother's choices. A thread of frustration she hadn't felt in a while flinched inside. It was time for them to learn why.

Silence again as Emilia continued reading. "Then the tone changes. She becomes almost angry. She says, 'you should return to live in Italy with your daughter. We can help you raise her and you won't have to do this by yourself. Each time you come to Italy it breaks my heart when you leave us. It takes me a long time to recover. Your place is here.' Then she says a few more things to convince Gianna." She looked up around the room. "Maybe the last letter will explain Gianna's side of things, but I'll read this second one first."

So far, there was nothing Julia didn't already know. She'd grown up listening to her mother complain about the pressure Nonna Lucia put on her to return to Italy, that raising a child alone in a foreign country wasn't good when she had a loving family that would help her. She'd heard it for many years, until one day, she stopped hearing anything at all about it.

"Here is the second letter. It looks like it was written by Lucia a month after the first one." Emilia opened the second letter and scanned through it. She sighed. "This one starts out urging Gianna to think about her daughter. A woman alone won't be able to provide for her as well if she's disconnected from her family. More pressure and some guilt." She lifted her eyes to Giuseppe. "We remember that, don't we, Giuseppe? She'd always turn on the guilt when we didn't do what she wanted. I shouldn't say that about our mother, but it's true."

Julia looked around the room. Giuseppe was nodding, but said nothing. Sergio, who hadn't said anything yet, looked uncomfortable. His face showed the strain of the recent events in the company. He wasn't directly involved in the outcome of the letters. He was there as the patriarch and to support Emilia, but maybe his reflections were far away. Paola's gaze flitted around the room as if her thoughts, too, were elsewhere.

There was silence as Emilia continued skimming the letter. "There's nothing new in this one, just more guilt. 'After all we did for you, taking you in—' not sure what that means. She was our sister. She wasn't taken in from anywhere." Emilia looked up again and shrugged. "Maybe this is all there is. Maybe there's no big revelation."

Finally, Sergio spoke. "What we don't know is if these letters are sequential, or if there were any phone calls or letters in between that could supply missing information."

At his comment, Julia remembered the loud, tearful phone call her mother had had with Lucia. She'd never seen her mother so upset. They'd argued in Italian for fifteen or twenty minutes. Her mother had hung up and sobbed, but she'd never told Julia why.

There likely was important information in that phone call. A call between two women, now both deceased. They'd never know.

Lucia hadn't been subtle in her pressure. Maybe she and Gianna hadn't gotten along. Her mother might have simply gotten tired of the nagging and had drawn a line. But it had been a harsh and definitive line with no return.

Emilia took a letter-opener and sliced through the final envelope. She unfolded the paper. This letter, too, was short. "This one is from Gianna and it was never sent." Emilia scanned the first side of the paper. "She explains to Lucia why she can't live in Italy. She's raised her daughter in the States and that is what she knows. She says they're happy in the States and was happy returning to Italy. *Was.* Something happened. I'll try to translate directly. The writing is becoming hard to read now. I believe Gianna was very upset when she wrote this. She says, 'After our phone call, I learned that I am not a De Luca, as I had always believed.'" Emilia stopped and her eyes raised to those in the room. Her face showed incomprehension. She lowered her eyes to the letter. "She says, 'All my life you never told me that my real parents had been killed and that you and Pappa Flavio had adopted me. Why didn't you tell me when I was a child? Do you know how difficult it is to learn this at my age? It makes me feel my whole life was a lie.'"

Julia's body went stiff as a hot flood coursed down her body. Her mother had been adopted?

Emilia continued reading. "'That likely explains why I felt you loved Emilia more than you loved me, once she was born. Why do you always ask me to come to Italy? I don't know whose family I belong to. Don't expect me to come there to live or to visit. I'll make my way with my daughter. We'll be fine. I will say, and this is full in my heart, even with tears, thank you for taking me in and raising me. Thank you for giving me a home. I will forever be grateful to you and Pappa for this. Yours, Gianna."

A deadly silence fell in the room for a few seconds. Then, "Why didn't we know this? Did anyone know this?" Emilia's voice became shrill.

Sergio flinched and looked at his wife with what seemed to be a mixture of irritation and concern.

"I know this." Giuseppe murmured simply without emotion and said nothing further. It was true?

Suddenly, Julia understood everything. The tearful argument on the phone when her mother learned the truth about her early life, her mother's fits of tears in the days that followed, and her final decision to cut ties with the family. Her mother wasn't a De Luca. *She* wasn't a De Luca. It shouldn't matter that her mother was adopted. It shouldn't. Yet, in that moment, it changed everything.

She rose and fled the room, as if her feet moved on their own accord. She fumbled through the door to the terrace and continued along the flagstones leading to the garden behind the house. The place where Craig had first kissed her. It was a welcoming place, calm and quiet, with only night noises of insects. A place far from the revelations in the house.

Julia collapsed on the bench. Tears wouldn't come, since her brain was still struggling to catch up. She rewound her entire life. None of it was true? She'd come across the ocean to reconnect with her blood family, the only family she had on earth. She thought she'd succeeded in that goal. But she was just as alone as when she'd started. She might as well be a stranger to them. She wasn't their family. She had no idea who she was.

Finally, tears burned and pushed through, trailing down her cheeks. After the initial incredulous burst, she fell back against the bench. Something inside her snapped and she felt a sickening flood of defeat rising like a noxious tide.

She closed her eyes, willing it to be different. *Lord, why did you bring me here? Why have I reconnected to this family that I'm not even a part of? Am I destined to be fatherless and alone all my life?* A sob escaped her throat as her tears multiplied.

Then she felt a presence beside her on the bench. She opened her eyes and turned to see Emilia. In the deepening dusk, her face was shadowed but Julia saw it was taut with tension.

Emilia swallowed. "Julia, I know it's a shock to hear what you heard tonight. It was a shock for me, too. I never knew that your mother had been adopted. Despite what she said, I always thought that *she* was the favorite, not me. I was actually envious of her most of my life." A small smile attempted to coax one from Julia. But it was too raw, too surprising. Too soon.

"My mother never found out until she was in her *forties*." Julia shifted on the bench. "If adopted children are told when they are young about their birth parents and the circumstances of their adoption, they grow up with it and it's a natural part of life. They know and it's fine. Mostly. I'm sure there are some cases where that isn't true. But to tell an adult—" she shook her head and splayed her hands upward, "it's too hard. I think my mother had an identity crisis." Like she herself was having.

"Yes, I think that's true." Emilia's voice was soft. "Your mother overreacted to being told so late in her life. And she found out in the midst of conflict with our mother. It didn't come out in a good way. But I assure you, I grew up with your mother and our mother loved her just as much as she loved Giuseppe and me. She never thought Gianna in any other way but as her own daughter. No one in the family ever had any idea she wasn't a De Luca." Emilia gripped Julia's forearm and waited until Julia looked into her eyes. "And it didn't matter. No one would have cared. Because she *became* a De Luca." Emilia held Julia's gaze for a long moment, as if willing her to embrace her statement.

At Emilia's words, Julia's heart slowed its wild pounding in her chest. She stared down at her hands. "I'm sure you're right about that. It would have been better if she'd never found out. She'd likely have remained a part of the family." They'd have continued visiting Florence, maintained a bond with the family. Julia wouldn't have felt bereft of relatives.

"Since it was revealed so clumsily and late by our mother, who can be harsh, as you heard in the letters, maybe that's true. It may have been better for her not to find out. It must have damaged her heart to the point that she cut contact. That's a shame, and I think it was a big mistake. Look at all she cut away from. She denied you the chance to see your family for all those years."

"But we—we aren't family."

"You're wrong, Julia. We *are* family. You are our family and we are yours. Do you think we would have cared if we'd known? No, we would not." Emilia shook her head emphatically. "Why is blood so important? There are blood families who don't care about each other and don't speak. They aren't a part of one another's lives. It means nothing to us that your mother was adopted. Because we were a *family*. Of course, we didn't know, except for Giuseppe, but it would not have made any difference. The same is true for you."

Emilia's words brought a tightness to Julia's throat and her eyes stung. She swallowed. "Really?" She turned to Emilia, whose face looked soft and relaxed for the first time. Her aunt nodded. "I know I'm acting like a six-year-old right now." She let out an embarrassed chuckle. "But all my life, I never knew my father. It was as though this Italian family of mine gave me a sense of belonging to someone besides my mother. It was a comfort for me.

For a while, it made it okay to not have a dad. Sometimes if feels like I don't have anyone."

Emilia reached out and squeezed Julia's hands in both of hers. "You had your mother, and that's a very big thing. It's true that the two of you were alone, but you were together. And I know she loved you very much and would do anything for you."

Julia nodded. "That's true, and I knew it. Sometimes I didn't appreciate her enough because she didn't give me a bigger family by remarrying. Now it all seems so stupid to have cared that much about brothers and sisters and cousins. Her love was a sure thing in my life, but I was always complaining about not having more." Needles of shame and regret pricked her insides.

"You don't have your mother anymore but you have us. I told you before that I was glad you came to us. I told you the truth. We won't let you go now." She smiled and a small fiery light lit her eyes with humor and challenge.

They both laughed. Emilia seemed like a completely different person than the crusty, suspicious woman Julia had met when she'd first arrived in Italy. Maybe there was more heart, more softness—and more hurt—there than she knew.

Emilia's gaze wandered out to the fruit trees in the garden. "I have to tell you something about myself, Julia. This will make you feel better." She turned her face toward Julia and looked her square in the eyes. "You know I am much younger than your mother and Giuseppe. He and I are nine years apart. A few years after Giuseppe and my brother Flavio, my mother wanted another child. She tried to have a child with my father, your Nonno Flavio. They tried for two years, and it seems that my father wasn't able to father other children. He let my mother know that if she became pregnant by someone else, he would recognize the child and raise it as his own.

No one would know. They had a sort of understanding. So, that's how I came to be born."

Julia's mouth dropped open. "You're not Flavio's daughter?" Emilia shook her head. "Did you know this as a child?"

"I overheard them talking one day. Then I started thinking about how I didn't look like my father in any respect. There were other things, too. Habits and character traits which I didn't share with Flavio. I concluded that it was true."

"Were you devastated?"

"Not devastated. It took me some time to work it out in my head. Eventually, I was able to talk to my mother about it and she confirmed it. But I knew she wanted a baby badly enough to do what she did. It was for that reason alone. It was not a simple extramarital affair. I saw how much she had wanted me and loved me." She leaned back on the bench and looked up at the sky. "So, you see, Julia, I'm not a De Luca either."

"Halfway, though." Julia smiled at her.

"Yes. But the De Lucas aren't royalty. It's just a family, like any other family. Blood isn't so important, as long as we have people who love us."

Her comment hit a soft spot inside. People who love us. She thought of her friends back home, and this new family she'd acquired. They didn't share her genes, but loved and accepted her just the same.

Emilia turned back to Julia with a sudden fierceness. "Julia, don't make the same mistake your mother did. Please."

Julia shook her head. "No, I won't. You're still my aunt Emilia. And I feel even closer to you now than before." The walls around Emilia had fallen down that night.

"Let's go inside now, shall we?"

Julia nodded and followed her back up the path and toward the house. Her heart and mind were so full, it would take a few days to sort it out. But for now, she'd join the family. *Her* family.

Giuseppe, Paola, and Sergio were already seated around the table on the terrace. Julia smiled at everyone, pricked with embarrassment at her outburst. They likely wondered what was so bad about being adopted. Now she knew. Nothing. Nothing at all. Emilia had been right. Love was more important than blood. And as she looked at the people around the table, she had already started to love them.

She slid into a chair just as Amara brought out a steaming urn of soup for the first course.

"*Il primo piatto. La zuppa di verdura,*" announced Amara. She set down the urn and began to scoop ladles of the green broth into their bowls.

Julia had already gotten accustomed to Amara's pronouncements before each course. Usually, each one was accompanied by a wonderful aroma.

Once they began eating, Julia looked across the table at Giuseppe who, she had learned, spoke pretty decent English. "Uncle Giuseppe, may I ask you a question?"

Her uncle inclined his head toward her. "*Si.*"

"Can you tell me anything about my mother's real parents? What happened to them?"

He wiped his mouth with a napkin. "The parents of Gianna were good friends of my parents, your *Nonno* and *Nonna*. As is our custom in Italy, we have *figliocci.*"

"These are called god-children in English, I believe," Sergio said. He turned to Giuseppe. "Many people have god-children, not just in Italy."

Giuseppe shrugged. "My parents were married not a long time when Gianna's parents both died in a car accident. I do not remember their names. I was not born and I do not know them. Gianna was the *figlioccia* of my parents, so they adopted her. I was born later, then Emilia."

Julia nodded. "Thank you, Giuseppe." Flavio and Lucia had been newlyweds who'd had to adopt a baby after the death of their friends. This knowledge settled into her mind like falling rain, watering her sketchy understanding of her mother's past.

"They were surprised and very sad about their good friends but very happy with Gianna. They think she like a treasure or a gift they suddenly received." Giuseppe stroked his Stalin mustache then said no more.

"This is very good soup, isn't it?" asked Emilia brightly, perhaps trying to change the subject. The peaceful expression had remained on her face, as though tight rubber bands had been removed, permitting her to relax and reveal her beauty. Maybe she'd grown up in Gianna's shadow and knowing the truth had released her.

"Yes, I like the soup a lot. I would love to have Amara's recipe." Julia took a long sip from the spoon, then another, suddenly ravenous. When she'd finished eating and swabbing the bowl with crusty bread, Amara swept in and whisked away all of the bowls. Julia looked at Sergio, who'd been quiet during the meal. "Sergio, can I ask another delicate question?" She'd been told she was family. She shouldn't take liberties, but she couldn't help herself.

He looked back at her with dark, serious eyes.

"How did you find out the identity of the spy?"

He let out a long sigh. "We had cameras and saw Marco going through Fabrizio's drawings. The film showed him taking photos. We had locked everything up, but since we wanted to catch the spy in the act, we unlocked Fabrizio's office as if it had been forgotten.

It was after hours. We knew it would have to be someone with a key. There are not many employees who have a key to the building, only the managers. It's very hard, very disappointing for me. Marco was almost like a son. He was the last person I would suspect."

Julia guessed by Sergio's unusually haggard appearance that the discovery was much more than just disappointing. His protégé had betrayed him. That was bound to be painful. "Did he admit to spying? And did he give any reasons?"

"He did admit it. He told me he had been desperate because he needed money for surgery for his father. I don't know if this is true. I told him I would have given him the money for his father. He didn't need to steal from me."

"What will happen now? Will Marco be arrested?"

Sergio shook his head. "No, I fired him but I won't have him arrested. He will have trouble working in the same industry. I will make sure of this."

Julia nodded. "Of course." Poor Valentina. Her perfect imagined future had been derailed by an act more treasonous than a simple break-up. But at least her cousin had been spared. She was thankful for that and Valentina would be, too, one day.

Amara brought in a platter of roasted chicken surrounded by root vegetables. More sumptuous aromas filled the air surrounding the table, then swirled off into the night. Julia sighed. She'd miss the family dinners.

Sergio thanked Amara then turned his attention back to Julia. "You are a businesswoman, Julia. It's a shame you know more about interior design than about shoes." He gave her a muted smile. "You could help us through this difficult passage we are in at De Luca."

"I wish I could. I'm guessing you're not talking now about the spying. Is this what Valentina and Luca were arguing about?" She'd taken a risk, but Sergio seemed to have trusted her by opening the discussion.

He nodded, not surprised that she was aware of her cousins' discontent. "I see what they are saying, but change is difficult. It can be expensive, too. But if we do not change, it will be more expensive and we will be obsolete. There are many, many shoe companies in Italy and across the world. We have no choice. I am lucky to have intelligent adult children who are modern in their thinking. They know the current trends, they know technology, and they know what the competition is doing. I have not valued their knowledge enough."

"I agree with you, Sergio. You are very lucky. If you let them use their special abilities and knowledge to help De Luca, they'll be very loyal and you'll be happy with the outcome." She smiled then. "Do Valentina and Luca know that you are starting to agree with them?"

Sergio grimaced. "I will tell them. When we finish with our problem with Marco, we'll discuss their ideas." He exchanged glances with Emilia. She set her hand on the table and he grasped it, the first sign of affection Julia had seen between them. Her throat tightened with emotion.

Sergio offered to drive Julia home. Before they left the villa, she said goodbye to Giuseppe, Paola, and Emilia, who stood in the hallway near the front door. Emilia pressed the letters back into her hands. "You should keep these, Julia. Thank you for bringing them. We can all put this situation behind us now and remember Gianna in the best possible light."

"Thank you for being willing to read them. You were very courageous. I'll see you tomorrow evening."

Emilia smiled then. "*Si*, for your farewell dinner. Be here before six and bring Stefano."

Stefano? She still hadn't heard from Craig and only responded to Emilia with a smile.

"And earlier in your visit, you said you had photos of your mother. Please bring them tomorrow when you come."

Emilia leaned toward her and for the first time, kissed her on each cheek. "We won't be sad at your farewell dinner because you'll come back to us."

Julia grinned. "*Sì*. I'll come back. I promise."

Chapter Nineteen

It was earlier than usual when Julia slipped into her customary seat at the coffee shop. Her last full day in Italy and she didn't want to miss a moment. As she sipped her cappuccino, the events of the previous evening lapped through her mind like a lazy river, returning again and again. It no longer bothered her that her mother had been adopted. But as Emilia had said, her mother had made a colossal mistake in cutting ties with a family who loved her. Julia wasn't planning to make the same mistake.

Although she valued her relationship with the De Lucas, she'd certainly blown the importance of having relatives far out of proportion, as Craig had said in an indirect way. Families had their problems, as she'd seen. And she was leaving tomorrow. They'd be separated by an ocean. They might keep in touch from time to time, but wouldn't be present in her daily life. The life she'd embrace the following day on another shore.

As she considered returning, a faint sense of preparation began inside, filament thoughts moving ahead to the near future. She was starting to miss home and wonder about her company, De Luca Interiors. She'd put off contacting Crystal or any of her other employees in the last two days because she wanted to keep the two worlds apart as long as possible.

One more day to savor. Maybe she'd hear from Craig that day. She'd thought about texting him again, sure the first one hadn't gone through, but amidst the turmoil of the previous evening, it hadn't crossed her mind until she was back at her hotel. Then, there was that *other* reason. On the off chance that he *had* gotten her message, she didn't want to write and say the same thing again and look desperate.

Besides that, if he'd been sincere about his feelings for her, he wouldn't even need her text message. He'd have contacted her. A hollow pain weighed down, smudging her contentment.

She shifted her thoughts deliberately toward home. It wouldn't do any good to think too much about Craig. Aside from that, thinking of home would begin her preparation for that inevitable transition. She felt ready, though, satisfied with her visit. Her home awaited her, her own bed, everything comfortable and familiar. Her local friends and acquaintances. Her special group of girlfriends. Her employees, all with whom she got along well.

Suddenly, she realized how many people were in her life who could, in a loose way, fit the definition of family, or at least a caring network. They didn't need to share bloodlines to be richly important to her. That realization pushed a wave of joy through her. She wasn't as alone as she'd always thought.

Then there was her church family, which she had yet to discover. She was determined to do that this fall. It was a priority. She would shove aside her fears and stereotypes and discover this group of people, her spiritual family. Of course, her spiritual family stretched across the entire planet. Her thoughts went to the woman in the museum. Though she'd never see that woman again, they'd connected on the lynchpin of their shared faith. A sister she'd met for the first time.

The word 'family' had a much broader definition, a more varied appearance than it previously had. No wonder she spent her life feeling so alone, with her limited, worn-out definition. *Open wide your mouth and I will fill it*. Julia recalled Marissa's quote, which created a thirst Julia hadn't known before. She'd known in her head and let it all go stale. For decades.

The glass wasn't just half-full, it was overflowing, and she hadn't seen it before now. She stood on a long, barren bridge between her current backslidden position and all that new faith had meant to her as a lonely college student. She was the one who'd let the joy of adoption—Julia stopped her coffee cup halfway to her mouth. *Adoption*. Suddenly, it was a beautiful word, pregnant with joy and opportunity. Back in college when she'd run into the arms of a loving God, she'd been struck more by the term 'adoption' than 'conversion', and it was a happy, transformative word to her. She'd all but forgotten those memories. She'd been adopted by God himself and that opened the door wide to *all* of him, the blessings of knowing him, the blessings of knowing his children and his world. It was all there for her. *Open wide your mouth and I will fill it*. Open up her heart. He'd fill it.

Julia realized that she was grinning so wide, it almost hurt, despite the fact that tears also stung her eyes. She'd always rationed out the big smiles for the rare occasions when one was merited, which didn't seem to be very often. Now, she knew she didn't need an approved reason, because she was flooded with reasons. Inundated with blessings, if only she'd open her eyes. The glass would never be empty again. It gushed like an eternal spring. *Oh, God, you're such a good Father. My true father.*

She wiped crumbs of a buttery *cornetta* from her lips and rose from the café table to rediscover the city for the last time, through the rosy filter of her new understanding of her life. She fell into step with the strings of shoppers and tourists and observed everything around her. The ochre and cinnamon-colored buildings with curved tile roofs, the square pavers on the ground where feet had trod for centuries, so many celebrations of color in flower boxes, planters, and manicured beds around the city. She smiled at a group of children passing by, then smiled at a flower vendor, but not until she first stopped to absorb the beauty of the petals and leaves of all the colors that surrounded her senses. Color, what a gift! And a valuable tool of her trade.

By the time she'd walked alongside her beloved river Arno, maybe for the last time, it was late morning. She'd been able to absorb the soft breeze under the ancient shade of oak trees and listen to the musical pattern of water from the fountains shooting upward and pattering down. The sun was high in the sky and she was perspiring from her extended walk on both sides of the river. She'd stop by her hotel to change into a tank top, then emerge again into the city to continue walking until time to prepare for her farewell dinner at the villa. She'd also look for a gelato stand for the last time. She *couldn't* miss that.

She turned down her street and as she approached her hotel, she saw him, punching a number into his phone. He was calling her. Casually dressed in a short-sleeve black polo with a pair of sunglasses stuck into the neckline, and a pair of jeans and sandals—he was killer-handsome. Her heart leaped as she watched him scrutinize the phone. A ring sounded in her purse and she pulled it out, a grin stretching across her face. "Craig?" she answered.

"Julia, I just got back—"

She walked toward him, the phone to her ear. Just then, he looked up and they locked eyes. Without dropping his gaze, he said, "I guess I can hang up now, huh?" They laughed.

Julia stopped in front of him and said into the phone, "Sure. Why don't you hang up now?" She disconnected her phone and slipped it back into her purse. They stood for a moment, looking at each other, silly grins on their faces.

"Julia." He opened his arms and enfolded her in them, a warm circle around her, firm and strong. She fit perfectly there against his chest. She breathed deeply. He smelled like soap and woodsy cologne. So good.

"I got your message last night. It made me happy." His voice was thick as he spoke into her hair.

She tilted her head up. "Last night? I sent it mid-morning yesterday." *It made him happy.*

"It must have gotten delayed, then. We're using an American phone system in Italy, so who knows what happened."

"You just got back this morning from France?"

"Yeah, I usually stay a couple days at my sister's. She lives in Toulouse and it's a direct flight from here. But I changed my return so I could see you before you left." His eyes searched her face as he spoke.

"You did?" she asked softly. "Thank you. I'm so glad you did."

He bent his head toward her and pressed into her lips lightly, then deeper. She pulled into him, lifting her face and tightening her arms around his neck. A groan escaped from his throat as his kiss became fervent. A minute passed. Julia reveled in his arms around her, his lips exploring hers, the taste of him.

He pulled back, his forehead against hers, and stared at her. "I missed you, Julia. I wasn't happy with myself when we parted company the other night. I'd miscommunicated somehow, but I didn't know how to make it right. Your text made it right. Told me it was okay, that I was okay."

Julia smiled. "I personally think you're *way* more than okay. And I'm so glad you came back."

"Of course, I'd come back."

"You never said how long you would be at your sister's, so I wasn't sure. I was afraid I might not see you before I left tomorrow."

"I wasn't about to let you leave before saying goodbye. I'm sorry I didn't communicate better about my sister and my plans."

True, it had left a void of confusion. But God had met her despite her lack of closure with Craig. Her current joy had engulfed her and answered her lifelong questions well before she found herself in Craig's arms, his green eyes searching hers.

Even Isabelle no longer haunted in the background.

As if reading her mind, Craig said, "I want you to know I spoke to Isabelle on the phone last night. I called her from France because I wanted to get this thing straight once and for all *before* seeing you again. I wanted to be able to tell you it was finished."

"I appreciate that. And it is?"

He nodded. "Yes, it's over. There was less and less on my side. Well, nothing at all, since meeting you. But I needed to tell her to stop hoping and trying."

"Did she mention me?"

"She did mention you, as if you were the reason. I told her clearly that although I cared for you, you were not the reason. I said that she and I were not meant to be together. I wanted her to find the right person for her and I knew it wasn't me. I apologized to her for any miscommunication or double message on my part."

"How did she respond?"

He grinned then. "She flicked it off as if it didn't matter to her. As if I were just one of her toys she'd gotten tired of." He laughed. "I'm glad she took that approach. Makes everything easier for both of us. Meaning, you and me."

"Her response let you off the hook and it also helped her save her pride. Very strategic of her." Julia grinned. "I'm glad you told her. For our sake and for yours."

He nodded. "I feel free now." Then he raised his eyebrows in an impish leer. "Free to go after Julia De Luca."

She laughed and he kissed her again.

When they drew apart, he asked, "Have you seen the Piazale Michelangelo yet?"

"Hmm, I've been all over the city but haven't gone there yet. I haven't even heard about it."

"I don't know how you haven't heard about it. Spending too much time at the De Luca villa and the gelaterias, I guess." He grinned at her. "It's the best view of the city, and many people say it's the most romantic spot in Florence. Let's go, I'll show you."

He took her hand and they headed up the street, took another turn and soon they were back at the south bank of the river. Julia had walked along the river on either side so many times since her arrival in Florence, but it was different with Craig beside her.

"This river was therapy for me during my trip." Julia looked out again across the Arno, its waters gently churning, and its many colorful bridges.

"As effective as gelato therapy?"

She laughed. "Yes, that too. I guess I deserve all the teasing about gelato. By the way, I haven't had my gelato today and it's my last day, so—"

"I get it. You need some. I'll sacrifice and have some with you." He pointed to a colorful awning on the next block. "There's a place on that corner there. You'll need a snack before our thirty-minute hike up that hill." Craig nodded his head to indicate a sizable crest ahead of them. "In answer to your unspoken questions, yes, it will be a workout and, yes, it will be worth it."

"I believe you. And if it's the best view and the most romantic, of course we should go."

After ordering gelato at the window of the open-air gelateria, they sat down at a tiny café table in view of a sputtering fountain. The hill they were to climb loomed up ahead like a tree-covered cliff. Julia was thankful for a gelato rest before attacking what looked like an athletic challenge. "Mmm. This is my last Florence gelato for who knows how long." Julia savored the creamy treat. She'd look up Italian gelaterias as soon as she got back to the States.

"Might be shorter than you think. I'm sure the De Lucas will be happy to see you back. Most of them, anyway."

Julia thought of Isabelle and was immensely thankful that her cousin hadn't been in the room the previous night when it was revealed that Gianna had been adopted. She'd have had all the ammunition she needed to make Julia's presence in the family tense. "Speaking of the De Lucas, I have something to tell you."

Craig looked at her, his green eyes luminescent in the direct sunlight, while his tongue kept working on his gelato.

"Before I came to Italy, I found three letters in my mom's things after she passed. Two were from my Nonna Lucia and one was from my mother, but had never been sent. I brought them with me in hopes that Valentina could translate them and I'd get clues as to why my mother suddenly deserted the family."

Craig nodded attentively as she spoke. She still couldn't believe he was right here next to her when she'd been sure she wouldn't see him before her flight the next day. "You've waited so long to find out," he said.

"The letters were in my suitcase all this time and I forgot about them. Just yesterday, I remembered. Thank God I remembered before leaving Italy. I contacted Emilia to see if she wanted to read them and she did. So much so that she came to Florence to pick me up and bring me back to the villa." Julia took a breath and a few final licks of her gelato. "When she read the letters I learned, in fact we all learned at the same time, that my mother was *adopted* by Flavio and Lucia early in their marriage. She was their god-daughter but her parents were killed in a car accident." Her few phrases seemed inadequate to convey the drama of that moment for both herself and Emilia.

His eyes widened and he stopped licking. He cocked his head. "Really? That means—"

She nodded. "That means I'm an adopted De Luca as well."

He held her eyes for a moment then shrugged. "So? I'm sure you know it doesn't matter to anyone. You're still a De Luca."

Julia smiled and wiped her mouth with a napkin. "That's true. I am a De Luca and it doesn't matter if I don't share their bloodline. It was a shock, of course, but since then, I've realized that family is made up of the people who love you."

Craig set his forearms on the table and stared at her. "I'm glad you're saying this, Julia. You were pretty intent on the family thing for a while. I was afraid you'd be let down once the De Lucas had fallen off their pedestal."

He grinned and reached up to move a lock of stray hair from her cheek. His fingers lingered there, sending a warm tingle through her body. He said, "You know my story. Having lots of relatives doesn't necessarily make a happy life. Sometimes they're difficult. The more of them there are, the harder it can be. Why do you think my sister moved all the way to France? No, I'm kidding about that. She fell in love with a Frenchman."

"Yeah, I've heard about how hard big families can be, as you've said yourself. It's tough for those in the middle, like you were. I know the De Lucas have their problems, too. With Marco, with Valentina and Luca. Not to diminish the importance of true families, of course. But all my life I've needed to learn this truth that families have problems and people without families or with small families, or people who don't have spouses or kids, can all find family in the people we choose along the way. Now at the ripe old age of forty-eight, I finally get it."

He leaned back and squinted at her. "You seem calmer and more open to me. I liked you before, but now, you're amazing." She was pretty sure she didn't deserve the look of admiration on his face, but she enjoyed it. She did feel happier. Lighter. Craig leaned forward and kissed her temple. She closed her eyes and breathed in his masculine scent.

"I do feel more peaceful. The glass seems super-full now."

"And I'll do my best to fill it even more." At his whispered promise, they locked eyes and shared a smile.

"I accept." She grinned at him. "I'd like to ask what you have in mind for that objective, but I'll wait and be surprised." Especially because he lived in Philadelphia.

"Surprises are good. Mine are, at any rate. Almost finished? We have a mountain to climb."

They left the gelato shop and turned toward a path leading to a wide stone staircase. It appeared to go straight up. Julia took a deep breath. Craig had said it would be worth it, so she was game.

"See that over there? It's the ancient city wall."

Julia's eyes followed his outstretched arm and she saw it, a thick stone wall that traced a barrier up along a slope. "I wonder how old that thing is. Do you think it's medieval?"

"I actually did a bit of research on that one time. The first wall was built before Christ. Over the centuries it was extended about six times, so the fragment we see here is from the thirteenth century. The rest of the wall was torn down during the eighteen-hundreds when the city grew."

"So, this is the only piece of it that's left?"

"Seems so. Here, let's take a selfie."

They turned around and he positioned the phone in front of them. It took Julia back to their very first posed photo on the crest of Montefioralle, that magical day which seemed so long ago.

Along the way up the wide stone staircase, they passed an enclosed garden with rose bushes festooned with pink and red blooms. The views of the city part-way up the hill were already worth several photos. Many tourists and locals had joined them on their ascent, which was beginning to feel like a pilgrimage. They slowed the pace as Craig told her about his sister and his trip to France.

"When are you flying back to the States?" Julia asked him.

"Three days after you. Tuesday. I changed that flight, too. I was thinking of staying longer, but I'm ready to get home."

"And no plans to move back to Italy?" She watched his reaction.

He cast a sideways glance in her direction. "No plans. Not alone, at any rate."

Huh. She'd have to think about that one. But for now, she gave him what she hoped was a sweet smile and said, "That's good news."

When they finally reached the top, Julia's back and neck were moist with perspiration. A throng of tourists filled the wide, flat area at the top of the stairway. Beyond the clusters of gawkers, she saw it. The panorama of the city of Florence. "Oh, Craig. That's fabulous." She hurried to the overlook and found a space among the tourists.

She felt breathless with the beauty of the city sprawling out before her, soaked in the rosy blush of late afternoon. From their position up on the hill, the river sparkled like a diamond necklace snaking under the bridges and flowing out of sight. She could see the red dome of the Duomo and the Santa Croce, the city wall, and

Ponte Vecchio. She gazed at the view, back and forth across the valley, absorbing the sight so that she could imprint it on her mind's eye until her next trip to Florence. Then she pulled out her phone and took several photos, some of the city alone, others of Craig alone, and a few selfies next to him. He took some photos of only her with his and her phones.

"We're quite the tourists, aren't we?" Craig chuckled and put away his phone. He pulled Julia close from behind, wrapping his arms around her, pressing her back against him as they both memorized the sight.

"We *are* tourists, but since this is our second home, I guess we're more than tourists." Whether they stayed together or not, it was a true statement for both of them.

Moments passed as they watched the afternoon sun blaze down, spreading a brandied glow across the sky. "You know you're invited to my farewell dinner tonight, right?"

"If you're inviting me, I accept. I'm sorry you're leaving, but I'll see you soon."

She turned in his arms, which circled around her like a wreath, and faced him. "You will?" Hope fluttered inside.

"I was going to ask if you're free next weekend. I have miles, so I booked a flight. Am I premature?"

She laughed. "Next weekend? Uh, no, you're not premature. You don't waste any time, but I like that. I'll have a week to regroup, so I'd love to see you."

He leaned forward and brushed her lips with his. "You can tell me the name of your town and I'll book a hotel. I'd like you to show me around the world of Julia."

"Gladly. I should be over jet lag by then." A bolt of heat did a giddy dance in her stomach, fanning out to fill her completely.

They pulled apart and both leaned against the stone wall overlook, silent for a few moments. Craig turned his head toward her. "I wanted to tell you, since you like big families so much, you'll have to meet mine one day. Four siblings, all married, most with kids, a few grand-kids, parents still alive, a grand-dad, a few aunts, uncles . . . They'll love you. We have over a hundred at family reunions."

Julia laughed. "Sounds like too much of a good thing."

Then it hit her. That wasn't even possible, too much of a good thing. Not in the life that she was beginning to live. "On second thought, why not? Sounds fun, actually."

She was ready now to live in the moment, receive it all by birthright, and laugh freely.

Because her glass was full.

I hope you enjoyed reading *Julia Redesigned*. If you did, please consider leaving a review at the online store where you bought it. It would help other readers discover my books and be encouraged by their inspiring truths. You can also sign up to receive updates about new books at www.Kyle-Hunter.com where you'll receive *Marissa Rewritten* (first book in this series) free just for signing up!

For more romantic stories that take you places . . .

Second Chance Series

In *The Second Chance Series*, you'll meet Marissa, Julia, Sydney, and Eden, four college friends who, twenty-five years later, renew their friendships as they find themselves empty nesters and single again. You'll love getting to know these women and following each one in her own book.

Marissa Rewritten (A Novella) #1

Author Marissa Thompson has had a writer's block since her husband died almost two years earlier. Her three closest friends are a comfort. Despite this, things are getting urgent as her career hangs by a thread and repairs on her historic home mount up. Prodded by desperation, Marissa heads to Wilmington, North Carolina for a Civil War research trip. She hopes for inspiration, but receives encouragement from a surprising source, a feisty character from her last novel.

Jarrod Lambert has already lost his wife. He's always been close with his college-age daughter, but she seems to be slipping further away from him. In an effort to reconnect with her, he makes an impulsive trip to see her in Wilmington.

Through an accident, Marissa and Jarrod meet and discover common ground. Will it be enough to overcome the obstacles standing between them?

Romance in Provence Series

The Provence Series takes you with Bree and Lauren, best friends and business partners, to one of the loveliest regions of France. It's not always idyllic in the land of lavender fields and cliffside villages. Join Bree and Lauren as each woman discovers her unique journey—and surprising romance.

Prodigals in Provence (Bree's story) #1

Bree and Lauren own and run Le Bon Voyage, a travel company specializing in tours to charming Provence, France.

Travis is a TV travel critic accustomed to crossing the globe to film documentaries and write books. But he's been in a spiritual desert ever since losing his marriage and ministry five years earlier.

Between film projects, Travis plans to accompany his elderly mother on a tour to Provence, a long-term dream for her. Bree tries unsuccessfully to block him, sure he's coming to spy on the struggling company for an exposé article.

A diverse group of tourists arrives at the rented villa to spend the week and discover the spectacular villages, vineyards, and history of the Luberon mountain region of Provence. Amidst a series of problems and relational tensions, Bree thinks she has all she can handle . . . until she becomes attracted to Travis.

As Bree and Travis are drawn together, will their hidden wounds drive them apart?

A Promise in Provence (Lauren's story) #2

Lauren is at a turning point. If only she knew *where* to turn. Her long-term relationship with Mark is fading fast. Instead, she feels drawn to Jean-Pierre, an attractive Frenchman she'd met the previous summer. When she's laid off from her job as a chef, she decides to go see him in Provence, France.

Mark can't get Lauren out of his heart, even though it's been close to a year since she asked him to give her space. When she goes to France, he's afraid he'll lose her for good. That is, until he decides to go there, too, as a last-ditch effort to win her back.

At first, Lauren is angry that Mark follows her to France. But a joint desire to help a young refugee boy leads them to work together. Lauren finds herself torn between the two men. Worse, she's confronted with obstacles in helping the boy and even greater obstacles within herself.

Stand Alone Novels that take you places . . .

One December

Is there any way to recapture what happened under the moon one December?

Nikki has loved Mike for as long as she can remember. Mike has his own past hurts to resolve, having lost both parents when he was fourteen. He's tried to escape the memories by starting a new life on the West Coast.

At Christmas, he comes back to New York for the first time in three years. He and Nikki rekindle the friendship they had as children and share their newfound faith. Under a Christmas moon, romantic sparks fly…but their mutual attraction takes an unexpected detour.

Nikki is devastated, believing the romance is over. She impulsively takes a one-year teaching opportunity in Paris to face her own fears and to get over Mike.

If they think they can run away from each other, they'd better think again.

"*One December* sizzles with romantic tension, taking the reader on a roller-coaster ride from New York to San Francisco, with a delightful detour in Paris. I couldn't put it down!"

– Elizabeth Musser, author of *The Secrets of the Cross* trilogy and *The Swan House.*

Circle Back Around

Hailey and her father haven't always seen eye to eye, especially in running the failing family textile mill. Frustrated, Hailey leaves the mill and her hometown in North Carolina to start a new life near her sister in Colorado. Only months later her father calls to ask a special favor. He needs heart surgery and asks Hailey to run the mill in his place.

Moving back would devastate Hailey's sister, Hope. Yet Hailey would have an opportunity to possibly save the mill, and at a time when her father needs her most. And maybe he'd even approve of her for the first time in her life.

Filled with self-doubt, Hailey returns to North Carolina and struggles to make a difference at the mill, facing more challenges than she bargained for. Her attractive neighbor, Alex, is almost enough to outweigh the difficulties, but she doesn't know that in the shadows lurks someone who wants to destroy both her *and* the mill.

Read Chapter One of all books at
www.Kyle-Hunter.com

Kyle Hunter writes inspirational romance and women's fiction that sometimes take her characters to faraway places. She lived in France for thirteen years. Currently, she lives in North Carolina where she writes fiction, non-fiction (under the pen name K. B. Oliver and the travel blog OliversFrance.com), and teaches French to adults.